PUFFIN CLASSICS

The Enchanted Castle

EDITH NESBIT (1858–1924) was a mischievous, tomboyish child who grew into an unconventional adult. With her husband, Hubert Bland, she was one of the founder members of the socialist Fabian Society; their household became a centre of the socialist and literary circles of the time. The chaos of their Bohemian home, managed by the restless 'Daisy' (as she was known to her friends), was regularly increased by the presence of numerous friends, among whom were George Bernard Shaw and H. G. Wells. Apart from their own children, Edith also raised two adopted children.

Her clothing, haircut, lifestyle and habit of expressing herself forcefully and in public proclaimed her to be a woman who was trying to break out of the mould which English society demanded at the time. She was no armchair socialist, however: in fact, despite her success as a writer, late in life her charitable deeds brought her close to bankruptcy.

E. Nesbit – she always used the plain initial for her writing, with the result that she was occasionally thought to be a man – turned late to children's writing, after a number of years as a successful writer of short pieces for adult magazines. Thanks to her success, she was approached by a popular children's magazine of the time to write pieces about her childhood.

This request opened up a rich vein. When Edith turned from describing the literal facts of her childhood to capturing in fictional form the happy and relaxed atmosphere she had known as a girl, the result was a series of children's books which have remained firm favourites and bestsellers for decades. One of her most admired abilities as a writer is the combination – often with more than a pinch of humour – of a real-life situation with elements of magical fantasy. *The Enchanted Castle* shows this combination at its best.

Some other Puffin Classics to enjoy

FIVE CHILDREN AND IT
THE MAGIC WORLD
THE STORY OF THE TREASURE SEEKERS
NEW TREASURE SEEKERS
THE PHOENIX AND THE CARPET
THE RAILWAY CHILDREN
THE STORY OF THE AMULET
THE WOULDBEGOODS
E. Nesbit

E. NESBIT

The Enchanted Castle

Illustrated by
H. R. MILLAR

PUFFIN BOOKS

PUFFIN BOOKS

Published by the Penguin Group
Penguin Books Ltd, 27 Wrights Lane, London W8 5TZ, England
Penguin Books USA Inc., 375 Hudson Street, New York, New York 10014, USA
Penguin Books Australia Ltd, Ringwood, Victoria, Australia
Penguin Books Canada Ltd, 10 Alcorn Avenue, Toronto, Ontario, Canada M4V 3B2
Penguin Books (NZ) Ltd, 182–190 Wairau Road, Auckland 10, New Zealand

Penguin Books Ltd, Registered Offices: Harmondsworth, Middlesex, England

First published 1907
First published in this edition by Ernest Benn Ltd 1956
Published in Puffin Books 1979
Reissued in this edition 1994
10

Filmset by Datix International Limited, Bungay, Suffolk
Printed in England by Clays Ltd, St Ives plc
Set in 11/14 pt Monophoto Plantin

To Margaret Ostler
with love from
E. Nesbit

Peggy, you came from the heath and moor,
And you brought their airs through my open door;
You brought the blossom of youth to blow
In the Latin Quarter of Soho.

For the sake of that magic I send you here
A tale of enchantments, Peggy dear,
– A bit of my work, and a bit of my heart . . .
The bit that you left when we had to part.

Royalty Chambers, Soho, W.
25 September 1907

1

There were three of them – Jerry, Jimmy, and Kathleen. Of course, Jerry's name was Gerald, and not Jeremiah, whatever you may think; and Jimmy's name was James; and Kathleen was never called by her name at all, but Cathy, or Catty, or Puss Cat, when her brothers were pleased with her, and Scratch Cat when they were not pleased. And they were at school in a little town in the West of England – the boys at one school, of course, and the girl at another, because the sensible habit of having boys and girls at the same school is not yet as common as I hope it will be some day. They used to see each other on Saturdays and Sundays at the house of a kind maiden lady; but it was one of those houses where it is impossible to play. You know the kind of house, don't you? There is a sort of a something about that kind of house that makes you hardly able even to talk to each other when you are left alone, and playing seems unnatural and affected. So they looked forward to the holidays, when they should all go home and be together all day long, in a house where playing was natural and conversation possible, and where the Hampshire forests and fields were full of interesting things to do and see. Their Cousin Betty was to be there too, and there were plans. Betty's school broke

up before theirs, and so she got to the Hampshire
home first, and the moment she got there she began
to have measles, so that my three couldn't go home at
all. You may imagine their feelings. The thought of
seven weeks at Miss Hervey's was not to be borne,
and all three wrote home and said so. This astonished
their parents very much, because they had always
thought it was so nice for the children to have dear
Miss Hervey's to go to. However, they were 'jolly
decent about it', as Jerry said, and after a lot of letters
and telegrams, it was arranged that the boys should
go and stay at Kathleen's school, where there were
now no girls left and no mistresses except the French
one.

'It'll be better than being at Miss Hervey's,' said
Kathleen, when the boys came round to ask Mademoiselle when it would be convenient for them to come;
'and, besides, our school's not half so ugly as yours.
We do have tablecloths on the tables and curtains at
the windows, and yours is all deal boards, and desks,
and inkiness.'

When they had gone to pack their boxes Kathleen
made all the rooms as pretty as she could with flowers
in jam jars – marigolds chiefly, because there was
nothing much else in the back garden. There were
geraniums in the front garden, and calceolarias and
lobelias; of course, the children were not allowed to
pick these.

'We ought to have some sort of play to keep us
going through the holidays,' said Kathleen, when tea
was over, and she had unpacked and arranged the
boys' clothes in the painted chests of drawers, feeling
very grown-up and careful as she neatly laid the differ-

ent sorts of clothes in tidy little heaps in the drawers. 'Suppose we write a book.'

'You couldn't,' said Jimmy.

'I didn't mean me, of course,' said Kathleen, a little injured; 'I meant us.'

'Too much fag,' said Gerald briefly.

'If we wrote a book,' Kathleen persisted, 'about what the insides of schools really *are* like, people would read it and say how clever we were.'

'More likely expel us,' said Gerald. 'No; we'll have an out-of-doors game – bandits, or something like that. It wouldn't be bad if we could get a cave and keep stores in it, and have our meals there.'

'There aren't any caves,' said Jimmy, who was fond of contradicting everyone. 'And, besides, your precious Mam'selle won't let us go out alone, as likely as not.'

'Oh, we'll see about that,' said Gerald. 'I'll go and talk to her like a father.'

'Like that?' Kathleen pointed the thumb of scorn at him, and he looked in the glass.

'To brush his hair and his clothes and to wash his face and hands was to our hero but the work of a moment,' said Gerald, and went to suit the action to the word.

It was a very sleek boy, brown and thin and interesting-looking, that knocked at the door of the parlour where Mademoiselle sat reading a yellow-covered book and wishing vain wishes. Gerald could always make himself look interesting at a moment's notice, a very useful accomplishment in dealing with strange grown-ups. It was done by opening his grey eyes rather wide, allowing the corners of his mouth to droop, and assuming a gentle, pleading expression, resembling that of the late little Lord Fauntleroy – who must, by the way, be quite old now, and an awful prig.

'Entrez!' said Mademoiselle, in shrill French accents. So he entered.

'Eh bien?' she said rather impatiently.

'I hope I am not disturbing you,' said Gerald, in whose mouth, it seemed, butter would not have melted.

'But no,' she said, somewhat softened. 'What is it that you desire?'

'I thought I ought to come and say how do you do,' said Gerald, 'because of you being the lady of the house.'

He held out the newly-washed hand, still damp and red. She took it.

'You are a very polite little boy,' she said.

'Not at all,' said Gerald, more polite than ever. 'I am so sorry for you. It must be dreadful to have us to look after in the holidays.'

'But not at all,' said Mademoiselle in her turn. 'I am sure you will be very good childrens.'

Gerald's look assured her that he and the others would be as near angels as children could be without ceasing to be human.

'We'll try,' he said earnestly.

'Can one do anything for you?' asked the French governess kindly.

'Oh, no, thank you,' said Gerald. 'We don't want to give you any trouble at all. And I was thinking it would be less trouble for you if we were to go out into the woods all day tomorrow and take our dinner with us – something cold, you know – so as not to be a trouble to the cook.'

'You are very considerate,' said Mademoiselle coldly. Then Gerald's eyes smiled; they had a trick of doing this when his lips were quite serious. Mademoiselle caught the twinkle, and she laughed and Gerald laughed too.

'Little deceiver!' she said. 'Why not say at once you want to be free of *surveillance,* how you say – overwatching – without pretending it is me you wish to please?'

'You have to be careful with grown-ups,' said Gerald, 'but it isn't all pretence either. We *don't* want to trouble you – and we don't want you to –'

'To trouble you. Eh bien! Your parents, they permit these days at woods?'

'Oh, yes,' said Gerald truthfully.

'Then I will not be more a dragon than the parents. I will forewarn the cook. Are you content?'

'Rather!' said Gerald. 'Mademoiselle, you are a dear.'

'A deer?' she repeated – 'a stag?'

'No, a – a *chérie,*' said Gerald – 'a regular A1 *chérie.* And you shan't repent it. Is there anything we can do for you – wind your wool, or find your spectacles, or –?'

'He thinks me a grandmother!' said Mademoiselle, laughing more than ever. 'Go then, and be not more naughty than you must.'

'Well, what luck?' the others asked.

'It's all right,' said Gerald indifferently. 'I told you it would be. The ingenuous youth won the regard of the foreign governess, who in her youth had been the beauty of her humble village.'

'I don't believe she ever was. She's too stern,' said Kathleen.

'Ah!' said Gerald, 'that's only because you don't know how to manage her. She wasn't stern with *me*.'

'I say, what a humbug you are though, aren't you?' said Jimmy.

'No, I'm a dip– what's-its-name? Something like an ambassador. Dipsoplomatist – that's what I am. Anyhow, we've got our day, and if we don't find a cave in it my name's not Jack Robinson.'

Mademoiselle, less stern than Kathleen had ever

seen her, presided at supper, which was bread and treacle spread several hours before, and now harder and drier than any other food you can think of. Gerald was very polite in handing her butter and cheese, and pressing her to taste the bread and treacle.

'Bah! it is like sand in the mouth – of a dryness! Is it possible this pleases you?'

'No,' said Gerald, 'it is not possible, but it is not polite for boys to make remarks about their food!'

She laughed, but there was no more dried bread and treacle for supper after that.

'How *do* you do it?' Kathleen whispered admiringly as they said good night.

'Oh, it's quite easy when you've once got a grown-up to see what you're after. You'll see, I shall drive her with a rein of darning cotton after this.'

Next morning Gerald got up early and gathered a little bunch of pink carnations from a plant which he found hidden among the marigolds. He tied it up with black cotton and laid it on Mademoiselle's plate. She smiled and looked quite handsome as she stuck the flowers in her belt.

'Do you think it's quite decent,' Jimmy asked later – 'sort of bribing people to let you do as you like with flowers and things and passing them the salt?'

'It's not that,' said Kathleen suddenly. '*I* know what Gerald means, only I never think of the things in time myself. You see, if you want grown-ups to be nice to you the least you can do is to be nice to them and think of little things to please them. I never think of any myself. Jerry does; that's why all the old ladies like him. It's not bribery. It's a sort of honesty – like paying for things.'

'Well, anyway,' said Jimmy, putting away the moral question, 'we've got a ripping day for the woods.'

They had.

The wide High Street, even at the busy morning hour almost as quiet as a dream-street, lay bathed in sunshine; the leaves shone fresh from last night's rain, but the road was dry, and in the sunshine the very dust of it sparkled like diamonds. The beautiful old houses, standing stout and strong, looked as though they were basking in the sunshine and enjoying it.

'But *are* there any woods?' asked Kathleen as they passed the market-place.

'It doesn't much matter about woods,' said Gerald dreamily, 'we're sure to find *something*. One of the chaps told me his father said when he was a boy there used to be a little cave under the bank in a lane near the Salisbury Road; but he said there was an enchanted castle there too, so perhaps the cave isn't true either.'

'If we were to get horns,' said Kathleen, 'and to blow them very hard all the way, we might find a magic castle.'

'If you've got the money to throw away on horns...' said Jimmy contemptuously.

'Well, I have, as it happens, so there!' said Kathleen. And the horns were bought in a tiny shop with a bulging window full of a tangle of toys and sweets and cucumbers and sour apples.

And the quiet square at the end of the town where the church is, and the houses of the most respectable people, echoed to the sound of horns blown long and loud. But none of the houses turned into enchanted castles.

So they went along the Salisbury Road, which was

very hot and dusty, so they agreed to drink one of the bottles of ginger-beer.

'We might as well carry the ginger-beer inside us as inside the bottle,' said Jimmy, 'and we can hide the bottle and call for it as we come back.'

Presently they came to a place where the road, as Gerald said, went two ways at once.

'*That* looks like adventures,' said Kathleen; and they took the right-hand road, and the next time they took a turning it was a left-hand one, so as to be quite fair, Jimmy said, and then a right-hand one and then a left, and so on, till they were completely lost.

'*Com*pletely,' said Kathleen; 'how jolly!'

And now trees arched overhead, and the banks of the road were high and bushy. The adventurers had long since ceased to blow their horns. It was too tiring to go on doing that, when there was no one to be annoyed by it.

'Oh, kriky!' observed Jimmy suddenly, 'let's sit down a bit and have some of our dinner. We might call it lunch, you know,' he added persuasively.

So they sat down in the hedge and ate the ripe red gooseberries that were to have been their dessert.

And as they sat and rested and wished that their boots did not feel so full of feet, Gerald leaned back against the bushes, and the bushes gave way so that he almost fell over backward. Something had yielded to the pressure of his back, and there was the sound of something heavy that fell.

'Oh, Jimminy!' he remarked, recovering himself suddenly; 'there's something hollow in there – the stone I was leaning against simply *went*!'

'I wish it was a cave,' said Jimmy; 'but of course it isn't.'

'If we blow the horns perhaps it will be,' said Kathleen, and hastily blew her own.

Gerald reached his hand through the bushes. 'I can't feel anything but air,' he said; 'it's just a hole full of emptiness.' The other two pulled back the bushes. There certainly was a hole in the bank. 'I'm going to go in,' observed Gerald.

'Oh, don't!' said his sister. 'I wish you wouldn't. Suppose there were snakes!'

'Not likely,' said Gerald, but he leaned forward and struck a match. 'It *is* a cave!' he cried, and put his knee on the mossy stone he had been sitting on, scrambled over it, and disappeared.

A breathless pause followed.

'You all right?' asked Jimmy.

'Yes; come on. You'd better come feet first – there's a bit of a drop.'

'I'll go next,' said Kathleen, and went – feet first, as advised. The feet waved wildly in the air.

'Look out!' said Gerald in the dark; 'you'll have my eye out. Put your feet *down*, girl, not up. It's no use trying to fly here – there's no room.'

He helped her by pulling her feet forcibly down and then lifting her under the arms. She felt rustling dry leaves under her boots, and stood ready to receive Jimmy, who came in head first, like one diving into an unknown sea.

'It *is* a cave,' said Kathleen.

'The young explorers,' explained Gerald, blocking up the hole of entrance with his shoulders, 'dazzled at first by the darkness of the cave, could see nothing.'

'Darkness doesn't dazzle,' said Jimmy.

'I wish we'd got a candle,' said Kathleen.

'Yes, it does,' Gerald contradicted – 'could see nothing. But their dauntless leader, whose eyes had grown used to the dark while the clumsy forms of the others were bunging up the entrance, had made a discovery.'

'Oh, what!' Both the others were used to Gerald's way of telling a story while he acted it, but they did sometimes wish that he didn't talk quite so long and so like a book in moments of excitement.

'He did not reveal the dread secret to his faithful followers till one and all had given him their word of honour to be calm.'

'We'll be calm all right,' said Jimmy impatiently.

'Well, then,' said Gerald, ceasing suddenly to be a book and becoming a boy, 'there's a light over there – look behind you!'

They looked. And there was. A faint greyness on the brown walls of the cave, and a brighter greyness cut off sharply by a dark line, showed that round a turning or angle of the cave there was daylight.

'Attention!' said Gerald; at least, that was what he meant, though what he said was ''Shun!' as becomes the son of a soldier. The others mechanically obeyed.

'You will remain at attention till I give the word "Slow march!" on which you will advance cautiously in open order, following your hero leader, taking care not to tread on the dead and wounded.'

'I wish you wouldn't!' said Kathleen.

'There aren't any,' said Jimmy, feeling for her hand in the dark; 'he only means, take care not to tumble over stones and things.'

Here he found her hand, and she screamed.

'It's only me,' said Jimmy. 'I thought you'd like me to hold it. But you're just like a girl.'

Their eyes had now begun to get accustomed to the darkness, and all could see that they were in a rough stone cave, that went straight on for about three or four yards and then turned sharply to the right.

'Death or victory!' remarked Gerald. 'Now, then – Slow march!'

He advanced carefully, picking his way among the loose earth and stones that were the floor of the cave.

'A sail, a sail!' he cried, as he turned the corner.

'How splendid!' Kathleen drew a long breath as she came out into the sunshine.

'I don't see any sail,' said Jimmy, following.

The narrow passage ended in a round arch all fringed with ferns and creepers. They passed through the arch into a deep, narrow gully whose banks were of stones, moss-covered; and in the crannies grew more ferns and long grasses. Trees growing on the top of the bank arched across, and the sunlight came through in changing patches of brightness, turning the gully to a roofed corridor of goldy-green. The path, which was of greeny-grey flagstones where heaps of leaves had drifted, sloped steeply down, and at the end of it was another round arch, quite dark inside, above which rose rocks and grass and bushes.

'It's like the outside of a railway tunnel,' said James.

'It's the entrance to the enchanted castle,' said Kathleen. 'Let's blow the horns.'

'Dry up!' said Gerald. 'The bold Captain, reproving the silly chatter of his subordinates –'

'I like that!' said Jimmy, indignant.

'I thought you would,' resumed Gerald – 'of his subordinates, bade them advance with caution and in silence, because after all there might be somebody about, and the other arch might be an ice-house or something dangerous.'

'What?' asked Kathleen anxiously.

'Bears, perhaps,' said Gerald briefly.

'There aren't any bears without bars – in England, anyway,' said Jimmy. 'They call bears bars in America,' he added absently.

'Quick march!' was Gerald's only reply.

And they marched. Under the drifted damp leaves the path was firm and stony to their shuffling feet. At the dark arch they stopped.

'There are steps down,' said Jimmy.

'It *is* an ice-house,' said Gerald.

'Don't let's,' said Kathleen.

'Our hero,' said Gerald, 'who nothing could dismay, raised the faltering hopes of his abject minions by saying that he was jolly well going on, and they could do as they liked about it.'

'If you call names,' said Jimmy, 'you can go on by yourself.' He added, 'So there!'

'It's part of the game, silly,' explained Gerald kindly. 'You can be Captain tomorrow, so you'd better hold your jaw now, and begin to think about what names you'll call us when it's your turn.'

Very slowly and carefully they went down the steps. A vaulted stone arched over their heads. Gerald struck a match when the last step was found to have no edge, and to be, in fact, the beginning of a passage, turning to the left.

'This,' said Jimmy, 'will take us back into the road.'

'Or under it,' said Gerald. 'We've come down eleven steps.'

They went on, following their leader, who went very slowly for fear, as he explained, of steps. The passage was very dark.

'I don't half like it!' whispered Jimmy.

Then came a glimmer of daylight that grew and grew, and presently ended in another arch that looked out over a scene so like a picture out of a book about Italy that everyone's breath was taken away, and they simply walked forward silent and staring. A short avenue of cypresses led, widening as it went, to a marble terrace that lay broad and white in the sunlight. The children, blinking, leaned their arms on the broad, flat balustrade and gazed. Immediately below them was a lake – just like a lake in 'The Beauties of Italy' – a lake with swans and an island and weeping willows; beyond it were green slopes dotted with groves of trees, and amid the trees gleamed the white limbs of statues. Against a little hill to the left was a round white building with pillars, and to the right a waterfall came tumbling down among mossy stones to splash into the lake. Steps fed from the terrace to the water, and other steps to the green lawns beside it. Away across the grassy slopes deer were feeding, and in the distance where the groves of trees thickened into what looked almost a forest were enormous shapes of grey stone, like nothing that the children had ever seen before.

'That chap at school –' said Gerald.

'It *is* an enchanted castle,' said Kathleen.

'I don't see any castle,' said Jimmy.

'What do you call that, then?' Gerald pointed to where, beyond a belt of lime-trees, white towers and turrets broke the blue of the sky.

'There doesn't seem to be anyone about,' said Kathleen, 'and yet it's all so tidy. I believe it is magic.'

'Magic mowing machines,' Jimmy suggested.

'If we were in a book it would be an enchanted castle – certain to be,' said Kathleen.

'It *is* an enchanted castle,' said Gerald in hollow tones.

'But there aren't any.' Jimmy was quite positive.

'How do you know? Do you think there's nothing in

the world but what *you've* seen?' His scorn was crushing.

'I think magic went out when people began to have steam-engines,' Jimmy insisted, 'and newspapers, and telephones and wireless telegraphing.'

'Wireless is rather like magic when you come to think of it,' said Gerald.

'Oh, *that* sort!' Jimmy's contempt was deep.

'Perhaps there's given up being magic because people didn't believe in it any more,' said Kathleen.

'Well, don't let's spoil the show with any silly old not believing,' said Gerald with decision. 'I'm going to believe in magic as hard as I can. This is an enchanted garden, and that's an enchanted castle, and I'm jolly well going to explore. The dauntless knight then led the way, leaving his ignorant squires to follow or not, just as they jolly well chose.' He rolled off the balustrade and strode firmly down towards the lawn, his boots making, as they went, a clatter full of determination.

The others followed. There never was such a garden – out of a picture or a fairy-tale. They passed quite close by the deer, who only raised their pretty heads to look, and did not seem startled at all. And after a long stretch of turf they passed under the heaped-up heavy masses of lime-trees and came into a rose-garden, bordered with thick, close-cut yew hedges, and lying red and pink and green and white in the sun, like a giant's many-coloured, highly-scented pocket-handkerchief.

'I know we shall meet a gardener in a minute, and he'll ask what we're doing here. And then what will you say?' Kathleen asked with her nose in a rose.

'I shall say we have lost our way, and it will be quite true,' said Gerald.

But they did not meet a gardener or anybody else, and the feeling of magic got thicker and thicker, till they were almost afraid of the sound of their feet in the great silent place. Beyond the rose garden was a yew hedge with an arch cut in it, and it was the beginning of a maze like the one in Hampton Court.

'Now,' said Gerald, 'you mark my words. In the middle of this maze we shall find the secret enchantment. Draw your swords, my merry men all, and hark forward tallyho in the utmost silence.'

Which they did.

It was very hot in the maze, between the close yew hedges, and the way to the maze's heart was hidden well. Again and again they found themselves at the black yew arch that opened on the rose garden, and they were all glad that they had brought large, clean pocket-handkerchiefs with them.

It was when they found themselves there for the fourth time that Jimmy suddenly cried, 'Oh, I wish –' and then stopped short very suddenly. 'Oh!' he added in quite a different voice, 'where's the dinner?' And then in a stricken silence they all remembered that the basket with the dinner had been left at the entrance of the cave. Their thoughts dwelt fondly on the slices of cold mutton, the six tomatoes, the bread and butter, the screwed-up paper of salt, the apple turnovers, and the little thick glass that one drank the ginger-beer out of.

'Let's go back,' said Jimmy, 'now this minute, and get our things and have our dinner.'

'Let's have one more try at the maze. I hate giving things up,' said Gerald.

'I *am* so hungry!' said Jimmy.

'Why didn't you say so before?' asked Gerald bitterly.

'I wasn't before.'

'Then you can't be now. You don't get hungry all in a minute. What's that?'

'That' was a gleam of red that lay at the foot of the yew hedge – a thin little line, that you would hardly have noticed unless you had been staring in a fixed and angry way at the roots of the hedge.

It was a thread of cotton. Gerald picked it up. One end of it was tied to a thimble with holes in it, and the other –

'There *is* no other end,' said Gerald, with firm

triumph. 'It's a clue – that's what it is. What price cold mutton now? I've always felt something magic would happen some day, and now it has.'

'I expect the gardener put it there,' said Jimmy.

'With a Princess's silver thimble on it? Look! there's a crown on the thimble.'

There was.

'Come,' said Gerald in low, urgent tones, 'if you are adventurers *be* adventurers; and anyhow, I expect someone has gone along the road and bagged the mutton hours ago.'

He walked forward, winding the red thread round his fingers as he went. And it *was* a clue, and it led them right into the middle of the maze. And in the very middle of the maze they came upon the wonder.

The red clue led them up two stone steps to a round grass plot. There was a sun-dial in the middle, and all round against the yew hedge a low, wide marble seat. The red clue ran straight across the grass and by the sun-dial, and ended in a small brown hand with jewelled rings on every finger. The hand was, naturally, attached to an arm, and that had many bracelets on it, sparkling with red and blue and green stones. The arm wore a sleeve of pink and gold brocaded silk, faded a little here and there but still extremely imposing, and the sleeve was part of a dress, which was worn by a lady who lay on the stone seat asleep in the sun. The rosy gold dress fell open over an embroidered petticoat of a soft green colour. There was old yellow lace the colour of scalded cream, and a thin white veil spangled with silver stars covered the face.

'It's the enchanted Princess,' said Gerald, now really impressed. 'I told you so.'

'It's the Sleeping Beauty,' said Kathleen. 'It is – look how old-fashioned her clothes are, like the pictures of Marie Antoinette's ladies in the history book. She has slept for a hundred years. Oh, Gerald, you're the eldest; you must be the Prince, and we never knew it.'

'She isn't really a Princess,' said Jimmy. But the others laughed at him, partly because his saying things like that was enough to spoil any game, and partly because they really were not at all sure that it was not a Princess who lay there as still as the sunshine. Every stage of the adventure – the cave, the wonderful gardens, the maze, the clue, had deepened the feeling of magic, till now Kathleen and Gerald were almost completely bewitched.

'Lift the veil up, Jerry,' said Kathleen in a whisper;

'if she isn't beautiful we shall know she can't be the Princess.'

'Lift it yourself,' said Gerald.

'I expect you're forbidden to touch the figures,' said Jimmy.

'It's not wax, silly,' said his brother.

'No,' said his sister, 'wax wouldn't be much good in this sun. And, besides, you can see her breathing. It's the Princess right enough.' She very gently lifted the edge of the veil and turned it back. The Princess's face was small and white between long plaits of black hair. Her nose was straight and her brows finely traced. There were a few freckles on cheekbones and nose.

'No wonder,' whispered Kathleen, 'sleeping all these years in all this sun!' Her mouth was not a rosebud. But all the same –

'Isn't she lovely!' Kathleen murmured.

'Not so dusty,' Gerald was understood to reply.

'Now, Jerry,' said Kathleen firmly, 'you're the eldest.'

'Of course I am,' said Gerald uneasily.

'Well, you've got to wake the Princess.'

'She's not a Princess,' said Jimmy, with his hands in the pockets of his knickerbockers; 'she's only a little girl dressed up.'

'But she's in long dresses,' urged Kathleen.

'Yes, but look what a little way down her frock her feet come. She wouldn't be any taller than Jerry if she was to stand up.'

'Now then,' urged Kathleen. 'Jerry, don't be silly. You've got to do it.'

'Do what?' asked Gerald, kicking his left boot with his right.

'Why, kiss her awake, of course.'

'Not me!' was Gerald's unhesitating rejoinder.

'Well, someone's got to.'

'She'd go for me as likely as not the minute she woke up,' said Gerald anxiously.

'I'd do it like a shot,' said Kathleen, 'but I don't suppose it 'ud make any difference me kissing her.'

She did it; and it didn't. The Princess still lay in deep slumber.

'Then you must, Jimmy. I dare say you'll do. Jump back quickly before she can hit you.'

'She won't hit him, he's such a little chap,' said Gerald.

'Little yourself!' said Jimmy. '*I* don't mind kissing her. I'm not a coward, like Some People. Only if I do, I'm going to be the dauntless leader for the rest of the day.'

'No, look here – hold on!' cried Gerald, 'perhaps I'd better –' But, in the meantime, Jimmy had planted a loud, cheerful-sounding kiss on the Princess's pale cheek, and now the three stood breathless, awaiting the result.

And the result was that the Princess opened large, dark eyes, stretched out her arms, yawned a little, covering her mouth with a small brown hand, and said, quite plainly and distinctly, and without any room at all for mistake:

'Then the hundred years are over? How the yew hedges have grown! Which of you is my Prince that aroused me from my deep sleep of so many long years?'

'I did,' said Jimmy fearlessly, for she did not look as

though she were going to slap anyone.

'My noble preserver!' said the Princess, and held out her hand. Jimmy shook it vigorously.

'But I say,' said he, 'you aren't really a Princess, are you?'

'Of course I am,' she answered; 'who else could I be? Look at my crown!' She pulled aside the spangled veil, and showed beneath it a coronet of what even Jimmy could not help seeing to be diamonds.

'But –' said Jimmy.

'Why,' she said, opening her eyes very wide, 'you must have known about my being here, or you'd never have come. How *did* you get past the dragons?'

Gerald ignored the question. 'I say,' he said, 'do you really believe in magic, and all that?'

'I ought to,' she said, 'if anybody does. Look, here's

the place where I pricked my finger with the spindle.'
She showed a little scar on her wrist.

'Then this really *is* an enchanted castle?'

'Of course it is,' said the Princess. 'How stupid you
are!' She stood up, and her pink brocaded dress lay in
bright waves about her feet.

'I said her dress would be too long,' said Jimmy.

'It was the right length when I went to sleep,'
said the Princess; 'it must have grown in the hundred
years.'

'I don't believe you're a Princess at all,' said Jimmy;
'at least –'

'Don't bother about believing it, if you don't
like,' said the Princess. 'It doesn't so much matter
what you believe as what I am.' She turned to the
others.

'Let's go back to the castle,' she said, 'and I'll show
you all my lovely jewels and things. Wouldn't you like
that?'

'Yes,' said Gerald with very plain hesitation. 'But –'

'But what?' The Princess's tone was impatient.

'But we're most awfully hungry.'

'Oh, so am I!' cried the Princess.

'We've had nothing to eat since breakfast.'

'And it's three now,' said the Princess, looking at
the sun-dial. 'Why, you've had nothing to eat for
hours and hours and hours. But think of me! I haven't
had anything to eat for a hundred years. Come along
to the castle.'

'The mice will have eaten everything,' said Jimmy
sadly. He saw now that she really *was* a Princess.

'Not they,' cried the Princess joyously. 'You forget
everything's enchanted here. Time simply stood still

for a hundred years. Come along, and one of you must carry my train, or I shan't be able to move now it's grown such a frightful length.'

2

When you are young so many things are difficult to believe, and yet the dullest people will tell you that they are true – such things, for instance, as that the earth goes round the sun, and that it is not flat but round. But the things that seem really likely, like fairy-tales and magic, are, so say the grown-ups, not true at all. Yet they are so easy to believe, especially when you see them happening. And, as I am always telling you, the most wonderful things happen to all sorts of people, only you never hear about them because the people think that no one will believe their stories, and so they don't tell them to any one except me. And they tell me, because they know that I can believe anything.

When Jimmy had awakened the Sleeping Princess, and she had invited the three children to go with her to her palace and get something to eat, they all knew quite surely that they had come into a place of magic happenings. And they walked in a slow procession along the grass towards the castle. The Princess went first, and Kathleen carried her shining train; then came Jimmy, and Gerald came last. They were all quite sure that they had walked right into the middle of a fairy-tale, and they were the more ready to believe it because they were so tired and hungry. They were, in fact, so hungry and tired that they hardly noticed where they were going, or observed the beauties of the formal gardens through which the pink-silk Princess was leading them. They were in a sort of dream, from which they only partially awakened to find themselves in a big hall, with suits of armour and old flags round the walls, the skins of beasts on the floor, and heavy oak tables and benches ranged along it.

The Princess entered, slow and stately, but once inside she twitched her sheeny train out of Jimmy's hand and turned to the three.

'You just wait here a minute,' she said, 'and mind you don't talk while I'm away. This castle is crammed with magic, and I don't know what will happen if you talk.' And with that, picking up the thick goldy-pink folds under her arms, she ran out, as Jimmy said afterwards, 'most unprincesslike', showing as she ran black stockings and black strap shoes.

Jimmy wanted very much to say that he didn't believe anything would happen, only he was afraid something would happen if he did, so he merely made a face and put out his tongue. The others pretended not to see this, which was much more crushing than anything they could have said. So they sat in silence, and Gerald ground the heel of his boot upon the marble floor. Then the Princess came back, very slowly and kicking her long skirts in front of her at every step. She could not hold them up now because of the tray she carried.

It was not a silver tray, as you might have expected, but an oblong tin one. She set it down noisily on the end of the long table and breathed a sigh of relief.

'Oh! it *was* heavy,' she said. I don't know what fairy feast the children's fancy had been busy with. Anyhow, this was nothing like it. The heavy tray held a loaf of bread, a lump of cheese, and a brown jug of water. The rest of its heaviness was just plates and mugs and knives.

'Come along,' said the Princess hospitably. 'I couldn't find anything but bread and cheese – but it doesn't matter, because everything's magic here, and unless you have some dreadful secret fault the bread and cheese will turn into anything you like. What *would* you like?' she asked Kathleen.

'Roast chicken,' said Kathleen, without hesitation.

The pinky Princess cut a slice of bread and laid it on a dish.

'There you are,' she said, 'roast chicken. Shall I carve it, or will you?'

'You, please,' said Kathleen, and received a piece of dry bread on a plate.

'Green peas?' asked the Princess, cut a piece of cheese and laid it beside the bread.

Kathleen began to eat the bread, cutting it up with knife and fork as you would eat chicken. It was no use owning that she didn't see any chicken and peas, or anything but cheese and dry bread, because that would be owning that she had some dreadful secret fault.

'If I have, it *is* a secret, even from me,' she told herself.

The others asked for roast beef and cabbage – and got it, she supposed, though to her it only looked like dry bread and Dutch cheese.

'I *do* wonder what my dreadful secret fault is,' she

thought, as the Princess remarked that, as for her, she could fancy a slice of roast peacock. 'This one,' she added, lifting a second mouthful of dry bread on her fork, 'is quite delicious.'

'It's a game, isn't it?' asked Jimmy suddenly.

'What's a game?' asked the Princess, frowning.

'Pretending it's beef – the bread and cheese, I mean.'

'A game? But it *is* beef. Look at it,' said the Princess, opening her eyes very wide.

'Yes, of course,' said Jimmy feebly. 'I was only joking.'

Bread and cheese is not perhaps so good as roast beef or chicken or peacock (I'm not sure about the peacock. I never tasted peacock, did you?); but bread and cheese is, at any rate, very much better than nothing when you have gone on having nothing since breakfast (gooseberries and gingerbeer hardly count) and it is long past your proper dinner-time. Everyone ate and drank and felt much better.

'Now,' said the Princess, brushing the breadcrumbs off her green silk lap, 'if you're sure you won't have any more meat you can come and see my treasures. Sure you won't take the least bit more chicken? No? Then follow me.'

She got up and they followed her down the long hall to the end where the great stone stairs ran up at each side and joined in a broad flight leading to the gallery above. Under the stairs was a hanging of tapestry.

'Beneath this arras,' said the Princess, 'is the door leading to my private apartments.' She held the tapestry up with both hands, for it was heavy, and showed a little door that had been hidden by it.

'The key,' she said, 'hangs above.'

And so it did, on a large rusty nail.

'Put it in,' said the Princess, 'and turn it.'

Gerald did so, and the great key creaked and grated in the lock.

'Now push,' she said; 'push hard, all of you.'

They pushed hard, all of them. The door gave way, and they fell over each other into the dark space beyond.

The Princess dropped the curtain and came after them, closing the door behind her.

'Look out!' she said; 'look out! there are two steps down.'

'Thank you,' said Gerald, rubbing his knee at the bottom of the steps. 'We found that out for ourselves.'

'I'm sorry,' said the Princess, 'but you can't have

hurt yourselves much. Go straight on. There aren't any more steps.'

They went straight on – in the dark.

'When you come to the door just turn the handle and go in. Then stand still till I find the matches. I know where they are.'

'Did they have matches a hundred years ago?' asked Jimmy.

'I meant the tinder-box,' said the Princess quickly. 'We always called it the matches. Don't you? Here, let me go first.'

She did, and when they had reached the door she was waiting for them with a candle in her hand. She thrust it on Gerald.

'Hold it steady,' she said, and undid the shutters of a long window, so that first a yellow streak and then a blazing great oblong of light flashed at them and the room was full of sunshine.

'It makes the candle look quite silly,' said Jimmy.

'So it does,' said the Princess, and blew out the candle. Then she took the key from the outside of the door, put it in the inside keyhole, and turned it.

The room they were in was small and high. Its domed ceiling was of deep blue with gold stars painted on it. The walls were of wood, panelled and carved, and there was no furniture in it whatever.

'This,' said the Princess, 'is my treasure chamber.' 'But where,' asked Kathleen politely, '*are* the treasures?'

'Don't you see them?' asked the Princess.

'No, we don't,' said Jimmy bluntly. 'You don't come that bread-and-cheese game with me – not twice over, you don't!'

'If you *really* don't see them,' said the Princess, 'I suppose I shall have to say the charm. Shut your eyes, please. And give me your word of honour you won't look till I tell you, and that you'll never tell anyone what you've seen.'

Their words of honour were something that the children would rather not have given just then, but they gave them all the same, and shut their eyes tight.

'Wiggadil yougadoo begadee leegadeeve nowgadow?' said the Princess rapidly; and they heard the swish of her silk train moving across the room. Then there was a creaking, rustling noise.

'She's locking us in!' cried Jimmy.

'Your word of honour,' gasped Gerald.

'Oh, do be quick!' moaned Kathleen.

'You may look,' said the voice of the Princess. And they looked. The room was not the same room, yet – yes, the starry-vaulted blue ceiling was there, and below it half a dozen feet of the dark panelling, but below that the walls of the room blazed and sparkled with white and blue and red and green and gold and silver. Shelves ran round the room, and on them were gold cups and silver dishes, and platters and goblets set with gems, ornaments of gold and silver, tiaras of diamonds, necklaces of rubies, strings of emeralds and pearls, all set out in unimaginable splendour against a background of faded blue velvet. It was like the Crown jewels that you see when your kind uncle takes you to the Tower, only there seemed to be far more jewels than you or anyone else has ever seen together at the Tower or anywhere else.

The three children remained breathless, open-mouthed, staring at the sparkling splendours all about them, while the Princess stood, her arm stretched out in a gesture of command, and a proud smile on her lips.

'My word!' said Gerald, in a low whisper. But no one spoke out loud. They waited as if spellbound for the Princess to speak.

She spoke.

'What price bread-and-cheese games now?' she asked triumphantly. 'Can I do magic, or can't I?'

'You can; oh, you can!' said Kathleen.

'May we – may we *touch*?' asked Gerald.

'All that's mine is yours,' said the Princess, with a generous wave of her brown hand, and added quickly, 'Only, of course, you mustn't take anything away with you.'

'We're not thieves!' said Jimmy. The others were already turning over the wonderful things on the blue velvet shelves.

'Perhaps not,' said the Princess, 'but you're a very unbelieving little boy. You think I can't see inside you, but I can. *I* know what you've been thinking.'

'What?' asked Jimmy.

'Oh, you know well enough,' said the Princess. 'You're thinking about the bread and cheese that I changed into beef, and about your secret fault. I say, let's all dress up and you be princes and princesses too.'

'To crown our hero,' said Gerald, lifting a gold crown with a cross on the top, 'was the work of a moment.' He put the crown on his head, and added a collar of SS and a zone of sparkling emeralds, which would not quite meet round his middle. He turned from fixing it by an ingenious adaptation of his belt to find the others already decked with diadems, necklaces, and rings.

'How splendid you look!' said the Princess, 'and how I wish your clothes were prettier. What ugly clothes people wear nowadays! A hundred years ago –'

Kathleen stood quite still with a diamond bracelet raised in her hand.

'I say,' she said. 'The King and Queen?'

'*What* King and Queen?' asked the Princess.

'Your father and mother, your sorrowing parents,'

said Kathleen. 'They'll have waked up by now. Won't they be wanting to see you, after a hundred years, you know?'

'Oh – ah – yes,' said the Princess slowly. 'I embraced my rejoicing parents when I got the bread and cheese. They're having their dinner. They won't expect me yet. Here,' she added, hastily putting a ruby bracelet on Kathleen's arm, 'see how splendid that is!'

Kathleen would have been quite content to go on all day trying on different jewels and looking at herself in the little silver-framed mirror that the Princess took from one of the shelves, but the boys were soon weary of this amusement.

'Look here,' said Gerald, 'if you're sure your father

and mother won't want you, let's go out and have a jolly good game of something. You could play besieged castles awfully well in that maze – unless you can do any more magic tricks.'

'You forget,' said the Princess, 'I'm grown up. I don't play games. And I don't like to do too much magic at a time, it's so tiring. Besides, it'll take us ever so long to put all these things back in their proper places.'

It did. The children would have laid the jewels just anywhere; but the Princess showed them that every necklace, or ring, or bracelet had its own home on the velvet – a slight hollowing in the shelf beneath, so that each stone fitted into its own little nest.

As Kathleen was fitting the last shining ornament into its proper place, she saw that part of the shelf near it held, not bright jewels, but rings and brooches and chains, as well as queer things that she did not know the names of, and all were of dull metal and odd shapes.

'What's all this rubbish?' she asked.

'Rubbish, indeed!' said the Princess. 'Why those are *all* magic things! This bracelet – anyone who wears it has got to speak the truth. This chain makes you as strong as ten men; if you wear this spur your horse will go a mile a minute; or if you're walking it's the same as seven-league boots.'

'What does this brooch do?' asked Kathleen, reaching out her hand. The princess caught her by the wrist.

'You mustn't touch,' she said; 'if anyone but me touches them all the magic goes out at once and never comes back. That brooch will give you any wish you like.'

'And this ring?' Jimmy pointed.

'Oh, that makes you invisible.'

'What's this?' asked Gerald, showing a curious buckle.

'Oh, that undoes the effect of all the other charms.'

'Do you mean *really*?' Jimmy asked. 'You're not just kidding?'

'Kidding indeed!' repeated the Princess scornfully. 'I should have thought I'd shown you enough magic to prevent you speaking to a Princess like *that*!'

'I say,' said Gerald, visibly excited. 'You might show us how some of the things act. Couldn't you give us each a wish?'

The Princess did not at once answer. And the minds of the three played with granted wishes – brilliant yet thoroughly reasonable – the kind of wish that never seems to occur to people in fairy-tales when they suddenly get a chance to have their three wishes granted.

'No,' said the Princess suddenly, 'no; I can't give wishes to *you*, it only gives me wishes. But I'll let you see the ring make *me* invisible. Only you must shut your eyes while I do it.'

They shut them.

'Count fifty,' said the Princess, 'and then you may look. And then you must shut them again, and count fifty, and I'll reappear.'

Gerald counted, aloud. Through the counting one could hear a creaking, rustling sound.

'Forty-seven, forty-eight, forty-nine, fifty!' said Gerald, and they opened their eyes.

They were alone in the room. The jewels had vanished and so had the Princess.

'She's gone out by the door, of course,' said Jimmy, but the door was locked.

'That *is* magic,' said Kathleen breathlessly.

'Maskelyne and Devant can do *that* trick,' said Jimmy. 'And I want my tea.'

'Your tea!' Gerald's tone was full of contempt. 'The lovely Princess,' he went on, 'reappear'd as soon as our hero had finished counting fifty. One, two, three, four –'

Gerald and Kathleen had both closed their eyes. But somehow Jimmy hadn't. He didn't mean to cheat, he just forgot. And as Gerald's count reached twenty he saw a panel under the window open slowly.

'Her,' he said to himself. 'I *knew* it was a trick!' and at once shut his eyes, like an honourable little boy.

On the word 'fifty' six eyes opened. And the panel was closed and there was no Princess.

'She hasn't pulled it off this time,' said Gerald.

'Perhaps you'd better count again,' said Kathleen.

'I believe there's a cupboard under the window,' said Jimmy, 'and she's hidden in it. Secret panel, you know.'

'You looked! that's cheating,' said the voice of the Princess so close to his ear that he quite jumped.

'I didn't cheat.'

'Where on earth – What ever –' said all three together. For still there was no Princess to be seen.

'Come back visible, Princess dear,' said Kathleen. 'Shall we shut our eyes and count again?'

'Don't be silly!' said the voice of the Princess, and it sounded very cross.

'We're *not* silly,' said Jimmy, and his voice was cross too. 'Why can't you come back and have done with it? You know you're only hiding.'

'Don't!' said Kathleen gently. 'She *is* invisible, you know.'

'So should I be if I got into the cupboard,' said Jimmy.

'Oh yes,' said the sneering tone of the Princess, 'you think yourselves very clever, I dare say. But *I* don't mind. We'll play that you *can't* see me, if you like.'

'Well, but we *can't*,' said Gerald. 'It's no use getting in a wax. If you're hiding, as Jimmy says, you'd better come out. If you've really turned invisible, you'd better make yourself visible again.'

'Do you really mean,' asked a voice quite changed, but still the Princess's, 'that you *can't* see me?'

'Can't you *see* we can't?' asked Jimmy rather unreasonably.

The sun was blazing in at the window; the eight-sided room was very hot, and everyone was getting cross.

'You can't *see* me?' There was the sound of a sob in the voice of the invisible Princess.

'*No*, I tell you,' said Jimmy, 'and I want my tea – and –'

What he was saying was broken off short, as one might break a stick of sealing wax. And then in the golden afternoon a really quite horrid thing happened: Jimmy suddenly leaned backwards, then forwards, his eyes opened wide and his mouth too. Backward and forward he went, very quickly and abruptly, then stood still.

'Oh, he's in a fit! Oh, Jimmy, dear Jimmy!' cried Kathleen, hurrying to him. 'What is it, dear, what is it?'

'It's *not* a fit,' gasped Jimmy angrily. 'She shook me.'

'Yes,' said the voice of the Princess, 'and I'll shake him again if he keeps on saying he can't see me.'

'You'd better shake *me*,' said Gerald angrily. 'I'm nearer your own size.'

And instantly she did. But not for long. The moment

Gerald felt hands on his shoulders he put up his own and caught those other hands by the wrists. And there he was, holding wrists that he couldn't see. It was a dreadful sensation. An invisible kick made him wince, but he held tight to the wrists.

'Cathy,' he cried, 'come and hold her legs; she's kicking me.'

'Where?' cried Kathleen, anxious to help. 'I don't *see* any legs.'

'This is her hands I've got,' cried Gerald. 'She *is* invisible right enough. Get hold of this hand, and then you can feel your way down to her legs.'

Kathleen did so. I wish I could make you understand how very, very uncomfortable and frightening it is to feel, in broad daylight, hands and arms that you can't see.

'I *won't* have you hold my legs,' said the invisible Princess, struggling violently.

'What are you so cross about?' Gerald was quite calm. 'You said you'd be invisible and you *are*.'

'I'm not.'

'You are really. Look in the glass.'

'I'm not; I can't be.'

'Look in the glass,' Gerald repeated, quite unmoved.

'Let go, then,' she said.

Gerald did, and the moment he had done so he found it impossible to believe that he really had been holding invisible hands.

'You're just pretending not to see me,' said the Princess anxiously, 'aren't you? Do say you are. You've had your joke with me. Don't keep it up. I don't like it.'

'On our sacred word of honour,' said Gerald, 'you're still invisible.'

There was a silence. Then, 'Come,' said the Princess. 'I'll let you out, and you can go. I'm tired of playing with you.'

They followed her voice to the door, and through it, and along the little passage into the hall. No one said anything. Everyone felt very uncomfortable.

'Let's get out of this,' whispered Jimmy as they got to the end of the hall.

But the voice of the Princess said: 'Come out this way; it's quicker. I think you're perfectly hateful. I'm sorry I ever played with you. Mother always told me not to play with strange children.'

A door abruptly opened, though no hand was seen to touch it. 'Come through, can't you!' said the voice of the Princess.

It was a little ante-room, with long, narrow mirrors between its long, narrow windows.

'Good-bye,' said Gerald. 'Thanks for giving us such a jolly time. Let's part friends,' he added, holding out his hand.

An unseen hand was slowly put in his, which closed on it, vice-like.

'Now,' he said, 'you've jolly well *got* to look in the glass and own that we're not liars.'

He led the invisible Princess to one of the mirrors, and held her in front of it by the shoulders.

'Now,' he said, 'you just look for yourself.'

There was a silence, and then a cry of despair rang through the room.

'Oh – oh – oh! I *am* invisible. Whatever shall I do?'

'Take the ring off,' said Kathleen, suddenly practical.

Another silence.

'I *can't*!' cried the Princess. 'It won't come off. But it can't be the ring; rings don't make you invisible.'

'You said this one did,' said Kathleen, 'and it has.'

'But it *can't*,' said the Princess. 'I was only playing at magic. I just hid in the secret cupboard – it was only a game. Oh, whatever *shall* I do?'

'A game?' said Gerald slowly; 'but you *can* do magic – the invisible jewels, and you made them come visible.'

'Oh, it's only a secret spring and the panelling slides up. Oh, what am I to do?'

Kathleen moved towards the voice and gropingly got her arms round a pink-silk waist that she couldn't see. Invisible arms clasped her, a hot invisible cheek was laid against hers, and warm invisible tears lay wet between the two faces.

'Don't cry, dear,' said Kathleen; 'let me go and tell the King and Queen.'

'The –?'

'Your royal father and mother.'

'Oh, *don't* mock me!' said the poor Princess. 'You *know* that was only a game, too, like –'

'Like the bread and cheese,' said Jimmy triumphantly. 'I knew *that* was!'

'But your dress and being asleep in the maze, and –'

'Oh, I dressed up for fun, because everyone's away at the fair, and I put the clue just to make it all more real. I was playing at Fair Rosamond first, and then I heard you talking in the maze, and I thought what fun; and now I'm invisible, and I shall never come right again, never – I know I shan't! It serves me right for lying, but I didn't really think you'd believe it –

not more than half, that is,' she added hastily, trying to be truthful.

'But if you're not the Princess, who *are* you?' asked Kathleen, still embracing the unseen.

'I'm – my aunt lives here,' said the invisible Princess. 'She may be home any time. Oh, what shall I do?'

'Perhaps she knows some charm –'

'Oh, nonsense!' said the voice sharply; 'she doesn't believe in charms. She *would* be so vexed. Oh, I daren't let her see me like this!' she added wildly. 'And all of you here, too. She'd be so dreadfully cross.'

The beautiful magic castle that the children had believed in now felt as though it were tumbling about their ears. All that was left was the invisibleness of the Princess. But that, you will own, was a good deal.

'I just said it,' moaned the voice, 'and it came true. I wish I'd never played at magic – I wish I'd never played at anything at all.'

'Oh, don't say that,' Gerald said kindly. 'Let's go out into the garden, near the lake, where it's cool, and we'll hold a solemn council. You'll like that, won't you?'

'Oh!' cried Kathleen suddenly, 'the buckle; that makes magic come undone!'

'It doesn't *really*,' murmured the voice that seemed to speak without lips. 'I only just *said* that.'

'You only "just said" about the ring,' said Gerald. 'Anyhow, let's try.'

'Not *you* – *me*,' said the voice. 'You go down to the Temple of Flora, by the lake. I'll go back to the jewel-room by myself. Aunt might see you.'

'She won't see *you*,' said Jimmy.

'Don't rub it in,' said Gerald. 'Where *is* the Temple of Flora?'

'That's the way,' the voice said; 'down those steps and along the winding path through the shrubbery. You can't miss it. It's white marble, with a statue goddess inside.'

The three children went down to the white marble Temple of Flora that stood close against the side of the little hill, and sat down in its shadowy inside. It had arches all round except against the hill behind the statue, and it was cool and restful.

They had not been there five minutes before the feet of a runner sounded loud on the gravel. A shadow, very black and distinct, fell on the white marble floor.

'Your shadow's not invisible, anyhow,' said Jimmy.

'Oh, bother my shadow!' the voice of the Princess replied. 'We left the key inside the door, and it's shut itself with the wind, and it's a spring lock!'

There was a heartfelt pause.

Then Gerald said, in his most business-like manner:

'Sit down, Princess, and we'll have a thorough good palaver about it.'

'I shouldn't wonder,' said Jimmy, 'if we was to wake up and find it was dreams.'

'No such luck,' said the voice.

'Well,' said Gerald, 'first of all, what's your name, and if you're not a Princess, who are you?'

'I'm – I'm,' said a voice broken with sobs, 'I'm the – housekeeper's – niece – at – the – castle – and my name's Mabel Prowse.'

'That's exactly what I thought,' said Jimmy, without a shadow of truth, because how could he? The others

were silent. It was a moment full of agitation and
confused ideas.

'Well, any how,' said Gerald, 'you belong here.'

'Yes,' said the voice, and it came from the floor, as
though its owner had flung herself down in the madness of despair. 'Oh yes, I belong here right enough,
but what's the use of belonging anywhere if you're
invisible?'

3

Those of my readers who have gone about much with an invisible companion will not need to be told how awkward the whole business is. For one thing, however much you may have been convinced that your companion *is* invisible, you will, I feel sure, have found yourself every now and then saying, 'This must be a dream!' or 'I *know* I shall wake up in half a sec!' And this was the case with Gerald, Kathleen, and Jimmy as they sat in the white marble Temple of Flora, looking out through its arches at the sunshiny park and listening to the voice of the enchanted Princess, who really was not a Princess at all, but just the housekeeper's niece, Mabel Prowse; though, as Jimmy said, 'she was enchanted, right enough'.

'It's no use talking,' she said again and again, and the voice came from an empty-looking space between two pillars; 'I never believed anything would happen, and now it has.'

'Well,' said Gerald kindly, 'can we do anything for you? Because, if not, I think we ought to be going.'

'Yes,' said Jimmy; 'I *do* want my tea!'

'Tea!' said the unseen Mabel scornfully. 'Do you mean to say you'd go off to your teas and leave me after getting me into this mess?'

'Well, of all the unfair Princesses I ever met!' Gerald began. But Kathleen interrupted.

'Oh, don't rag her,' she said. 'Think how horrid it must be to be invisible!'

'I don't think,' said the hidden Mabel, 'that my aunt likes me very much as it is. She wouldn't let me go to the fair because I'd forgotten to put back some old trumpery shoe that Queen Elizabeth wore – I got it out from the glass case to try it on.'

'Did it fit?' asked Kathleen, with interest.

'Not it – much too small,' said Mabel. 'I don't believe it ever fitted anyone.'

'I do want my tea!' said Jimmy.

'I do really think perhaps we ought to go,' said Gerald. 'You see, it isn't as if we could do anything for you.'

'You'll have to tell your aunt,' said Kathleen kindly.

'No, no, no!' moaned Mabel invisibly; 'take me with you. I'll leave her a note to say I've run away to sea.'

'Girls don't run away to sea.'

'They might,' said the stone floor between the pillars, 'as stowaways, if nobody wanted a cabin boy – cabin girl, I mean.'

'I'm sure you oughtn't,' said Kathleen firmly.

'Well, what *am* I to do?'

'Really,' said Gerald, 'I don't know what the girl *can* do. Let her come home with us and have –'

'Tea – oh, yes,' said Jimmy, jumping up.

'And have a good council.'

'After tea,' said Jimmy.

'But her aunt'll find she's gone.'

'So she would if I stayed.'

'Oh, come on,' said Jimmy.

'But the aunt'll think something's happened to her.'

'So it has.'

'And she'll tell the police, and they'll look everywhere for me.'

'They'll never find you,' said Gerald. 'Talk of impenetrable disguises!'

'I'm sure,' said Mabel, 'aunt would much rather never see me again than see me like this. She'd never get over it; it might kill her – she has spasms as it is. I'll write to her, and we'll put it in the big letter-box at the gate as we go out. Has anyone got a bit of pencil and a scrap of paper?'

Gerald had a note-book, with leaves of the shiny kind which you have to write on, not with a blacklead pencil, but with an ivory thing with a point of real lead. And it won't write on any other paper except the kind that is in the book, and this is often very annoying when you are in a hurry. Then was seen the strange spectacle of a little ivory stick, with a leaden point, standing up at an odd, impossible-looking slant, and moving along all by itself as ordinary pencils do when you are writing with them.

'May we look over?' asked Kathleen.

There was no answer. The pencil went on writing.

'Mayn't we look over?' Kathleen said again.

'Of course you may!' said the voice near the paper. 'I nodded, didn't I? Oh, I forgot, my nodding's invisible too.'

The pencil was forming round, clear letters on the page torn out of the note-book. This is what it wrote: –

'DEAR AUNT, –

'I am afraid you will not see me again for some time. A lady in a motor-car has adopted me, and we are going straight to the coast and then in a ship. It is useless to try to follow me. Farewell, and may you be happy. I hope you enjoyed the fair.

'MABEL.'

'But that's all lies,' said Jimmy bluntly.

'No, it isn't; it's fancy,' said Mabel. 'If I said I've become invisible, she'd think that was a lie, anyhow.'

'Oh, *come* along,' said Jimmy; 'you can quarrel just as well walking.'

Gerald folded up the note as a lady in India had taught him to do years before, and Mabel led them by another and very much nearer way out of the park. And the walk home was a great deal shorter, too, than the walk out had been.

The sky had clouded over while they were in the Temple of Flora, and the first spots of rain fell as they got back to the house, very late indeed for tea.

Mademoiselle was looking out of the window, and came herself to open the door.

'But it is that you are in lateness, in lateness!' she cried. 'You have had a misfortune – no? All goes well?'

'We are very sorry indeed,' said Gerald. 'It took us longer to get home than we expected. I do hope you haven't been anxious. I have been thinking about you most of the way home.'

'Go, then,' said the French lady, smiling; 'you shall have them in the same time – the tea and the supper.'

Which they did.

'How *could* you say you were thinking about her all the time?' said a voice just by Gerald's ear, when Mademoiselle had left them alone with the bread and butter and milk and baked apples. 'It was just as much a lie as me being adopted by a motor lady.'

'No, it wasn't,' said Gerald, through bread and butter. 'I *was* thinking about whether she'd be in a wax or not. So there!'

There were only three plates, but Jimmy let Mabel have his, and shared with Kathleen. It was rather horrid to see the bread and butter waving about in the air, and bite after bite disappearing from it apparently by no human agency; and the spoon rising with apple in it and returning to the plate empty. Even the tip of the spoon disappeared as long as it was in Mabel's unseen mouth; so that at times it looked as though its bowl had been broken off.

Everyone was very hungry, and more bread and butter had to be fetched. Cook grumbled when the plate was filled for the third time.

'I tell you what,' said Jimmy; 'I did want my tea.'

'I tell *you* what,' said Gerald; 'it'll be jolly difficult to give Mabel any breakfast. Mademoiselle will be here then. She'd have a fit if she saw bits of forks with bacon on them vanishing, and then the forks coming back out of vanishment, and the bacon lost for ever.'

'We shall have to buy things to eat and feed our poor captive in secret,' said Kathleen.

'Our money won't last long,' said Jimmy, in gloom. 'Have *you* got any money?'

He turned to where a mug of milk was suspended in the air without visible means of support.

'I've not got much money,' was the reply from near the milk, 'but I've got heaps of ideas.'

'We must talk about everything in the morning,' said Kathleen. 'We must just say good night to Mademoiselle, and then you shall sleep in my bed, Mabel. I'll lend you one of my nightgowns.'

'I'll get my own tomorrow,' said Mabel cheerfully.

'You'll go back to get things?'

'Why not? Nobody can see me. I think I begin to see all sorts of amusing things coming along. It's not half bad being invisible.'

It was extremely odd, Kathleen thought, to see the Princess's clothes coming out of nothing. First the gauzy veil appeared hanging in the air. Then the sparkling coronet suddenly showed on the top of the chest of drawers. Then a sleeve of the pinky gown showed, then another, and then the whole gown lay on the floor in a glistening ring as the unseen legs of

Mabel stepped out of it. For each article of clothing became visible as Mabel took it off. The nightgown, lifted from the bed, disappeared a bit at a time.

'Get into bed,' said Kathleen, rather nervously.

The bed creaked and a hollow appeared in the pillow. Kathleen put out the gas and got into bed; all this magic had been rather upsetting, and she was just the least bit frightened, but in the dark she found it was not so bad. Mabel's arms went round her neck the moment she got into bed, and the two little girls kissed in the kind darkness, where the visible and the invisible could meet on equal terms.

'Good night,' said Mabel. 'You're a darling, Cathy; you've been most awfully good to me, and I shan't forget it. I didn't like to say so before the boys, because I know boys think you're a muff if you're grateful. But I *am*. Good night.'

Kathleen lay awake for some time. She was just getting sleepy when she remembered that the maid who would call them in the morning would see those wonderful Princess clothes.

'I'll have to get up and hide them,' she said. 'What a bother!'

And as she lay thinking what a bother it was she happened to fall asleep, and when she woke again it was bright morning, and Eliza was standing in front of the chair where Mabel's clothes lay, gazing at the pink Princess-frock that lay on the top of her heap and saying, 'Law!'

'Oh, don't touch, *please*!' Kathleen leaped out of bed as Eliza was reaching out her hand.

'Where on earth did you get hold of that?'

'We're going to use it for acting,' said Kathleen, on

the desperate inspiration of the moment. 'It's lent me for that.'

'You might show *me*, miss,' suggested Eliza.

'Oh, please not!' said Kathleen, standing in front of the chair in her nightgown. 'You shall see us act when we are dressed up. There! And you won't tell anyone, will you?'

'Not if you're a good little girl,' said Eliza. 'But you be sure to let me see when you *do* dress up. But where –'

Here a bell rang and Eliza had to go, for it was the postman, and she particularly wanted to see him.

'And now,' said Kathleen, pulling on her first stocking, 'we shall have to *do* the acting. Everything seems very difficult.'

'Acting isn't,' said Mabel; and an unsupported stocking waved in the air and quickly vanished. 'I shall love it.'

'You forget,' said Kathleen gently, 'invisible actresses can't take part in plays unless they're magic ones.'

'Oh,' cried a voice from under a petticoat that hung in the air, 'I've got *such* an idea!'

'Tell it us after breakfast,' said Kathleen, as the water in the basin began to splash about and to drip from nowhere back into itself. 'And oh! I do wish you hadn't written such whoppers to your aunt. I'm sure we oughtn't to tell lies for anything.'

'What's the use of telling the truth if nobody believes you?' came from among the splashes.

'I don't know,' said Kathleen, 'but I'm sure we ought to tell the truth.'

'*You* can, if you like,' said a voice from the folds of a

towel that waved lonely in front of the wash-hand stand.

'All right. We will, then, first thing after brek – *your* brek, I mean. You'll have to wait up here till we can collar something and bring it up to you. Mind you dodge Eliza when she comes to make the bed.'

The invisible Mabel found this a fairly amusing game; she further enlivened it by twitching out the corners of tucked-up sheets and blankets when Eliza wasn't looking.

'Drat the clothes!' said Eliza; 'anyone 'ud think the things was bewitched.'

She looked about for the wonderful Princess clothes she had glimpsed earlier in the morning. But Kathleen had hidden them in a perfectly safe place – under the mattress, which she knew Eliza never turned.

Eliza hastily brushed up from the floor those bits of fluff which come from goodness knows where in the best regulated houses. Mabel, very hungry and exasperated at the long absence of the others at their breakfast, could not forbear to whisper suddenly in Eliza's ear:

'Always sweep under the mats.'

The maid started and turned pale. 'I must be going silly,' she murmured; 'though it's just what mother always used to say. Hope I ain't going dotty, like Aunt Emily. Wonderful what you can fancy, ain't it?'

She took up the hearth-rug all the same, swept under it, and under the fender. So thorough was she, and so pale, that Kathleen, entering with a chunk of bread raided by Gerald from the pantry window, exclaimed:

'Not done yet. I say, Eliza, you do look ill! What's the matter?'

'I thought I'd give the room a good turn-out,' said Eliza, still very pale.

'Nothing's happened to upset you?' Kathleen asked. She had her own private fears.

'Nothing – only my fancy, miss,' said Eliza. 'I always was fanciful from a child – dreaming of the pearly gates and them little angels with nothing on only their heads and wings – so cheap to dress, I always think, compared with children.'

When she was got rid of, Mabel ate the bread and drank water from the tooth-mug.

'I'm afraid it tastes of cherry tooth-paste rather,' said Kathleen apologetically.

'It doesn't matter,' a voice replied from the tilted mug; 'it's more interesting than water. I should think red wine in ballads was rather like this.'

'We've got leave for the day again,' said Kathleen, when the last bit of bread had vanished, 'and Gerald feels like I do about lies. So we're going to tell your aunt where you really are.'

'She won't believe you.'

'That doesn't matter, if we speak the truth,' said Kathleen primly.

'I expect you'll be sorry for it,' said Mabel; 'but come on – and, I say, do be careful not to shut me in the door as you go out. You nearly did just now.'

In the blazing sunlight that flooded the High Street four shadows to three children seemed dangerously noticeable. A butcher's boy looked far too earnestly at the extra shadow, and his big, liver-coloured lurcher snuffed at the legs of that shadow's mistress and whined uncomfortably.

'Get behind me,' said Kathleen; 'then our two shadows will look like one.'

But Mabel's shadow, very visible, fell on Kathleen's back, and the ostler of the Davenant Arms looked up to see what big bird had cast that big shadow.

A woman driving a cart with chickens and ducks in it called out:

'Halloa, missy, ain't you blacked yer back, neither! What you been leaning up against?'

Everyone was glad when they got out of the town.

Speaking the truth to Mabel's aunt did not turn out at all as anyone – even Mabel – expected. The aunt was discovered reading a pink novelette at the window of the housekeeper's room, which, framed in clematis and green creepers, looked out on a nice little courtyard to which Mabel led the party.

'Excuse me,' said Gerald, 'but I believe you've lost your niece?'

'Not lost, my boy,' said the aunt, who was spare and tall, with a drab fringe and a very genteel voice.

'We could tell you something about her,' said Gerald.

'Now,' replied the aunt, in a warning voice, 'no complaints, please. My niece has gone, and I am sure no one thinks less than I do of her little pranks. If she's played any tricks on you it's only her light-hearted way. Go away, children, I'm busy.'

'Did you get her note?' asked Kathleen.

The aunt showed rather more interest than before, but she still kept her finger in the novelette.

'Oh,' she said, 'so you witnessed her departure? Did she seem glad to go?'

'Quite,' said Gerald truthfully.

'Then I can only be glad that she is provided for,' said the aunt. 'I dare say you were surprised. These romantic adventures do occur in our family. Lord Yalding selected me out of eleven applicants for the post of housekeeper here. I've not the slightest doubt the child was changed at birth and her rich relatives have claimed her.'

'But aren't you going to do anything – tell the police, or –'

'Shish!' said Mabel.

'*I* won't shish,' said Jimmy. 'Your Mabel's invisible – that's all it is. She's just beside me now.'

'I detest untruthfulness,' said the aunt severely, 'in all its forms. Will you kindly take that little boy away? I am quite satisfied about Mabel.'

'*Well*,' said Gerald, 'you *are* an aunt and no mistake! But what will Mabel's father and mother say?'

'Mabel's father and mother are dead,' said the aunt calmly, and a little sob sounded close to Gerald's ear.

'All right,' he said, 'we'll be off. But don't you go saying we didn't tell you the truth, that's all.'

'You have told me nothing,' said the aunt, 'none of you, except that little boy, who has told me a silly falsehood.'

'We meant well,' said Gerald gently. 'You don't mind our having come through the grounds, do you? We're very careful not to touch anything.'

'No visitors are allowed,' said the aunt, glancing down at her novel rather impatiently.

'Ah! but you wouldn't count *us* visitors,' said Gerald in his best manner. 'We're friends of Mabel's. Our father's Colonel of the — th.'

'Indeed!' said the aunt.

'And our aunt's Lady Sandling, so you can be sure we wouldn't hurt anything on the estate.'

'I'm sure you wouldn't hurt a fly,' said the aunt absently. 'Good-bye. Be good children.'

'And on this they got away quickly.

'Why,' said Gerald, when they were outside the little court, 'your aunt's as mad as a hatter. Fancy not caring what becomes of you, and fancy believing that rot about the motor lady!'

'I knew she'd believe it when I wrote it,' said Mabel modestly. 'She's not mad, only she's always reading novelettes. *I* read the books in the big library. Oh, it's such a jolly room – such a queer smell, like boots, and old leather books sort of powdery at the edges. I'll take you there some day. Now your consciences are all right about my aunt, I'll tell you my great idea. Let's get down to the Temple of Flora. I'm glad you got aunt's permission for the grounds. It would be so awkward for you to have to be always dodging behind bushes when one of the gardeners came along.'

'Yes,' said Gerald modestly, 'I thought of that.'

The day was as bright as yesterday had been, and from the white marble temple the Italian-looking landscape looked more than ever like a steel engraving coloured by hand, or an oleographic imitation of one of Turner's pictures.

When the three children were comfortably settled on the steps that led up to the white statue, the voice of the fourth child said sadly: 'I'm not ungrateful, but I'm rather hungry. And you can't be always taking things for me through your larder window. If you like, I'll go back and live in the castle. It's supposed to be haunted. I suppose I could haunt it as well as anyone else. I am a sort of ghost now, you know. I will if you like.'

'Oh no,' said Kathleen kindly; 'you must stay with us.'

'But about food. I'm not ungrateful, really I'm not, but breakfast is breakfast, and bread's only bread.'

'If you could get the ring off, you could go back.'

'Yes,' said Mabel's voice, 'but you see, I can't. I tried again last night in bed, and again this morning. And it's like stealing, taking things out of your larder – even if it's only bread.'

'Yes, it is,' said Gerald, who had carried out this bold enterprise.

'Well, now, what we must do is to earn some money.'

Jimmy remarked that this was all very well. But Gerald and Kathleen listened attentively.

'What I mean to say,' the voice went on, 'I'm really sure is all for the best, me being invisible. We shall have adventures – you see if we don't.'

' "Adventures," said the bold buccaneer, "are not always profitable." ' It was Gerald who murmured this.

'This one will be, anyhow, you see. Only you mustn't all go. Look here, if Jerry could make himself look common –'

'That ought to be easy,' said Jimmy. And Kathleen told him not to be so jolly disagreeable.

'I'm not,' said Jimmy, 'only –'

'Only he has an inside feeling that this Mabel of yours is going to get us into trouble,' put in Gerald. 'Like La Belle Dame Sans Merci, and he does not want to be found in future ages alone and palely loitering in the middle of sedge and things.'

'I won't get you into trouble, indeed I won't,' said the voice. 'Why, we're a band of brothers for life, after the way you stood by me yesterday. What I mean is – Gerald can go to the fair and do conjuring.'

'He doesn't know any,' said Kathleen.

'*I* should do it really,' said Mabel, 'but Jerry could look like doing it. Move things without touching them and all that. But it wouldn't do for all three of you to go. The more there are of children the younger they look, I think, and the more people wonder what they're doing all alone by themselves.'

'The accomplished conjurer deemed these the words of wisdom,' said Gerald; and answered the dismal 'Well, but what about us?' of his brother and sister by suggesting that they should mingle unsuspected with the crowd. 'But don't let on that you know me,' he said; 'and try to look as if you belonged to some of the grown-ups at the fair. If you don't, as likely as not you'll have the kind policemen taking the little lost children by the hand and leading them home to their stricken relations – French governess, I mean.'

'Let's go *now*,' said the voice that they never could get quite used to hearing, coming out of different parts of the air as Mabel moved from one place to another. So they went.

The fair was held on a waste bit of land, about half a mile from the castle gates. When they got near enough to hear the steam-organ of the merry-go-round, Gerald suggested that as he had ninepence he should go ahead and get something to eat, the amount spent to be paid back out of any money they might make by conjuring. The others waited in the shadows of a deep-banked lane, and he came back, quite soon, though long after they had begun to say what a long time he had been gone. He brought some Barcelona nuts, red-streaked apples, small sweet yellow pears, pale pasty ginger-bread, a whole quarter of a pound of peppermint bullseyes, and two bottles of ginger-beer.

'It's what they call an investment,' he said, when Kathleen said something about extravagance. 'We shall

all need special nourishing to keep our strength up, especially the bold conjurer.'

They ate and drank. It was a very beautiful meal, and the far-off music of the steam-organ added the last touch of festivity to the scene. The boys were never tired of seeing Mabel eat, or rather of seeing the strange, magic-looking vanishment of food which was all that showed of Mabel's eating. They were entranced by the spectacle, and pressed on her more than her just share of the feast, just for the pleasure of seeing it disappear.

'My aunt!' said Gerald, again and again; 'that ought to knock 'em!'

It did.

Jimmy and Kathleen had the start of the others, and when they got to the fair they mingled with the crowd, and were as unsuspected as possible.

They stood near a large lady who was watching the coconut shies, and presently saw a strange figure with its hands in its pockets strolling across the trampled yellowy grass among the bits of drifting paper and the sticks and straws that always litter the ground of an English fair. It was Gerald, but at first they hardly knew him. He had taken off his tie, and round his head, arranged like a turban, was the crimson school-scarf that had supported his white flannels. The tie, one supposed, had taken on the duties of the handkerchief. And his face and hands were a bright black, like very nicely polished stoves!

Everyone turned to look at him.

'He's just like a conjurer!' whispered Jimmy. 'I don't suppose it'll ever come off, do you?'

They followed him at a distance, and when he went

close to the door of a small tent, against whose door-post a long-faced melancholy woman was lounging, they stopped and tried to look as though they belonged to a farmer who strove to send up a number by banging with a big mallet on a wooden block.

Gerald went up to the woman.

'Taken much?' he asked, and was told, but not harshly, to go away with his impudence.

'I'm in business myself,' said Gerald, 'I'm a con-jurer, from India.'

'Not you!' said the woman; 'you ain't no conjurer. Why, the backs of yer ears is all white.'

'Are they?' said Gerald. 'How clever of you to see that!' He rubbed them with his hands. 'That better?'

'That's all right. What's your little game?'

'Conjuring, really and truly,' said Gerald. 'There's smaller boys than me put on to it in India. Look here, I owe you one for telling me about my ears. If you like to run the show for me I'll go shares. Let me have your tent to perform in, and you do the patter at the door.'

'Lor' love you! I can't do no patter. And you're getting at me. Let's see you do a bit of conjuring, since you're so clever an' all.'

'Right you are,' said Gerald firmly. 'You see this apple? Well, I'll make it move slowly through the air, and then when I say "Go!" it'll vanish.'

'Yes – into your mouth! Get away with your non-sense.'

'You're too clever to be so unbelieving,' said Gerald. 'Look here!'

He held out one of the little apples, and the woman saw it move slowly and unsupported along the air.

'Now – *go!*' cried Gerald, to the apple, and it went. 'How's that?' he asked, in tones of triumph.

The woman was glowing with excitement, and her eyes shone. 'The best I ever see!' she whispered. 'I'm on, mate, if you know any more tricks like that.'

'Heaps,' said Gerald confidently; 'hold out your hand.' The woman held it out; and from nowhere, as it seemed, the apple appeared and was laid on her hand. The apple was rather damp.

She looked at it a moment, and then whispered:

'Come on! there's to be no one in it but just us two. But not in the tent. You take a pitch here, 'longside the tent. It's worth twice the money in the open air.'

'But people won't pay if they can see it all for nothing.'

'Not for the first turn, but they will after – you see. And you'll have to do the patter.'

'Will you lend me your shawl?' Gerald asked. She unpinned it – it was a red and black plaid – and he spread it on the ground as he had seen Indian conjurers do, and seated himself cross-legged behind it.

'I mustn't have anyone behind me, that's all,' he said; and the woman hastily screened off a little enclosure for him by hanging old sacks to two of the guy-ropes of the tent. 'Now I'm ready,' he said. The woman got a drum from the inside of the tent and beat it. Quite soon a little crowd had collected.

'Ladies and gentlemen,' said Gerald, 'I come from India, and I can do a conjuring entertainment the like of which you've never seen. When I see two shillings on the shawl I'll begin.'

'I dare say you will!' said a bystander; and there were several short, disagreeable laughs.

'Of course,' said Gerald, 'if you can't afford two shillings between you' – there were about thirty people in the crowd by now – 'I say no more.'

Two or three pennies fell on the shawl, then a few more then the fall of copper ceased.

'Ninepence,' said Gerald. 'Well, I've got a generous nature. You'll get such a ninepennyworth as you've never had before. I don't wish to deceive you – I have an accomplice, but my accomplice is invisible.'

The crowd snorted.

'By the aid of that accomplice,' Gerald went on, 'I will read any letter that any of you may have in your pocket. If one of you will just step over the rope and stand beside me, my invisible accomplice will read that letter over his shoulder.'

A man stepped forward, a ruddy-faced, horsy-looking person. He pulled a letter from his pocket and stood plain in the sight of all, in a place where everyone saw that no one could see over his shoulder.

'Now!' said Gerald. There was a moment's pause. Then from quite the other side of the enclosure came a faint, faraway, sing-song voice. It said:

'"Sir, – Yours of the fifteenth duly to hand. With regard to the mortgage on your land, we regret our inability —"'

'Stow it!' cried the man, turning threateningly on Gerald.

He stepped out of the enclosure explaining that there was nothing of that sort in his letter; but nobody believed him, and a buzz of interested chatter began in the crowd, ceasing abruptly when Gerald began to speak.

'Now,' said he, laying the nine pennies down on the shawl, 'you keep your eyes on those pennies, and one by one you'll see them disappear.'

And of course they did. Then one by one they were laid down again by the invisible hand of Mabel. The crowd clapped loudly. 'Bravo!' 'That's something like!' 'Show us another!' cried the people in the front rank. And those behind pushed forward.

'Now,' said Gerald, 'you've seen what I can do, but I don't do any more till I see five shillings on this carpet.'

And in two minutes seven-and-threepence lay there and Gerald did a little more conjuring.

When the people in front didn't want to give any more money, Gerald asked them to stand back and let the others have a look in. I wish I had time to tell you of all the tricks he did – the grass round his enclosure was absolutely trampled off by the feet of the people who thronged to look at him. There is really hardly any limit to the wonders you can do if you have an invisible accomplice. All sorts of things were made to move about, apparently by themselves, and even to vanish – into the folds of Mabel's clothing. The woman stood by, looking more and more pleasant as she saw the money come tumbling in, and beating her shabby drum every time Gerald stopped conjuring.

The news of the conjurer had spread all over the fair. The crowd was frantic with admiration. The man who ran the coconut shies begged Gerald to throw in his lot with him; the owner of the rifle gallery offered him free board and lodging and go shares; and a brisk, broad lady, in stiff black silk and a violet bonnet, tried to engage him for the forthcoming Bazaar for Reformed Bandsmen.

And all this time the others mingled with the crowd – quite unobserved, for who could have eyes for anyone but Gerald? It was getting quite late, long past tea-time, and Gerald, who was getting very tired indeed, and was quite satisfied with his share of the money, was racking his brains for a way to get out of it.

'How are we to hook it?' he murmured, as Mabel made his cap disappear from his head by the simple process of taking it off and putting it in her pocket. 'They'll never let us get away. I didn't think of that before.'

'Let me think!' whispered Mabel; and next moment she said, close to his ear: 'Divide the money, and give her something for the shawl. Put the money on it and say . . .' She told him what to say.

Gerald's pitch was in the shade of the tent; otherwise, of course, everyone would have seen the shadow of the invisible Mabel as she moved about making things vanish.

Gerald told the woman to divide the money, which she did honestly enough.

'Now,' he said, while the impatient crowd pressed closer and closer, 'I'll give you five bob for your shawl.'

'Seven-and-six,' said the woman mechanically.

'Righto!' said Gerald, putting his heavy share of the money in his trouser pocket.

'This shawl will now disappear,' he said, picking it up. He handed it to Mabel, who put it on; and, of course, it disappeared. A roar of applause went up from the audience.

'Now,' he said, 'I come to the last trick of all. I shall take three steps backwards and vanish.' He took three steps backwards, Mabel wrapped the invisible shawl round him, and – he did not vanish. The shawl, being invisible, did not conceal him in the least.

'Yah!' cried a boy's voice in the crowd. 'Look at 'im! 'E knows 'e can't do it.'

'I wish I could put you in my pocket,' said Mabel. The crowd was crowding closer. At any moment they might touch Mabel, and then anything might happen – simply anything. Gerald took hold of his hair with both hands, as his way was when he was anxious or discouraged. Mabel, in invisibility, wrung her hands, as people are said to do in books; that is, she clasped them and squeezed very tight.

'Oh!' she whispered suddenly, 'it's loose. I can get it off.'

'Not –'

'Yes – the ring.'

'Come on, young master. Give us summat for our money,' a farm labourer shouted.

'I will,' said Gerald. 'This time I really will vanish. Slip round into the tent,' he whispered to Mabel.

'Push the ring under the canvas. Then slip out at the back and join the others. When I see you with them I'll disappear. Go slow, and I'll catch you up.'

'It's me,' said a pale and obvious Mabel in the ear of Kathleen. 'He's got the ring; come on, before the crowd begins to scatter.'

As they went out of the gate they heard a roar of surprise and annoyance rise from the crowd, and knew that this time Gerald really *had* disappeared.

They had gone a mile before they heard footsteps on the road, and looked back. No one was to be seen.

Next moment Gerald's voice spoke out of clear, empty-looking space.

'Halloa!' it said gloomily.

'How horrid!' cried Mabel; 'you did make me jump! Take the ring off; it makes me feel quite creepy, you being nothing but a voice.'

'So did you us,' said Jimmy.

'Don't take it off yet,' said Kathleen, who was really rather thoughtful for her age, 'because you're still blackleaded, I suppose, and you might be recognized, and eloped with by gipsies, so that you should go on doing conjuring for ever and ever.'

'I should take it off,' said Jimmy; 'it's no use going about invisible, and people seeing us with Mabel and saying we've eloped with her.'

'Yes,' said Mabel impatiently, 'that would be simply silly. And, besides, I want my ring.'

'It's not yours any more than ours, anyhow,' said Jimmy.

'Yes, it is,' said Mabel.

'Oh, stow it!' said the weary voice of Gerald beside her. 'What's the use of jawing?'

'I want the ring,' said Mabel, rather mulishly.

'Want' – the words came out of the still evening air – 'want must be your master. You can't have the ring. *I can't get it off!*'

4

The difficulty was not only that Gerald had got the ring on and couldn't get it off, and was therefore invisible, but that Mabel, who had been invisible and therefore possible to be smuggled into the house, was now plain to be seen and impossible for smuggling purposes.

The children would have not only to account for the apparent absence of one of themselves, but for the obvious presence of a perfect stranger.

'I can't go back to aunt. I can't and I won't,' said Mabel firmly, 'not if I was visible twenty times over.'

'She'd smell a rat if you did,' Gerald owned – 'about the motor-car, I mean, and the adopting lady. And what we're to say to Mademoiselle about you –!' He tugged at the ring.

'Suppose you told the truth,' said Mabel meaningly.

'She wouldn't believe it,' said Cathy; 'or, if she did, she'd go stark, staring, raving mad.'

'No,' said Gerald's voice, 'we daren't *tell* her. But she's really rather decent. Let's ask her to let you stay the night because it's too late for you to get home.'

'That's all right,' said Jimmy, 'but what about you?'

'I shall go to bed,' said Gerald, 'with a bad headache. Oh, *that's* not a lie! I've got one right enough. It's the sun, I think. I know blacklead attracts the concentration of the sun.'

'More likely the pears and the gingerbread,' said Jimmy unkindly. 'Well, let's get along. I wish it was me was invisible. I'd do something different from going to bed with a silly headache, I know that.'

'What would you do?' asked the voice of Gerald just behind him.

'Do keep in one place, you silly cuckoo!' said Jimmy. 'You make me feel all jumpy.' He had indeed jumped rather violently. 'Here, walk between Cathy and me.'

'What *would* you do?' repeated Gerald, from that apparently unoccupied position.

'I'd be a burglar,' said Jimmy.

Cathy and Mabel in one breath reminded him how wrong burgling was, and Jimmy replied:

'Well, then – a detective.'

'There's got to be something to detect before you can begin detectiving,' said Mabel.

'Detectives don't always detect things,' said Jimmy, very truly. 'If I couldn't be any other kind I'd be a baffled detective. You could be one all right, and have no end of larks just the same. Why don't you do it?'

'It's exactly what I *am* going to do,' said Gerald. 'We'll go round by the police-station and see what they've got in the way of crimes.'

They did, and read the notices on the board outside. Two dogs had been lost, a purse, and a portfolio of papers 'of no value to any but the owner'. Also Houghton Grange had been broken into and a quantity of silver plate stolen. 'Twenty pounds reward offered for any information that may lead to the recovery of the missing property.'

'That burglary's my lay,' said Gerald; 'I'll detect that. Here comes Johnson,' he added; 'he's going off duty. Ask him about it. The fell detective, being invisible, was unable to pump the constable, but the young brother of our hero made the inquiries in quite a creditable manner. Be creditable, Jimmy.'

Jimmy hailed the constable.

'Halloa, Johnson!' he said.

And Johnson replied: 'Halloa, young shaver!'

'Shaver yourself!' said Jimmy, but without malice.

'What are you doing this time of night?' the constable asked jocosely. 'All the dicky birds is gone to their little nesteses.'

'We've been to the fair,' said Kathleen. 'There was a conjurer there. I wish you could have seen him.'

'Heard about him,' said Johnson; 'all fake, you know. The quickness of the 'and deceives the hi.'

Such is fame. Gerald, standing in the shadow, jingled the loose money in his pocket to console himself.

'What's that?' the policeman asked quickly.

'Our money jingling,' said Jimmy, with perfect truth.

'It's well to be some people,' Johnson remarked; 'wish I'd got my pockets full to jingle with.'

'Well, why haven't you?' asked Mabel. 'Why don't you get that twenty pounds reward?'

'I'll tell you why I don't. Because in this 'ere realm of liberty, and Britannia ruling the waves, you ain't allowed to arrest a chap on suspicion, even if you know puffickly well who done the job.'

'What a shame!' said Jimmy warmly. 'And who *do* you think did it?'

'I don't think – I know.' Johnson's voice was ponderous as his boots. 'It's a man what's known to the police on account of a heap o' crimes he's done, but we never can't bring it 'ome to 'im, nor yet get sufficient evidence to convict.'

'Well,' said Jimmy, 'when I've left school I'll come to you and be apprenticed, and be a detective. Just now I think we'd better get home and detect our supper. Good night!'

They watched the policeman's broad form disappear through the swing door of the police-station; and as it settled itself into quiet again the voice of Gerald was heard complaining bitterly.

'You've no more brains than a halfpenny bun,' he said; 'no details about how and when the silver was taken.'

'But he told us he knew,' Jimmy urged.

'Yes, that's all you've got out of him. A silly policeman's silly idea. Go home and detect your precious supper! It's all you're fit for.'

'What'll you do about supper?' Mabel asked.

'Buns!' said Gerald, 'halfpenny buns. They'll make me think of my dear little brother and sister. Perhaps you've got enough sense to buy buns? I can't go into a shop in this state.'

'Don't you be so disagreeable,' said Mabel with spirit. 'We did our best. If I were Cathy you should whistle for your nasty buns.'

'If you were Cathy the gallant young detective would have left home long ago. Better the cabin of a tramp steamer than the best family mansion that's got a brawling sister in it,' said Gerald. 'You're a bit of an outsider at present, my gentle maiden. Jimmy and Cathy know well enough when their bold leader is chaffing and when he isn't.'

'Not when we can't see your face we don't,' said Cathy, in tones of relief. 'I really thought you were in a flaring wax, and so did Jimmy, didn't you?'

'Oh, rot!' said Gerald. 'Come on! This way to the bun shop.'

They went. And it was while Cathy and Jimmy were in the shop and the others were gazing through the glass at the jam tarts and Swiss rolls and Victoria sandwiches and Bath buns under the spread yellow muslin in the window, that Gerald discoursed in Mabel's ear of the plans and hopes of one entering on a detective career.

'I shall keep my eyes open tonight, I can tell you,' he began. 'I shall keep my eyes skinned, and no jolly error. The invisible detective may not only find out about the purse and the silver, but detect some crime that isn't even done yet. And I shall hang about until I see some suspicious-looking characters leave the town, and follow them furtively and catch them red-handed, with their hands full of priceless jewels, and hand them over.'

'Oh!' cried Mabel, so sharply and suddenly that Gerald was roused from his dream to express sympathy.

'Pain?' he said quite kindly. 'It's the apples – they were rather hard.'

'Oh, it's not that,' said Mabel very earnestly. 'Oh, how awful! I never thought of that before.'

'Never thought of *what*?' Gerald asked impatiently.

'The window.'

'What window?'

'The panelled-room window. At home, you know – at the castle. That settles it – I *must* go home. We left it open and the shutters as well, and all the jewels and things there. Auntie'll never go in; she never does. That settles it; I *must* go home – now – this minute.'

Here the others issued from the shop, bun-bearing, and the situation was hastily explained to them.

'So you see I must go,' Mabel ended.

And Kathleen agreed that she must.

But Jimmy said he didn't see what good it would do. 'Because the key's inside the door, anyhow.'

'She *will* be cross,' said Mabel sadly. 'She'll have to get the gardeners to get a ladder and –'

'Hooray!' said Gerald. 'Here's me! Nobler and more secret than gardeners or ladders was the invisible Jerry. I'll climb in at the window – it's all ivy, I know I could – and shut the window and the shutters all sereno, put the key back on the nail, and slip out unperceived the back way, threading my way through the maze of unconscious retainers. There'll be plenty of time. I don't suppose burglars begin their fell work until the night is far advanced.'

'Won't you be afraid?' Mabel asked. 'Will it be safe – suppose you were caught?'

'As houses. I can't be,' Gerald answered, and wondered that the question came from Mabel and not from Kathleen, who was usually inclined to fuss a little annoyingly about the danger and folly of adventures.

But all Kathleen said was, 'Well, good-bye; we'll come and see you tomorrow, Mabel. The floral temple at half-past ten. I hope you won't get into an awful row about the motor-car lady.'

'Let's detect our supper now,' said Jimmy.

'All right,' said Gerald a little bitterly. It is hard to enter on an adventure like this and to find the sympathetic interest of years suddenly cut off at the meter, as it were. Gerald felt that he ought, at a time like this, to have been the centre of interest. And he wasn't. They could actually talk about supper. Well, let them. He didn't care! He spoke with sharp sternness: 'Leave the pantry window undone for me to get in by when I've done my detecting. Come on, Mabel.' He caught her hand. 'Bags I the buns, though,' he added, by a happy afterthought, and snatching the bag, pressed it on Mabel, and the sound of four boots echoed on the pavement of the High Street as the outlines of the running Mabel grew small with distance.

Mademoiselle was in the drawing-room. She was sitting by the window in the waning light reading letters.

'Ah, *vous voici*!' she said unintelligibly. 'You are again late; and my little Gerald, where is he?'

This was an awful moment. Jimmy's detective scheme had not included any answer to this inevitable question. The silence was unbroken till Jimmy spoke.

'He *said* he was going to bed because he had a headache.' And this, of course, was true.

'This poor Gerald!' said Mademoiselle. 'Is it that I should mount him some supper?'

'He never eats anything when he's got one of his headaches,' Kathleen said. And this also was the truth.

Jimmy and Kathleen went to bed, wholly untroubled by anxiety about their brother, and Mademoiselle pulled out the bundle of letters and read them amid the ruins of the simple supper.

'It is ripping being out late like this,' said Gerald through the soft summer dusk.

'Yes,' said Mabel, a solitary-looking figure plodding along the high-road. 'I do hope auntie won't be *very* furious.'

'Have another bun,' suggested Gerald kindly, and a sociable munching followed.

It was the aunt herself who opened to a very pale and trembling Mabel the door which is appointed for the entrances and exits of the domestic staff at Yalding Towers. She looked over Mabel's head first, as if she expected to see someone taller. Then a very small voice said:

'Aunt!'

The aunt started back, then made a step towards Mabel.

'You naughty, naughty girl!' she cried angrily; 'how could you give me such a fright? I've a good mind to keep you in bed for a week for this, miss. Oh, Mabel, thank Heaven you're safe!' And with that the aunt's arms went round Mabel and Mabel's round the aunt in such a hug as they had never met in before.

'But you didn't seem to care a bit this morning,' said Mabel, when she had realized that her aunt really had been anxious, really was glad to have her safe home again.

'How do you know?'

'I was there listening. Don't be angry, auntie.'

'I feel as if I could never be angry with you again, now I've got you safe,' said the aunt surprisingly.

'But how was it?' Mabel asked.

'My dear,' said the aunt impressively, 'I've been in a sort of trance. I think I must be going to be ill. I've always been fond of you, but I didn't want to spoil you. But yesterday, about half-past three, I was talking about you to Mr Lewson, at the fair, and quite suddenly I felt as if you didn't matter at all. And I felt the same when I got your letter and when those children came. And today in the middle of tea I suddenly woke up and realized that you were gone. It was awful. I think I must be going to be ill. Oh, Mabel, why did you do it?'

'It was – a joke,' said Mabel feebly. And then the two went in and the door was shut.

'That's most uncommon odd,' said Gerald, outside; 'looks like more magic to me. I don't feel as if we'd got to the bottom of this yet, by any manner of means. There's more about this castle than meets the eye.'

There certainly was. For this castle happened to be – but it would not be fair to Gerald to tell you more about it than he knew on that night when he went alone and invisible through the shadowy great grounds of it to look for the open window of the panelled room. He knew that night no more than I have told you; but as he went along the dewy lawns and through the groups of shrubs and trees, where pools lay like giant looking-glasses reflecting the quiet stars, and the white limbs of statues gleamed against a background of shadow, he began to feel – well, not excited, not surprised, not anxious, but – different.

The incident of the invisible Princess had surprised, the incident of the conjuring had excited, and the sudden decision to be a detective had brought its own anxieties; but all these happenings, though wonderful and unusual, had seemed to be, after all, inside the circle of possible things – wonderful as the chemical experiments are where two liquids poured together make fire, surprising as legerdemain, thrilling as a juggler's display, but nothing more. Only now a new feeling came to him as he walked through those gardens; by day those gardens were like dreams, at night they were like visions. He could not see his feet as he walked, but he saw the movement of the dewy grass-blades that his feet displaced. And he had that extra-ordinary feeling so difficult to describe, and yet so real and so unforgettable – the feeling that he was in another world, that had covered up and hidden the old world as a carpet covers a floor. The floor was there all right, underneath, but what he walked on was the carpet that covered it – and that carpet was drenched in magic, as the turf was drenched in dew.

The feeling was very wonderful; perhaps you will feel it some day. There are still some places in the world where it can be felt, but they grow fewer every year.

The enchantment of the garden held him.

'I'll not go in yet,' he told himself; 'it's too early. And perhaps I shall never be here at night again. I suppose it *is* the night that makes everything look so different.'

Something white moved under a weeping willow; white hands parted the long, rustling leaves. A white figure came out, a creature with horns and goat's legs and the head and arms of a boy. And Gerald was not afraid. That was the most wonderful thing of all, though he would never have owned it. The white thing stretched its limbs, rolled on the grass, righted itself and frisked away across the lawn. Still something white gleamed under the willow; three steps nearer and Gerald saw that it was the pedestal of a statue – empty.

'They come alive,' he said; and another white shape came out of the Temple of Flora and disappeared in the laurels. 'The statues come alive.'

There was a crunching of the little stones in the gravel of the drive. Something enormously long and darkly grey came crawling towards him, slowly, heavily. The moon came out just in time to show its shape. It was one of those great lizards that you see at the Crystal Palace, made in stone, of the same awful size which they were millions of years ago when they were masters of the world, before Man was.

'It can't see me,' said Gerald. 'I am not afraid. *It's* come to life, too.'

As it writhed past him he reached out a hand and touched the side of its gigantic tail. It was of stone. It had not 'come alive', as he had fancied, but *was* alive in its stone. It turned, however, at the touch; but

Gerald also had turned, and was running with all his speed towards the house. Because at that stony touch Fear had come into the garden and almost caught him. It was Fear that he ran from, and not the moving stone beast.

He stood panting under the fifth window; when he had climbed to the window-ledge by the twisted ivy that clung to the wall, he looked back over the grey slope – there was a splashing at the fish-pool that had mirrored the stars – the shape of the great stone beast was wallowing in the shallows among the lily-pads.

Once inside the room, Gerald turned for another look. The fish-pond lay still and dark, reflecting the moon. Through a gap in the drooping willow the moonlight fell on a statue that stood calm and motionless on its pedestal. Everything was in its place now in the garden. Nothing moved or stirred.

'How extraordinarily rum!' said Gerald. 'I shouldn't have thought you *could* go to sleep walking through a garden and dream – like that.'

He shut the window, lit a match, and closed the shutters. Another match showed him the door. He turned the key, went out, locked the door again, hung the key on its usual nail, and crept to the end of the passage. Here he waited, safe in his invisibility, till the dazzle of the matches should have gone from his eyes, and he be once more able to find his way by the moonlight that fell in bright patches on the floor through the barred, unshuttered windows of the hall.

'Wonder where the kitchen is,' said Gerald. He had quite forgotten that he was a detective. He was only anxious to get home and tell the others about that extraordinarily odd dream that he had had in the

gardens. 'I suppose it doesn't matter *what* doors I open. I'm invisible all right still, I suppose? Yes; can't see my hand before my face.' He held up a hand for the purpose. 'Here goes!'

He opened many doors, wandered into long rooms with furniture dressed in brown holland covers that looked white in that strange light, rooms with chandeliers hanging in big bags from the high ceilings, rooms whose walls were alive with pictures, rooms whose walls were deadened with rows on rows of old books, state bedrooms in whose great plumed four-posters Queen Elizabeth had no doubt slept. (That Queen, by the way, must have been very little at home, for she seems to have slept in every old house in England.) But he could not find the kitchen. At last a door opened on stone steps that went up – there was a narrow stone passage – steps that went down – a door with a light under it. It was, somehow, difficult to put out one's hand to that door and open it.

'Nonsense!' Gerald told himself, 'don't be an ass! Are you invisible, or aren't you?'

Then he opened the door, and someone inside said something in a sudden rough growl.

Gerald stood back, flattened against the wall, as a man sprang to the doorway and flashed a lantern into the passage.

'All right,' said the man, with almost a sob of relief. 'It was only the door swung open, it's that heavy – that's all.'

'Blow the door!' said another growling voice; 'blessed if I didn't think it was a fair cop that time.'

They closed the door again. Gerald did not mind. In fact, he rather preferred that it should be so. He didn't like the look of those men. There was an air of threat about them. In their presence even invisibility seemed too thin a disguise. And Gerald had seen as much as he wanted to see. He had seen that he had been right about the gang. By wonderful luck – beginner's luck, a card-player would have told him – he had discovered a burglary on the very first night of his detective career. The men were taking silver out of two great chests, wrapping it in rags, and packing it in baize sacks. The door of the room was of iron six inches thick. It was, in fact, the strong-room, and these men had picked the lock. The tools they had done it with lay on the floor, on a neat cloth roll, such as wood-carvers keep their chisels in.

'Hurry up!' Gerald heard. 'You needn't take all night over it.'

The silver rattled slightly. 'You're a rattling of them trays like bloomin' castanets,' said the gruffest voice. Gerald turned and went away, very carefully and very quickly. And it is a most curious thing that, though he couldn't find the way to the servants' wing when he had nothing else to think of, yet now, with his mind full, so to speak, of silver forks and silver cups, and the question of who might be coming after him down those twisting passages, he went straight as an arrow to the door that led from the hall to the place he wanted to get to.

As he went the happenings took words in his mind.

'The fortunate detective,' he told himself, 'having succeeded beyond his wildest dreams, himself left the spot in search of assistance.'

But what assistance? There were, no doubt, men in the house, also the aunt; but he could not warn them.

He was too hopelessly invisible to carry any weight
with strangers. The assistance of Mabel would not be
of much value. The police? Before they could be got –
and the getting of them presented difficulties – the
burglars would have cleared away with their sacks of
silver.

Gerald stopped and thought hard; he held his head
with both hands to do it. You know the way – the
same as you sometimes do for simple equations or the
dates of the battles of the Civil War.

Then with pencil, note-book, a window-ledge, and

all the cleverness he could find at the moment, he wrote:

'You know the room where the silver is. Burglars are burgling it, the thick door is picked. Send a man for police. I will follow the burglars if they get away ere police arrive on the spot.'

He hesitated a moment, and ended –

'From a Friend – this is not a sell.'

This letter, tied tightly round a stone by means of a shoelace, thundered through the window of the room where Mabel and her aunt, in the ardour of reunion, were enjoying a supper of unusual charm – stewed plums, cream, spongecakes, custard in cups, and cold bread-and-butter pudding.

Gerald, in hungry invisibility, looked wistfully at the supper before he threw the stone. He waited till the shrieks had died away, saw the stone picked up, the warning letter read.

'Nonsense!' said the aunt, growing calmer. 'How wicked! Of course it's a hoax.'

'Oh! do send for the police, like he says,' wailed Mabel.

'Like who says?' snapped the aunt.

'Whoever it is,' Mabel moaned.

'Send for the police at once,' said Gerald, outside, in the manliest voice he could find. 'You'll only blame yourself if you don't. I can't do any more for you.'

'I – I'll set the dogs on you!' cried the aunt.

'Oh, auntie, *don't*!' Mabel was dancing with agitation. 'It's true – I know it's true. Do – do wake Bates!'

'I don't believe a word of it,' said the aunt. No more did Bates when, owing to Mabel's persistent worry-ings, he was awakened. But when he had seen the paper, and had to choose whether he'd go to the strong-room and see that there really wasn't anything to believe or go for the police on his bicycle, he chose the latter course.

When the police arrived the strong-room door stood ajar, and the silver, or as much of it as the three men could carry, was gone.

Gerald's note-book and pencil came into play again later on that night. It was five in the morning before he crept into bed, tired out and cold as a stone.

'Master Gerald!' – it was Eliza's voice in his ears – 'it's seven o'clock and another fine day, and there's been another burglary – My cats alive!' she screamed, as she drew up the blind and turned towards the bed; 'look at his bed, all crocked with black, and him not there! Oh, Jimminy!' It was a scream this time. Kath-leen came running from her room; Jimmy sat up in his bed and rubbed his eyes.

'Whatever is it?' Kathleen cried.

'I dunno when I 'ad such a turn.' Eliza sat down heavily on a box as she spoke. 'First thing his bed all empty and black as the chimley back, and him not in it, and then when I looks again he *is* in it all the time. I must be going silly. I thought as much when I heard them haunting angel voices yesterday morning. But I'll tell Mam'selle of you, my lad, with your tricks, you may rely on that. Blacking yourself all over and crocking up your clean sheets and pillow-cases. It's going back of beyond, this is.'

'Look here,' said Gerald slowly; 'I'm going to tell you something.'

Eliza simply snorted, and that was rude of her; but then, she had had a shock and had not got over it.

'Can you keep a secret?' asked Gerald, very earnest through the grey of his partly rubbed-off blacklead.

'Yes,' said Eliza.

'Then keep it and I'll give you two bob.'

'But what was you going to tell me?'

'That. About the two bob and the secret. And you keep your mouth shut.'

'I didn't ought to take it,' said Eliza, holding out her hand eagerly. 'Now you get up, and mind you wash all the corners, Master Gerald.'

'Oh, I'm so glad you're safe,' said Kathleen, when Eliza had gone.

'You didn't seem to care much last night,' said Gerald coldly.

'I can't think how I let you go. I didn't care last night. But when I woke this morning and remembered!'

'There, that'll do – it'll come off on you,' said Gerald through the reckless hugging of his sister.

'How did you get visible?' Jimmy asked.

'It just happened when she called me – the ring came off.'

'Tell us all about everything,' said Kathleen.

'Not yet,' said Gerald mysteriously.

'Where's the ring?' Jimmy asked after breakfast. '*I* want to have a try now.'

'I – I forgot it,' said Gerald; 'I expect it's in the bed somewhere.'

But it wasn't. Eliza had made the bed.

'I'll swear there ain't no ring there,' she said. 'I should 'a' seen it if there had 'a' been.'

5

'Search and research proving vain,' said Gerald, when every corner of the bedroom had been turned out and the ring had not been found, 'the noble detective hero of our tale remarked that he would have other fish to fry in half a jiff, and if the rest of you want to hear about last night . . .'

'Let's keep it till we get to Mabel,' said Kathleen heroically.

'The assignation was ten-thirty, wasn't it? Why shouldn't Gerald gas as we go along? I don't suppose anything very much happened, anyhow.' This, of course, was Jimmy.

'That shows,' remarked Gerald sweetly, 'how much *you* know. The melancholy Mabel will await the tryst without success, as far as this one is concerned. "Fish, fish, other fish – other fish I fry!"' he warbled to the tune of 'Cherry Ripe', till Kathleen could have pinched him.

Jimmy turned coldly away, remarking, 'When you've quite done.'

But Gerald went on singing –

'"Where the lips of Johnson smile,
There's the land of Cherry Isle.

> Other fish, other fish,
> Fish I fry.
> Stately Johnson, come and buy!"'

'How can you,' asked Kathleen, 'be so aggravating?'

'I don't know,' said Gerald, returning to prose. 'Want of sleep or intoxication – of success, I mean. Come where no one can hear us.

> 'Oh, come to some island where no one can hear,
>   And beware of the keyhole that's glued to an ear,'

he whispered, opened the door suddenly, and there, sure enough, was Eliza, stooping without. She flicked feebly at the wainscot with a duster, but concealment was vain.

'You know what listeners never hear,' said Jimmy severely.

'I didn't, then – so there!' said Eliza, whose listening ears were crimson. So they passed out, and up the High Street, to sit on the churchyard wall and dangle their legs. And all the way Gerald's lips were shut into a thin, obstinate line.

'*Now*,' said Kathleen. 'Oh, Jerry, don't be a goat! I'm simply dying to hear what happened.'

'That's better,' said Gerald, and he told his story. As he told it some of the white mystery and magic of the moonlit gardens got into his voice and his words, so that when he told of the statues that came alive, and the great beast that was alive through all its stone, Kathleen thrilled responsive, clutching his arm, and even Jimmy ceased to kick the wall with his boot heels, and listened open-mouthed.

Then came the thrilling tale of the burglars, and the warning letter flung into the peaceful company of Mabel, her aunt, and the bread-and-butter pudding. Gerald told the story with the greatest enjoyment and such fullness of detail that the church clock chimed half-past eleven as he said, 'Having done all that human agency could do, and further help being despaired of, our gallant young detective – Hullo, there's Mabel!'

There was. The tail-board of a cart shed her almost at their feet.

'I couldn't wait any longer,' she explained, 'when you didn't come. And I got a lift. Has anything more happened? The burglars had gone when Bates got to the strong-room.'

'You don't mean to say all that wheeze is *real*?' Jimmy asked.

'Of course it's real,' said Kathleen. 'Go on, Jerry. He's just got to where he threw the stone into your bread-and-butter pudding, Mabel. Go on.'

Mabel climbed on to the wall. 'You've got visible again quicker than I did,' she said.

Gerald nodded and resumed:

'Our story must be told in as few words as possible, owing to the fish-frying taking place at twelve, and it's past the half-hour now. Having left his missive to do its warning work, Gerald de Sherlock Holmes sped back, wrapped in invisibility, to the spot where by the light of their dark-lanterns the burglars were still – still burgling with the utmost punctuality and despatch. I didn't see any sense in running into danger, so I just waited outside the passage where the steps are – you know?'

Mabel nodded.

'Presently they came out, very cautiously, of course, and looked about them. They didn't see me – so deeming themselves unobserved they passed in silent Indian file along the passage – one of the sacks of silver grazed my front part – and out into the night.'

'But which way?'

'Through the little looking-glass room where you looked at yourself when you were invisible. The hero followed swiftly on his invisible tennis-shoes. The three miscreants instantly sought the shelter of the groves and passed stealthily among the rhododendrons and across the park, and' – his voice dropped and he looked straight before him at the pinky convolvulus netting a heap of stones beyond the white dust of the road – 'the stone things that come alive, they kept looking out from between bushes and under trees – and *I* saw them all right, but they didn't see me. They saw the burglars though, right enough; but the burglars couldn't see them. Rum, wasn't it?'

'The stone things?' Mabel had to have them explained to her.

'*I* never saw them come alive,' she said, 'and I've been in the gardens in the evening as often as often.'

'*I* saw them,' said Gerald stiffly.

'I know, I know,' Mabel hastened to put herself right with him; 'what I mean to say is I shouldn't wonder if they're only visible when you're *in*visible – the liveness of them, I mean, not the stoniness.'

Gerald understood, and I'm sure I hope you do.

'I shouldn't wonder if you're right,' he said. 'The castle garden's enchanted right enough; but what I should like to know is *how* and why. I say, come on,

I've got to catch Johnson before twelve. We'll walk as far as the market and then we'll have to run for it.'

'But go on with the adventure,' said Mabel. 'You can talk as we go. Oh, do – it is so awfully thrilling!'

This pleased Gerald, of course.

'Well, I just followed, you know, like in a dream, and they got out the cavy way – you know, where we got in – and I jolly well thought I'd lost them; I had to wait till they'd moved off down the road so that they shouldn't hear me rattling the stones, and I had to tear to catch them up. I took my shoes off – I expect my stockings are done for. And I followed and followed and followed and they went through the place where the poor people live, and right down to the river. And – I say, we must run for it.'

So the story stopped and the running began.

They caught Johnson in his own back-yard washing at a bench against his own back-door.

'Look here, Johnson,' Gerald said, 'what'll you give me if I put you up to winning that fifty pounds reward?'

'Halves,' said Johnson promptly, 'and a clout 'long-side your head if you was coming any of your nonsense over me.'

'It's *not* nonsense,' said Gerald very impressively. 'If you'll let us in I'll tell you all about it. And when you've caught the burglars and got the swag back you just give me a quid for luck. I won't ask for more.'

'Come along in, then,' said Johnson, 'if the young ladies'll excuse the towel. But I bet you *do* want something more off of me. Else why not claim the reward yourself?'

'Great is the wisdom of Johnson – he speaks winged

words.' The children were all in the cottage now, and the door was shut. 'I want you never to let on who told you. Let them think it was your own unaided pluck and far-sightedness.

'Sit you down,' said Johnson, 'and if you're kidding you'd best send the little gells home afore I begin on you.'

'I am not kidding,' replied Gerald loftily, 'never less. And anyone but a policeman would see why I don't want anyone to know it was me. I found it out at dead of night, in a place where I wasn't supposed to be; and there'd be a beastly row if they found out at home about me being out nearly all night. *Now* do you see, my bright-eyed daisy?'

Johnson was now too interested, as Jimmy said afterwards, to mind what silly names he was called. He said he did see – and asked to see more.

'Well, don't you ask any questions, then. I'll tell you all it's good for you to know. Last night about eleven I was at Yalding Towers. No – it doesn't matter how I got there or what I got there for – and there was a window open and I got in, and there was a light. And it was in the strong-room, and there were three men, putting silver in a bag.'

'Was it you give the warning, and they sent for the police?' Johnson was leaning eagerly forward, a hand on each knee.

'Yes, that was me. You can let them think it was you, if you like. You were off duty, weren't you?'

'I was,' said Johnson, 'in the arms of Murphy –'

'Well, the police didn't come quick enough. But *I* was there – a lonely detective. And I followed them.'

'You did?'

'And I saw them hide the booty and I know the other stuff from Houghton's Court's in the same place, and I heard them arrange about when to take it away.'

'Come and show me where,' said Johnson, jumping up so quickly that his Windsor arm-chair fell over backwards, with a crack, on the red-brick floor.

'Not so,' said Gerald calmly; 'if you go near the spot before the appointed time you'll find the silver, but you'll never catch the thieves.'

'You're right there.' The policeman picked up his chair and sat down in it again. 'Well?'

'Well, there's to be a motor to meet them in the lane beyond the boat-house by Sadler's Rents at one o'clock tonight. They'll get the things out at half-past twelve and take them along in a boat. So now's your chance to fill your pockets with chink and cover yourself with honour and glory.'

'So help me!' – Johnson was pensive and doubtful still – 'so help me! you *couldn't* have made all this up out of your head.'

'Oh yes, I could. But I didn't. Now look here. It's the chance of your lifetime, Johnson! A quid for me, and a still tongue for you, and the job's done. Do you agree?'

'Oh, *I* agree right enough,' said Johnson. 'I *agree*. But if you're coming any of your larks –'

'Can't you *see* he isn't?' Kathleen put in impatiently. 'He's not a liar – we none of us are.'

'If you're not on, say so,' said Gerald, 'and I'll find another policeman with more sense.'

'I could split about you being out all night,' said Johnson.

'But you wouldn't be so ungentlemanly,' said Mabel brightly. 'Don't you be so unbelieving, when we're trying to do you a good turn.'

'If I were you,' Gerald advised, 'I'd go to the place where the silver is, with two other men. You could make a nice little ambush in the wood-yard – it's close there. And I'd have two or three more men up trees in the lane to wait for the motor-car.'

'You ought to have been in the force, you ought,' said Johnson admiringly; 'but s'pose it *was* a hoax!'

'Well, then you'd have made an ass of yourself – I don't suppose it ud be the first time,' said Jimmy.

'Are you on?' said Gerald in haste. 'Hold your jaw, Jimmy, you idiot!'

'*Yes*,' said Johnson.

'Then when you're on duty you go down to the wood-yard, and the place where you see me blow my nose is *the* place. The sacks are tied with string to the posts under the water. You just stalk by in your dignified beauty and make a note of the spot. That's where glory waits you, and when Fame elates you and you're a sergeant, please remember me.'

Johnson said he was blessed. He said it more than once, and then remarked that he was on, and added that he must be off that instant minute.

Johnson's cottage lies just out of the town beyond the blacksmith's forge and the children had come to it through the wood. They went back the same way, and then down through the town, and through its narrow, unsavoury streets to the towing-path by the timber yard. Here they ran along the trunks of the big trees, peeped into the saw-pit, and – the men were away at dinner and this was a favourite play place of every boy within miles – made themselves a see-saw with a fresh cut, sweet-smelling pine plank and an elm-root.

'What a ripping place!' said Mabel, breathless on the seesaw's end. 'I believe I like this better than pretending games or even magic.'

'So do I,' said Jimmy. 'Jerry, don't keep sniffing so – you'll have no nose left.'

'I can't help it,' Gerald answered; 'I daren't use my hankey for fear Johnson's on the lookout somewhere unseen. I wish I'd thought of some other signal.' Sniff! 'No, nor I shouldn't want to now if I hadn't got not to. That's what's so rum. The moment I got down here and remembered what I'd said about the signal I began to have a cold – and – Thank goodness! here he is.'

The children, with a fine air of unconcern, abandoned the see-saw.

'Follow my leader!' Gerald cried, and ran along a barked oak trunk, the others following. In and out and round about ran the file of children, over heaps of logs, under the jutting ends of piled planks, and just as the policeman's heavy boots trod the towing-path Gerald halted at the end of a little landing-stage of rotten boards, with a rickety handrail, cried 'Pax!' and blew his nose with loud fervour.

'Morning,' he said immediately.

'Morning,' said Johnson. 'Got a cold, aint you?'

'Ah! I shouldn't have a cold if I'd got boots like yours,' returned Gerald admiringly. 'Look at them. Anyone ud know your fairy footstep a mile off. How do you ever get near enough to anyone to arrest them?' He skipped off the landing-stage, whispered as he passed Johnson, 'Courage, promptitude, and dispatch. That's the place,' and was off again, the active leader of an active procession.

'We've brought a friend home to dinner,' said Kathleen, when Eliza opened the door. 'Where's Mademoiselle?'

'Gone to see Yalding Towers. Today's show day, you know. An' just you hurry over your dinners. It's my afternoon out, and my gentleman friend don't like it if he's kept waiting.'

'All right, we'll eat like lightning,' Gerald promised. 'Set another place, there's an angel.'

They kept their word. The dinner – it was minced

veal and potatoes and rice-pudding, perhaps the dullest food in the world – was over in a quarter of an hour.

'And now,' said Mabel, when Eliza and a jug of hot water had disappeared up the stairs together, 'where's the ring? I ought to put it back.'

'I haven't had a turn yet,' said Jimmy. 'When we find it Cathy and I ought to have turns same as you and Gerald did.'

'When you find it –?' Mabel's pale face turned paler between her dark locks.

'I'm very sorry – we're all very sorry,' began Kathleen, and then the story of the losing had to be told.

'You couldn't have looked properly,' Mabel protested. 'It can't have vanished.'

'You don't know what it can do – no more do we. It's no use getting your quills up, fair lady. Perhaps vanishing itself is just what it does do. You see, it came off my hand in the bed. We looked everywhere.'

'Would you mind if *I* looked?' Mabel's eyes implored her little hostess. 'You see, if it's lost it's my fault. It's almost the same as stealing. That Johnson would say it was just the same. I know he would.'

'Let's all look again,' said Cathy, jumping up. 'We *were* rather in a hurry this morning.'

So they looked, and they looked. In the bed, under the bed, under the carpet, under the furniture. They shook the curtains, they explored the corners, and found dust and flue, but no ring. They looked, and they looked. Everywhere they looked. Jimmy even looked fixedly at the ceiling, as though he thought the ring might have bounced up there and stuck. But it hadn't.

'Then,' said Mabel at last, 'your housemaid must have stolen it. That's all. I shall tell her I think so.'

And she would have done it too, but at that moment the front door banged and they knew that Eliza had gone forth in all the glory of her best things to meet her 'gentleman friend'.

'It's no use' – Mabel was almost in tears; 'look here – will you leave me alone? Perhaps you others looking distracts me. And I'll go over every inch of the room by myself.'

'Respecting the emotion of their guest, the kindly charcoal-burners withdrew,' said Gerald. And they closed the door softly from the outside on Mabel and her search.

They waited for her, of course – politeness demanded it, and besides, they had to stay at home to let Mademoiselle in; though it was a dazzling day, and Jimmy had just remembered that Gerald's pockets were full of the money earned at the fair, and that nothing had yet been bought with that money, except a few buns in which he had had no share. And of course they waited impatiently.

It seemed about an hour, and was really quite ten minutes, before they heard the bedroom door open and Mabel's feet on the stairs.

'She hasn't found it,' Gerald said.

'How do you know?' Jimmy asked.

'The way she walks,' said Gerald. You can, in fact, almost always tell whether the thing has been found that people have gone to look for by the sound of their feet as they return. Mabel's feet said 'No go' as plain as they could speak. And her face confirmed the cheerless news.

A sudden and violent knocking at the back door prevented anyone from having to be polite about how sorry they were, or fanciful about being sure the ring would turn up soon.

All the servants except Eliza were away on their holidays, so the children went together to open the door, because, as Gerald said, if it was the baker they could buy a cake from him and eat it for dessert. 'That kind of dinner sort of *needs* dessert,' he said.

But it was not the baker. When they opened the

door they saw in the paved court where the pump is, and the dust-bin, and the water-butt, a young man, with his hat very much on one side, his mouth open under his fair bristly moustache, and his eyes as nearly round as human eyes can be. He wore a suit of a bright mustard colour, a blue necktie, and a goldish watch-chain across his waistcoat. His body was thrown back and his right arm stretched out towards the door, and his expression was that of a person who is being dragged somewhere against his will. He looked so strange that Kathleen tried to shut the door in his face, murmuring, 'Escaped insane.' But the door would not close. There was something in the way.

'Leave go of me!' said the young man.

'Ho yus! I'll leave go of you!' It was the voice of Eliza – but no Eliza could be seen.

'Who's got hold of you?' asked Kathleen.

'*She* has, miss,' replied the unhappy stranger.

'Who's she?' asked Kathleen, to gain time, as she afterwards explained, for she now knew well enough that what was keeping the door open was Eliza's unseen foot.

'My fyongsay, miss. At least it sounds like her voice, and it feels like her bones, but something's come over me, miss, an' I can't see her.'

'That's what he keeps on saying,' said Eliza's voice. "'E's my gentleman friend; is 'e gone dotty, or is it me?'

'Both, I shouldn't wonder,' said Jimmy.

'Now,' said Eliza, 'you call yourself a man; you look me in the face and say you can't see me.'

'Well – I can't,' said the wretched gentleman friend.

'If *I'd* stolen a ring,' said Gerald, looking at the sky,

'I should go indoors and be quiet, not stand at the back door and make an exhibition of myself.'

'Not much exhibition about her,' whispered Jimmy; 'good old ring!'

'I haven't stolen *any*thing,' said the gentleman friend. 'Here, you leave me be. It's my eyes has gone wrong. Leave go of me, d'ye hear?'

Suddenly his hand dropped and he staggered back against the water-butt. Eliza had 'left go' of him. She pushed past the children, shoving them aside with her invisible elbows. Gerald caught her by the arm with one hand, felt for her ear with the other, and whispered, 'You stand still and don't say a word. If you do – well, what's to stop me from sending for the police?'

Eliza did not know what there was to stop him. So she did as she was told, and stood invisible and silent, save for a sort of blowing, snorting noise peculiar to her when she was out of breath.

The mustard-coloured young man had recovered his balance, and stood looking at the children with eyes, if possible, rounder than before.

'What *is* it?' he gasped feebly. 'What's up? What's it all about?'

'If you don't know, I'm afraid we can't tell you,' said Gerald politely.

'Have I been talking very strange-like?' he asked, taking off his hat and passing his hand over his forehead.

'Very,' said Mabel.

'I hope I haven't said anything that wasn't good manners,' he said anxiously.

'Not at all,' said Kathleen. 'You only said your

fiancée had hold of your hand, and that you couldn't see her.'

'No more I can.'

'No more can we,' said Mabel.

'But I couldn't have dreamed it, and then come along here making a penny show of myself like this, could I?'

'You know best,' said Gerald courteously.

'But,' the mustard-coloured victim almost screamed, 'do you mean to tell me . . .'

'I don't mean to tell you anything,' said Gerald quite truly, 'but I'll give you a bit of advice. You go home and lie down a bit and put a wet rag on your head. You'll be all right tomorrow.'

'But I haven't –'

'*I* should,' said Mabel; 'the sun's very hot, you know.'

'I feel all right now,' he said, 'but – well, I can only say I'm sorry, that's all I can say. I've never been taken like this before, miss. I'm not subject to it – don't you think that. But I could have sworn Eliza – Aint she gone out to meet me?'

'Eliza's indoors,' said Mabel. 'She can't come out to meet anybody today.'

'You won't tell her about me carrying on this way, will you, miss? It might set her against me if she thought I was liable to fits, which I never was from a child.'

'We won't tell Eliza anything about you.'

'And you'll overlook the liberty?'

'Of course. We know you couldn't help it,' said Kathleen. 'You go home and lie down. I'm sure you must need it. Good afternoon.'

'Good afternoon, I'm sure, miss,' he said dreamily. 'All the same I can feel the print of her finger-bones on my hand while I'm saying it. And you won't let it get round to my boss – my employer I mean? Fits of all sorts are against a man in any trade.'

'No, no, no, it's all right – *good-bye*,' said everyone. And a silence fell as he went slowly round the water-butt and the green yard-gate shut behind him. The silence was broken by Eliza.

'Give me up!' she said. 'Give me up to break my heart in a prison cell!'

There was a sudden splash, and a round wet drop lay on the doorstep.

'Thunder shower,' said Jimmy; but it was a tear from Eliza.

'Give me up,' she went on, 'give me up' – splash – 'but don't let me be took here in the town where I'm known and respected' – splash. 'I'll walk ten miles to be took by a strange police – not Johnson as keeps company with my own cousin' – splash. 'But I do thank you for one thing. You didn't tell Elf as I'd stolen the ring. And I didn't' – splash – 'I only sort of borrowed it, it being my day out, and my gentleman friend such a toff, like you can see for yourselves.'

The children had watched, spellbound, the interesting tears that became visible as they rolled off the invisible nose of the miserable Eliza. Now Gerald roused himself, and spoke.

'It's no use your talking,' he said. 'We can't see you!'

'That's what *he* said,' said Eliza's voice, 'but –'

'You can't see yourself,' Gerald went on. 'Where's your hand?'

Eliza, no doubt, tried to see it, and of course failed; for instantly, with a shriek that might have brought the police if there had been any about, she went into a violent fit of hysterics. The children did what they could, everything that they had read of in books as suitable to such occasions, but it is extremely difficult to do the right thing with an invisible housemaid in strong hysterics and her best clothes. That was why the best hat was found, later on, to be completely ruined, and why the best blue dress was never quite itself again. And as they were burning bits of the feather dusting-brush as nearly under Eliza's nose as they could guess, a sudden spurt of flame and a horrible smell, as the flame died between the quick hands of Gerald, showed but too plainly that Eliza's feather boa had tried to help.

It did help. Eliza 'came to' with a deep sob and said, 'Don't burn me real ostrich stole; I'm better now.'

They helped her up and she sat down on the bottom step, and the children explained to her very carefully and quite kindly that she really was invisible, and that if you steal – or even borrow – rings you can never be sure what will happen to you.

'But 'ave I got to go on stopping like this,' she moaned, when they had fetched the little mahogany looking-glass from its nail over the kitchen sink, and convinced her that she was really invisible, 'for ever and ever? An' we was to a bin married come Easter. No one won't marry a gell as 'e can't see. It ain't likely.'

'No, not for ever and ever,' said Mabel kindly, 'but you've got to go through with it – like measles. I expect you'll be all right tomorrow.'

'Tonight, *I* think,' said Gerald.

'We'll help you all we can, and not tell anyone,' said Kathleen.

'Not even the police,' said Jimmy.

'Now let's get Mademoiselle's tea ready,' said Gerald.

'And ours,' said Jimmy.

'No,' said Gerald, 'we'll have our tea *out*. We'll have a picnic and we'll take Eliza. I'll go out and get the cakes.'

'*I* shan't eat no cake, Master Jerry,' said Eliza's

voice, 'so don't you think it. You'd see it going down inside my chest. It wouldn't be what I should call nice of me to have cake showing through me in the open air. Oh, it's a dreadful judgement – just for a borrow!'

They reassured her, set the tea, deputed Kathleen to let in Mademoiselle – who came home tired and a little sad, it seemed – waited for her and Gerald and the cakes, and started off for Yalding Towers.

'Picnic parties aren't allowed,' said Mabel.

'Ours will be,' said Gerald briefly. 'Now, Eliza, you catch on to Kathleen's arm and I'll walk behind to conceal your shadow. My aunt! take your hat off; it makes your shadow look like I don't know what. People will think we're the county lunatic asylum turned loose.'

It was then that the hat, becoming visible in Kathleen's hand, showed how little of the sprinkled water had gone where it was meant to go – on Eliza's face.

'Me best 'at,' said Eliza, and there was a silence with sniffs in it.

'Look here,' said Mabel, 'you cheer up. Just you think this is all a dream. It's just the kind of thing you might dream if your conscience had got pains in it about the ring.'

'But will I wake up again?'

'Oh yes, you'll wake up again. Now we're going to bandage your eyes and take you through a very small door, and don't you resist, or we'll bring a policeman into the dream like a shot.'

I have not time to describe Eliza's entrance into the cave. She went head first: the girls propelled and the boys received her. If Gerald had not thought of tying her hands someone would certainly have been

scratched. As it was Mabel's hand was scraped between
the cold rock and a passionate boot-heel. Nor will I
tell you all that she said as they led her along the fern-
bordered gully and through the arch into the wonder-
land of Italian scenery. She had but little language left
when they removed her bandage under a weeping
willow where a statue of Diana, bow in hand, stood
poised on one toe, a most unsuitable attitude for ar-
chery, I have always thought.

'Now,' said Gerald, 'it's all over – nothing but
niceness now and cake and things.'

'It's time we did have our tea,' said Jimmy. And it
was.

Eliza, once convinced that her chest, though invisible, was not transparent, and that her companions
could not by looking through it count how many buns
she had eaten, made an excellent meal. So did the
others. If you want really to enjoy your tea, have
minced veal and potatoes and rice-pudding for dinner,
with several hours of excitement to follow, and take
your tea late.

The soft, cool green and grey of the garden were
changing – the green grew golden, the shadows black,
and the lake where the swans were mirrored upside
down, under the Temple of Phoebus, was bathed in
rosy light from the little fluffy clouds that lay opposite
the sunset.

'It *is* pretty,' said Eliza, 'just like a picture-postcard,
aint it? – the tuppenny kind.'

'I ought to be getting home,' said Mabel.

'I can't go home like this. I'd stay and be a savage
and live in that white hut if it had any walls and
doors,' said Eliza.

'She means the Temple of Dionysus,' said Mabel, pointing to it.

The sun set suddenly behind the line of black fir-trees on the top of the slope, and the white temple, that had been pink, turned grey.

'It would be a very nice place to live in even as it is,' said Kathleen.

'Draughty,' said Eliza, 'and law, what a lot of steps to clean! What they make houses for without no walls to 'em? Who'd live in –' She broke off, stared, and added: 'What's that?'

'What?'

'That white thing coming down the steps. Why, it's a young man in statooary.'

'The statues do come alive here, after sunset,' said Gerald in very matter-of-fact tones.

'I see they do.' Eliza did not seem at all surprised or alarmed. 'There's another of 'em. Look at them little wings to his feet like pigeons.'

'I expect that's Mercury,' said Gerald.

'It's "Hermes" under the statue that's got wings on its feet,' said Mabel, 'but –'

'*I* don't see any statues, said Jimmy. 'What are you punching me for?'

'Don't you see?' Gerald whispered; but he need not have been so troubled, for all Eliza's attention was with her wandering eyes that followed hither and thither the quick movements of unseen statues. 'Don't you see? The statues come alive when the sun goes down – and you can't see them unless you're invisible – and *I* – if you *do* see them you're not frightened – unless you *touch* them.'

'Let's get her to touch one and see,' said Jimmy.

'''E's lep' into the water,' said Eliza in a rapt voice. 'My, can't he swim neither! And the one with the pigeons' wings is flying all over the lake having larks with 'im. I do call that pretty. It's like cupids as you see on wedding-cakes. And here's another of 'em, a little chap with long ears and a baby deer galloping alongside! An' look at the lady with the biby, throwing it up and catching it like as if it was a ball. I wonder she ain't afraid. But it's pretty to see 'em.'

The broad park lay stretched before the children in growing greyness and a stillness that deepened. Amid the thickening shadows they could see the statues gleam white and motionless. But Eliza saw other things. She watched in silence presently, and they watched silently, and the evening fell like a veil that grew heavier and blacker. And it was night. And the moon came up above the trees.

'Oh,' cried Eliza suddenly, 'here's the dear little boy with the deer – he's coming right for me, bless his heart!'

Next moment she was screaming, and her screams grew fainter and there was the sound of swift boots on gravel.

'Come on!' cried Gerald; 'she touched it, and then she was frightened. Just like I was. Run! she'll send everyone in the town mad if she gets there like that. Just a voice and boots! Run! Run!'

They ran. But Eliza had the start of them. Also when she ran on the grass they could not hear her footsteps and had to wait for the sound of leather on far-away gravel. Also she was driven by fear, and fear drives fast.

She went, it seemed, the nearest way, invisibly

through the waxing moonlight, seeing she only knew what amid the glades and groves.

'I'll stop here; see you tomorrow,' gasped Mabel, as the loud pursuers followed Eliza's clatter across the terrace. 'She's gone through the stable yard.'

'The back way,' Gerald panted as they turned the corner of their own street, and he and Jimmy swung in past the water-butt.

An unseen but agitated presence seemed to be fumbling with the locked back-door. The church clock struck the half-hour.

'Half-past nine,' Gerald had just breath to say. 'Pull at the ring. Perhaps it'll come off now.'

He spoke to the bare doorstep. But it was Eliza, dishevelled, breathless, her hair coming down, her collar crooked, her dress twisted and disordered, who suddenly held out a hand – a hand that they could see; and in the hand, plainly visible in the moonlight, the dark circle of the magic ring.

''Alf a mo!' said Eliza's gentleman friend next morning. He was waiting for her when she opened the door with pail and hearthstone in her hand. 'Sorry you couldn't come out yesterday.'

'So'm I.' Eliza swept the wet flannel along the top step. 'What did you do?'

'I 'ad a bit of a headache,' said the gentleman friend. 'I laid down most of the afternoon. What were you up to?'

'Oh, nothing pertickler,' said Eliza.

'Then it was all a dream,' she said, when he was gone; 'but it'll be a lesson to me not to meddle with

anybody's old ring again in a hurry.'

'So they didn't tell 'er about me behaving like I did,' said he as he went – 'sun, I suppose – like our Army in India. I hope I ain't going to be liable to it, that's all!'

6

Johnson was the hero of the hour. It was he who had tracked the burglars, laid his plans, and recovered the lost silver. He had not thrown the stone – public opinion decided that Mabel and her aunt must have been mistaken in supposing that there was a stone at all. But he did not deny the warning letter. It was Gerald who went out after breakfast to buy the news-paper, and who read aloud to the others the two columns of fiction which were the *Liddlesby Observer*'s report of the facts. As he read every mouth opened wider and wider, and when he ceased with 'this gifted fellow-townsman with detective instincts which out-rival those of Messrs Lecoq and Holmes, and whose promotion is now assured', there was quite a blank silence.

'Well,' said Jimmy, breaking it, 'he doesn't stick it on neither, does he?'

'I feel,' said Kathleen, 'as if it was our fault – as if it was us had told all these whoppers; because if it hadn't been for you they couldn't have, Jerry. How could he say all that?'

'Well,' said Gerald, trying to be fair, 'you know, after all, the chap had to say something. I'm glad I –' He stopped abruptly.

'You're glad you what?'

'No matter,' said he, with an air of putting away affairs of state. 'Now, what are we going to do today? The faithful Mabel approaches; she will want her ring. And you and Jimmy want it too. Oh, I know. Mademoiselle hasn't had any attention paid to her for more days than our hero likes to confess.'

'I wish you wouldn't always call yourself "our hero",' said Jimmy; 'you aren't mine, anyhow.'

'You're both of you *mine*,' said Kathleen hastily.

'Good little girl.' Gerald smiled annoyingly. 'Keep baby brother in a good temper till Nursie comes back.'

'You're not going out without us?' Kathleen asked in haste.

> '"I haste away,
> 'Tis market day,"'

sang Gerald,

> '"And in the market there
> Buy roses for my fair."

If you want to come too, get your boots on, and look slippy about it.'

'I don't want to come,' said Jimmy, and sniffed.

Kathleen turned a despairing look on Gerald.

'Oh, James, James,' said Gerald sadly, 'how difficult you make it for me to forget that you're my little brother! If ever I treat you like one of the other chaps, and rot you like I should Turner or Moberley or any of my pals – well, this is what comes of it.'

'You don't call them your baby brothers,' said Jimmy, and truly.

'No; and I'll take precious good care I don't call you it again. Come on, my hero and heroine. The devoted Mesrour is your salaaming slave.'

The three met Mabel opportunely at the corner of the square where every Friday the stalls and the awnings and the green umbrellas were pitched, and poultry, pork, pottery, vegetables, drapery, sweets, toys, tools, mirrors, and all sorts of other interesting merchandise were spread out on trestle tables, piled on carts whose horses were stabled and whose shafts were held in place by piled wooden cases, or laid out, as in the case of crockery and hardware, on the bare flagstones of the market-place.

The sun was shining with great goodwill, and, as Mabel remarked, 'all Nature looked smiling and gay.' There were a few bunches of flowers among the vegetables, and the children hesitated, balanced in choice.

'Mignonette is sweet,' said Mabel.

'Roses are roses,' said Kathleen.

'Carnations are tuppence,' said Jimmy; and Gerald, sniffing among the bunches of tightly-tied tea-roses, agreed that this settled it.

So the carnations were bought, a bunch of yellow ones, like sulphur, a bunch of white ones like clotted cream, and a bunch of red ones like the cheeks of the doll that Kathleen never played with. They took the carnations home, and Kathleen's green hair-ribbon came in beautifully for tying them up, which was hastily done on the doorstep.

Then discreetly Gerald knocked at the door of the

drawing-room, where Mademoiselle seemed to sit all day.

'Entrez!' came her voice; and Gerald entered. She was not reading, as usual, but bent over a sketch-book; on the table was an open colour-box of un-English appearance, and a box of that slate-coloured liquid so familiar alike to the greatest artist in watercolours and to the humblest child with a sixpenny paint-box.

'With all of our loves,' said Gerald, laying the flowers down suddenly before her.

'But it is that you are a dear child. For this it must that I embrace you – no?' And before Gerald could explain that he was too old, she kissed him with little quick French pecks on the two cheeks.

'Are you painting?' he asked hurriedly, to hide his annoyance at being treated like a baby.

'I achieve a sketch of yesterday,' she answered; and before he had time to wonder what yesterday would look like in a picture she showed him a beautiful and exact sketch of Yalding Towers.

'Oh, I say – ripping!' was the critic's comment. 'I say, mayn't the others come and see?' The others came, including Mabel, who stood awkwardly behind the rest, and looked over Jimmy's shoulder.

'I say, you are clever,' said Gerald respectfully.

'To what good to have the talent, when one must pass one's life at teaching the infants?' said Mademoiselle.

'It must be fairly beastly,' Gerald owned.

'You, too, see the design?' Mademoiselle asked Mabel, adding: 'A friend from the town, yes?'

'How do you do?' said Mabel politely. 'No, I'm not from the town. I live at Yalding Towers.'

The name seemed to impress Mademoiselle very much. Gerald anxiously hoped in his own mind that she was not a snob.

'Yalding Towers,' she repeated, 'but this is very extraordinary. Is it possible that you are then of the family of Lord Yalding?'

'He hasn't any family,' said Mabel; 'he's not married.'

'I would say are you – how you say? – cousin – sister – niece?'

'No,' said Mabel, flushing hotly, 'I'm nothing grand at all. I'm Lord Yalding's housekeeper's niece.'

'But you know Lord Yalding, is it not?'

'No,' said Mabel, 'I've never seen him.'

'He comes then never to his château?'

'Not since I've lived there. But he's coming next week.'

'Why lives he not there?' Mademoiselle asked.

'Auntie says he's too poor,' said Mabel, and proceeded to tell the tale as she had heard it in the housekeeper's room: how Lord Yalding's uncle had left all the money he could leave away from Lord Yalding to Lord Yalding's second cousin, and poor Lord Yalding had only just enough to keep the old place in repair, and to live very quietly indeed somewhere else, but not enough to keep the house open or to live there; and how he couldn't sell the house because it was 'in tale'.

'What is it then – in tail?' asked Mademoiselle.

'In a tale that the lawyers write out,' said Mabel, proud of her knowledge and flattered by the deep interest of the French governess; 'and when once they've put your house in one of their tales you can't sell it or give it away, but you have to leave it to your son, even if you don't want to.'

'But how his uncle could he be so cruel – to leave him the château and no money?' Mademoiselle asked; and Kathleen and Jimmy stood amazed at the sudden keenness of her interest in what seemed to them the dullest story.

'Oh, I can tell you that too,' said Mabel. 'Lord Yalding wanted to marry a lady his uncle didn't want him to, a barmaid or a ballet lady or something, and he wouldn't give her up, and his uncle said, "Well then," and left everything to the cousin.'

'And you say he is not married.'

'No – the lady went into a convent; I expect she's bricked-up alive by now.'

'Bricked –?'

'In a wall, you know,' said Mabel, pointing explain-ingly at the pink and gilt roses of the wall-paper, 'shut up to kill them. That's what they do to you in convents.'

'Not at all,' said Mademoiselle; 'in convents are very kind good women; there is but one thing in convents that is detestable – the locks on the doors. Sometimes people cannot get out, especially when they are very young and their relations have placed them there for their welfare and happiness. But brick – how you say it? – enwalling ladies to kill them. No – it does itself never. And this Lord – he did not then seek his lady?'

'Oh, yes – he sought her right enough,' Mabel assured her; 'but there are millions of convents, you know, and he had no idea where to look, and they sent back his letters from the post-office, and –'

'Ciel!' cried Mademoiselle, 'but it seems that one knows all in the housekeeper's saloon.'

'Pretty well all,' said Mabel simply.

'And you think he will find her? No?'

'Oh, he'll find her all right,' said Mabel, 'when he's old and broken down, you know – and dying; and then a gentle sister of charity will soothe his pillow, and just when he's dying she'll reveal herself and say: "My own lost love!" and his face will light up with a wonderful joy and he'll expire with her beloved name on his parched lips.'

Mademoiselle's was the silence of sheer astonish-ment. 'You do the prophecy, it appears?' she said at last.

'Oh no,' said Mabel, 'I got that out of a book. I can

tell you lots more fatal love stories any time you like.'

The French governess gave a little jump, as though she had suddenly remembered something.

'It is nearly dinner-time,' she said. 'Your friend – Mabelle, yes – will be your convivial, and in her honour we will make a little feast. My beautiful flowers – put them to the water, Kathleen. I run to buy the cakes. Wash the hands, all, and be ready when I return.'

Smiling and nodding to the children, she left them, and ran up the stairs.

'Just as if she was young,' said Kathleen.

'She *is* young,' said Mabel. 'Heaps of ladies have offers of marriage when they're no younger than her. I've seen lots of weddings too, with much older brides. And why didn't you tell me she was so beautiful?'

'*Is* she?' asked Kathleen.

'Of course she is; and what a darling to think of cakes for me, and calling me a convivial!'

'Look here,' said Gerald, 'I call this jolly decent of her. You know, governesses never have more than the meanest pittance, just enough to sustain life, and here she is spending her little all on us. Supposing we just don't go out today, but play with her instead. I expect she's most awfully bored really.'

'Would she really like it?' Kathleen wondered. 'Aunt Emily says grown-ups never really like playing. They do it to please us.'

'They little know,' Gerald answered, 'how often we do it to please them.'

'We've got to do that dressing-up with the Princess

clothes anyhow – we said we would,' said Kathleen. 'Let's treat her to that.'

'Rather near tea-time,' urged Jimmy, 'so that there'll be a fortunate interruption and the play won't go on for ever.'

'I suppose all the things are safe?' Mabel asked.

'Quite. I told you where I put them. Come on, Jimmy; let's help lay the table. We'll get Eliza to put out the best china.'

They went.

'It was lucky,' said Gerald, struck by a sudden thought, 'that the burglars didn't go for the diamonds in the treasure-chamber.'

'They couldn't,' said Mabel almost in a whisper; 'they didn't know about them. I don't believe anybody knows about them, except me – and you, and you're sworn to secrecy.' This, you will remember, had been done almost at the beginning. 'I know aunt doesn't know. I just found out the spring by accident. Lord Yalding's kept the secret well.'

'I wish I'd got a secret like that to keep,' said Gerald.

'If the burglars *do* know,' said Mabel, 'it'll all come out at the trial. Lawyers make you tell everything you know at trials, and a lot of lies besides.'

'There won't be any trial,' said Gerald, kicking the leg of the piano thoughtfully.

'No trial?'

'It said in the paper,' Gerald went on slowly, '"The miscreants must have received warning from a confederate, for the admirable preparations to arrest them as they returned for their ill-gotten plunder were unavailing. But the police have a clue."'

'What a pity!' said Mabel.

'You needn't worry – they haven't got any old clue,' said Gerald, still attentive to the piano leg.

'I didn't mean the clue; I meant the confederate.'

'It's a pity you think he's a pity, because he was *me*,' said Gerald, standing up and leaving the piano leg alone. He looked straight before him, as the boy on the burning deck may have looked.

'I couldn't help it,' he said. 'I know you'll think I'm a criminal, but I couldn't do it. I don't know how detectives can. I went over a prison once, with father; and after I'd given the tip to Johnson I remembered that, and I just couldn't. I know I'm a beast, and not worthy to be a British citizen.'

'I think it was rather nice of you,' said Mabel kindly. 'How did you warn them?'

'I just shoved a paper under the man's door – the one that I knew where he lived – to tell him to lie low.'

'Oh! do tell me – what did you put on it exactly?' Mabel warmed to this new interest.

'It said: "The police know all except your names. Be virtuous and you are safe. But if there's any more burgling I shall split and you may rely on that from a friend." I know it was wrong, but I couldn't help it. Don't tell the others. They wouldn't understand why I did it. I don't understand it myself.'

'I do,' said Mabel: 'it's because you've got a kind and noble heart.'

'Kind fiddlestick, my good child!' said Gerald, suddenly losing the burning boy expression and becoming in a flash entirely himself. 'Cut along and wash your hands; you're as black as ink.'

'So are you,' said Mabel, 'and I'm not. It's dye with

me. Auntie was dyeing a blouse this morning. It told you how in *Home Drivel* – and she's as black as ink too, and the blouse is all streaky. Pity the ring won't make just parts of you invisible – the dirt, for instance.'

'Perhaps,' Gerald said unexpectedly, 'it won't make even all of you invisible again.'

'Why not? You haven't been doing anything to it – have you?' Mabel sharply asked.

'No; but didn't you notice you were invisible twenty-one hours; I was fourteen hours invisible, and Eliza only seven – that's seven less each time. And now we've come to –'

'How frightfully good you are at sums!' said Mabel, awe-struck.

'You see, it's got seven hours less each time, and seven from seven is nought; it's got to be something different this time. And then afterwards – it can't be minus seven, because I don't see how – unless it made you more visible – thicker, you know.'

'*Don't!*' said Mabel; 'you make my head go round.'

'And there's another odd thing,' Gerald went on; 'when you're invisible your relations don't love you. Look at your aunt, and Cathy never turning a hair at me going burgling. We haven't got to the bottom of that ring yet. Crikey! here's Mademoiselle with the cakes. Run, bold bandits – wash for your lives!'

They ran.

It was not cakes only; it was plums and grapes and jam tarts and soda-water and raspberry vinegar, and chocolates in pretty boxes and 'pure, thick, rich' cream in brown jugs, also a big bunch of roses. Mademoiselle was strangely merry, for a governess. She served out

the cakes and tarts with a liberal hand, made wreaths
of the flowers for all their heads – she was not eating
much herself – drank the health of Mabel, as the guest
of the day, in the beautiful pink drink that comes from
mixing raspberry vinegar and soda-water, and actually
persuaded Jimmy to wear his wreath, on the ground
that the Greek gods as well as the goddesses always
wore wreaths at a feast.

There never was such a feast provided by any
French governess since French governesses began.
There were jokes and stories and laughter. Jimmy
showed all those tricks with forks and corks and
matches and apples which are so deservedly popular.
Mademoiselle told them stories of her own schooldays
when she was 'a quite little girl with two tight tresses
– so,' and when they could not understand the tresses,
called for paper and pencil and drew the loveliest
little picture of herself when she was a child with two
short fat pig-tails sticking out from her head like
knitting-needles from a ball of dark worsted. Then
she drew pictures of everything they asked for, till
Mabel pulled Gerald's jacket and whispered: 'The
acting!'

'Draw us the front of a theatre,' said Gerald tactfully,
'a French theatre.'

'They are the same thing as the English theatres,'
Mademoiselle told him.

'Do you like acting – the theatre, I mean?'

'But yes – I love it.'

'All right,' said Gerald briefly. 'We'll act a play for
you – now – this afternoon if you like.'

'Eliza will be washing up,' Cathy whispered, 'and
she was promised to see it.'

'Or this evening,' said Gerald 'and please, Mademoiselle, may Eliza come in and look on?'

'But certainly,' said Mademoiselle; 'amuse yourselves well, my children.'

'But it's *you*,' said Mabel suddenly, 'that we want to
amuse. Because we love you very much – don't we, all
of you?'

'Yes,' the chorus came unhesitatingly. Though the
others would never have thought of saying such a
thing on their own account. Yet, as Mabel said it, they
found to their surprise that it was true.

'Tiens!' said Mademoiselle, 'you love the old French
governess? Impossible,' and she spoke rather in-
distinctly.

'You're not old,' said Mabel; 'at least not so very,'
she added brightly, 'and you're as lovely as a Princess.'

'Go then, flatteress!' said Mademoiselle, laughing;
and Mabel went. The others were already half-way up
the stairs.

Mademoiselle sat in the drawing-room as usual, and
it was a good thing that she was not engaged in serious
study, for it seemed that the door opened and shut
almost ceaselessly all throughout the afternoon. Might
they have the embroidered antimacassars and the sofa
cushions? Might they have the clothes-line out of the
washhouse? Eliza said they mightn't, but might they?
Might they have the sheepskin hearth-rugs? Might
they have tea in the garden, because they had almost
got the stage ready in the dining-room, and Eliza
wanted to set tea? Could Mademoiselle lend them any
coloured clothes – scarves or dressing-gowns, or anything bright? Yes, Mademoiselle could, and did – silk

things, surprisingly lovely for a governess to have. Had Mademoiselle any rouge? They had always heard that French ladies – No. Mademoiselle hadn't – and to judge by the colour of her face, Mademoiselle didn't need it. Did Mademoiselle think the chemist sold rouge – or had she any false hair to spare? At this challenge Mademoiselle's pale fingers pulled out a dozen hairpins, and down came the loveliest blue-black hair, hanging to her knees in straight, heavy lines.

'No, you terrible infants,' she cried. 'I have not the false hair, nor the rouge. And my teeth – you want them also, without doubt?'

She showed them in a laugh.

'I *said* you were a Princess,' said Mabel, 'and now I know. You're Rapunzel. Do always wear your hair like that! May we have the peacock fans, please, off the mantelpiece, and the things that loop back the curtains, and all the handkerchiefs you've got?'

Mademoiselle denied them nothing. They had the fans and the handkerchiefs and some large sheets of expensive drawing-paper out of the school cupboard, and Mademoiselle's best sable paint-brush and her paint-box.

'Who would have thought,' murmured Gerald, pensively sucking the brush and gazing at the paper mask he had just painted, 'that she was such a brick in disguise? I wonder why crimson lake always tastes just like Liebig's Extract.'

Everything was pleasant that day somehow. There are some days like that, you know, when everything goes well from the very beginning; all the things you want are in their places, nobody misunderstands you, and all that you do turns out admirably. How different from those other days which we all know too well, when your shoe-lace breaks, your comb is mislaid, your brush spins on its back on the floor and lands under the bed where you can't get at it – you drop the soap, your buttons come off, an eyelash gets into your eye, you have used your last clean handkerchief, your collar is frayed at the edge and cuts your neck, and at the very last moment your suspender breaks, and there is no string. On such a day as this you are naturally late for breakfast, and everyone thinks you did it on purpose. And the day goes on and on, getting worse and worse – you mislay your exercise-book, you drop your arithmetic in the mud, your pencil breaks, and when you open your knife to sharpen the pencil you split your nail. On such a day you jam your thumb in doors, and muddle the messages you are sent on by grown-ups. You upset your tea, and your bread-and-butter won't hold together for a moment. And when at last you get to bed – usually in disgrace – it is no comfort at all to you to know that not a single bit of it is your own fault.

This day was not one of those days, as you will have noticed. Even the tea in the garden – there was a bricked bit by a rockery that made a steady floor for the tea-table – was most delightful, though the thoughts of four out of the five were busy with the coming play, and the fifth had thoughts of her own that had had nothing to do with tea or acting.

Then there was an interval of slamming doors, interesting silences, feet that flew up and down stairs.

It was still good daylight when the dinner-bell rang – the signal had been agreed upon at tea-time, and carefully explained to Eliza. Mademoiselle laid down her book and passed out of the sunset-yellowed hall into the faint yellow gaslight of the dining-room. The giggling Eliza held the door open before her, and followed her in. The shutters had been closed – streaks of daylight showed above and below them. The green-and-black tablecloths of the school dining-tables were supported on the clothes-line from the backyard. The line sagged in a graceful curve, but it answered its purpose of supporting the curtains which concealed that part of the room which was the stage.

Rows of chairs had been placed across the other end of the room – all the chairs in the house, as it seemed – and Mademoiselle started violently when she saw that fully half a dozen of these chairs were occupied. And by the queerest people, too: an old woman with a poke bonnet tied under her chin with a red handkerchief, a lady in a large straw hat wreathed in flowers and the oddest hands that stuck out over the chair in front of her, several men with strange, clumsy figures, and all with hats on.

'But,' whispered Mademoiselle, through the chinks of the tablecloths, 'you have then invited other friends? You should have asked me, my children.'

Laughter and something like a 'hurrah' answered her from behind the folds of the curtaining table-cloths.

'All right, Mademoiselle Rapunzel,' cried Mabel; 'turn the gas up. It's only part of the entertainment.'

Eliza, still giggling, pushed through the lines of chairs, knocking off the hat of one of the visitors as she did so, and turned up the three incandescent burners.

Mademoiselle looked at the figure seated nearest to her, stooped to look more closely, half laughed, quite screamed, and sat down suddenly.

'Oh!' she cried, 'they are not alive!'

Eliza, with a much louder scream, had found out the same thing and announced it differently. 'They ain't got no insides,' said she. The seven members of the audience seated among the wilderness of chairs had, indeed, no insides to speak of. Their bodies were

bolsters and rolled-up blankets, their spines were broom-handles, and their arm and leg bones were hockey sticks and umbrellas. Their shoulders were the wooden crosspieces that Mademoiselle used for keeping her jackets in shape; their hands were gloves stuffed out with handkerchiefs; and their faces were the paper masks painted in the afternoon by the untutored brush of Gerald, tied on to the round heads made of the ends of stuffed bolster-cases. The faces were really rather dreadful. Gerald had done his best, but even after his best had been done you would hardly have known they were faces, some of them, if they hadn't been in the positions which faces usually occupy, between the collar and the hat. Their eyebrows were furious with lamp-black frowns – their eyes the size, and almost the shape, of five-shilling pieces, and on their lips and cheeks had been spent much crimson lake and nearly the whole of a half-pan of vermilion.

'You have made yourself an auditors, yes? Bravo!' cried Mademoiselle, recovering herself and beginning to clap. And to the sound of that clapping the curtain went up – or, rather, apart. A voice said, in a breathless, choked way, 'Beauty and the Beast,' and the stage was revealed.

It was a real stage too – the dining-tables pushed close together and covered with pink-and-white counterpanes. It was a little unsteady and creaky to walk on, but very imposing to look at. The scene was simple, but convincing. A big sheet of cardboard, bent square, with slits cut in it and a candle behind, represented, quite transparently, the domestic hearth; a round hat-tin of Eliza's, supported on a stool with a night-light under it, could not have been mistaken, save by wilful malice, for anything but a copper. A waste-paper basket with two or three school dusters and an overcoat in it, and a pair of blue pyjamas over the back of a chair, put the finishing touch to the scene. It did not need the announcement from the wings, 'The laundry at Beauty's home.' It was so plainly a laundry and nothing else.

In the wings: 'They look just like a real audience, don't they?' whispered Mabel. 'Go on, Jimmy – don't forget the Merchant has to be pompous and use long words.'

Jimmy, enlarged by pillows under Gerald's best overcoat which had been intentionally bought with a view to his probable growth during the two years which it was intended to last him, a Turkish towel turban on his head and an open umbrella over it, opened the first act in a simple and swift soliloquy:

'I am the most unlucky merchant that ever was. I was once the richest merchant in Bagdad, but I lost all my ships, and now I live in a poor house that is all to bits; you can see how the rain comes through the roof, and my daughters take in washing. And –'

The pause might have seemed long, but Gerald rustled in, elegant in Mademoiselle's pink dressing-gown and the character of the eldest daughter.

'A nice drying day,' he minced. 'Pa dear, put the umbrella the other way up. It'll save us going out in the rain to fetch water. Come on, sisters, dear father's got us a new wash-tub. Here's luxury!'

Round the umbrella, now held the wrong way up, the three sisters knelt and washed imaginary linen. Kathleen wore a violet skirt of Eliza's, a blue blouse of her own, and a cap of knotted handkerchiefs. A white nightdress girt with a white apron and two red carnations in Mabel's black hair left no doubt as to which of the three was Beauty.

The scene went very well. The final dance with waving towels was all that there is of charming, Mademoiselle said; and Eliza was so much amused that, as she said, she got quite a nasty stitch along of laughing so hearty.

You know pretty well what Beauty and the Beast would be like acted by four children who had spent the afternoon in arranging their costumes and so had left no time for rehearsing what they had to say. Yet it delighted them, and it charmed their audience. And what more can any play do, even Shakespeare's? Mabel, in her Princess clothes, was a resplendent Beauty; and Gerald a Beast who wore the drawing-room hearthrugs with an air of indescribable distinction. If Jimmy was not a talkative merchant, he made it up with a stoutness practically unlimited, and Kathleen surprised and delighted even herself by the quickness with which she changed from one to the other of the minor characters – fairies, servants, and messengers. It was at the end of the second act that Mabel, whose costume, having reached the height of elegance, could not be bettered and therefore did not need to be changed, said to Gerald, sweltering under the weighty magnificence of his beast-skin:

'I say, you might let us have the ring back.'

'I'm going to,' said Gerald, who had quite forgotten it. 'I'll give it you in the next scene. Only don't lose it, or go putting it on. You might go out all together and never be seen again, or you might get seven times as visible as anyone else, so that all the rest of us would look like shadows beside you, you'd be so thick, or –'

'Ready!' said Kathleen, bustling in, once more a wicked sister.

Gerald managed to get his hand into his pocket under his hearthrug, and when he rolled his eyes in agonies of sentiment, and said, 'Farewell, dear Beauty! Return quickly, for if you remain long absent from your faithful beast he will assuredly perish,' he pressed a ring into her hand and added: 'This is a magic ring that will give you anything you wish. When you desire to return to your own disinterested beast, put on the ring and utter your wish. Instantly you will be by my side.'

Beauty-Mabel took the ring, and it was *the* ring.

The curtains closed to warm applause from two pairs of hands.

The next scene went splendidly. The sisters were almost *too* natural in their disagreeableness, and Beauty's annoyance when they splashed her Princess's dress with real soap and water was considered a miracle of good acting. Even the merchant rose to something more than mere pillows, and the curtain fell on his pathetic assurance that in the absence of his dear Beauty he was wasting away to a shadow. And again two pairs of hands applauded.

'Here, Mabel, catch hold,' Gerald appealed from under the weight of a towel-horse, the tea-urn, the tea-tray, and the green baize apron of the boot boy, which together with four red geraniums from the landing, the pampas-grass from the drawing-room fireplace, and the india rubber plants from the drawing-room window were to represent the fountains and garden of the last act. The applause had died away.

'I wish,' said Mabel, taking on herself the weight of the tea-urn, 'I wish those creatures we made were alive. We should get something like applause then.'

'I'm jolly glad they aren't,' said Gerald, arranging the baize and the towel-horse. 'Brutes! It makes me feel quite silly when I catch their paper eyes.'

The curtains were drawn back. There lay the hearthrug-coated beast, in flat abandonment among the tropic beauties of the garden, the pampas-grass shrubbery, the indiarubber plant bushes, the geranium-trees and the urn fountain. Beauty was ready to make her great entry in all the thrilling splendour of despair. And then suddenly it all happened.

Mademoiselle began it: she applauded the garden scene – with hurried little clappings of her quick French hands. Eliza's fat red palms followed heavily, and then – someone else was clapping, six or seven people, and their clapping made a dull padded sound. Nine faces instead of two were turned towards the stage, and seven out of the nine were painted, pointed paper faces. And every hand and every face was alive. The applause grew louder as Mabel glided forward, and as she paused and looked at the audience her unstudied pose of horror and amazement drew forth applause louder still; but it was not loud enough to drown the shrieks of Mademoiselle and Eliza as they rushed from the room, knocking chairs over and crushing each other in the doorway. Two distant doors banged, Mademoiselle's door and Eliza's door.

'Curtain! curtain! quick!' cried Beauty-Mabel, in a voice that wasn't Mabel's or the Beauty's. 'Jerry – those things *have* come alive. Oh, whatever *shall* we do?'

Gerald in his hearthrugs leaped to his feet. Again that flat padded applause marked the swish of cloths on clothes-line as Jimmy and Kathleen drew the curtains.

'What's up?' they asked as they drew.

'You've done it this time!' said Gerald to the pink, perspiring Mabel. 'Oh, bother these strings!'

'Can't you burst them? *I've* done it?' retorted Mabel. 'I like that!'

'More than I do,' said Gerald.

'Oh, it's all right,' said Mabel. 'Come on. We must go and pull the things to pieces – then they *can't* go on being alive.'

'It's your fault, anyhow,' said Gerald with every possible absence of gallantry. 'Don't you see? It's turned into a wishing ring. I *knew* something different was going to happen. Get my knife out of my pocket – this string's in a knot. Jimmy, Cathy, those Ugly-Wuglies have come alive – because Mabel wished it. Cut out and pull them to pieces.'

Jimmy and Cathy peeped through the curtain and recoiled with white faces and staring eyes. 'Not me!' was the brief rejoinder of Jimmy. Cathy said, 'Not much!' And she meant it, anyone could see that.

And now, as Gerald, almost free of the hearthrugs, broke his thumb-nail on the stiffest blade of his knife, a thick rustling and a sharp, heavy stumping sounded beyond the curtain.

'They're going out!' screamed Kathleen – '*walking* out – on their umbrella and broomstick legs. You can't stop them, Jerry, they're too awful!'

'Everybody in the town'll be insane by tomorrow night if we *don't* stop them,' cried Gerald. 'Here, give me the ring – I'll unwish them.'

He caught the ring from the unresisting Mabel,
cried, 'I wish the Uglies *weren't* alive,' and tore
through the door. He saw, in fancy, Mabel's wish
undone, and the empty hall strewed with limp bolsters,
hats, umbrellas, coats and gloves, prone abject proper-
ties from which the brief life had gone out for ever.
But the hall was crowded with live things, strange
things – all horribly short as broom sticks and umbrellas are short. A limp hand gesticulated. A pointed
white face with red cheeks looked up at him, and wide

red lips said something, he could not tell what. The voice reminded him of the old beggar down by the bridge who had no roof to his mouth. These creatures had no roofs to their mouths, of course – they had no –

'Aa oo ré o me me oo a oo ho el?' said the voice again. And it had said it four times before Gerald could collect himself sufficiently to understand that this horror – alive, and most likely quite uncontrollable – was saying, with a dreadful calm, polite persistence:

'Can you recommend me to a good hotel?'

7

'Can you recommend me to a good hotel?' The speaker had no inside to his head. Gerald had the best of reasons for knowing it. The speaker's coat had no shoulders inside it – only the cross-bar that a jacket is slung on by careful ladies. The hand raised in interrogation was not a hand at all; it was a glove lumpily stuffed with pocket-handkerchiefs; and the arm attached to it was only Kathleen's school umbrella. Yet the whole thing was alive, and was asking a definite, and for anybody else, anybody who really *was* a body, a reasonable question.

With a sensation of inward sinking, Gerald realized that now or never was the time for him to rise to the occasion. And at the thought he inwardly sank more deeply than before. It seemed impossible to rise in the very smallest degree.

'I beg your pardon' was absolutely the best he could do; and the painted, pointed paper face turned to him once more, and once more said: –

'Aa oo ré o me me oo a oo ho el?'

'You want a hotel?' Gerald repeated stupidly, 'a *good* hotel?'

'A oo ho el,' reiterated the painted lips.

'I'm awfully sorry,' Gerald went on – one can always

be polite, of course, whatever happens, and politeness came naturally to him – 'but all our hotels shut so early – about eight, I think.'

'Och em er,' said the Ugly-Wugly. Gerald even now does not understand how that practical joke – hastily wrought of hat, overcoat, paper face and limp hands – could have managed, by just being alive, to become perfectly respectable, apparently about fifty years old, and obviously well known and respected in his own suburb – the kind of man who travels first class and smokes expensive cigars. Gerald knew this time, without need of repetition, that the Ugly-Wugly had said:

'Knock 'em up.'

'You can't,' Gerald explained; 'they're all stone deaf – every single person who keeps a hotel in this town. It's –' he wildly plunged – 'it's a County Council law. Only deaf people are allowed to keep hotels. It's because of the hops in the beer,' he found himself adding; 'you know, hops are so good for ear-ache.'

'I o wy ollo oo,' said the respectable Ugly-Wugly; and Gerald was not surprised to find that the thing did 'not quite follow him'.

'It is a little difficult at first,' he said. The other Ugly-Wuglies were crowding round. The lady in the poke bonnet said – Gerald found he was getting quite clever at understanding the conversation of those who had no roofs to their mouths:

'If not a hotel, a lodging.'

'My lodging is on the cold ground,' sang itself unbidden and unavailing in Gerald's ear. Yet stay – was it unavailing?

'I do know a lodging,' he said slowly, 'but –' The

tallest of the Ugly-Wuglies pushed forward. He was dressed in the old brown overcoat and top-hat which always hung on the school hat-stand to discourage possible burglars by deluding them into the idea that there was a gentleman-of-the-house, and that he was at home. He had an air at once more sporting and less reserved than that of the first speaker, and anyone could see that he was not quite a gentleman.

'Wa I wo oo oh,' he began, but the lady Ugly-Wugly in the flower-wreathed hat interrupted him. She spoke more distinctly than the others, owing, as Gerald found afterwards, to the fact that her mouth had been drawn *open*, and the flap cut from the aperture had been folded back – so that she really had something like a roof to her mouth, though it was only a paper one.

'What *I* want to know,' Gerald understood her to say, 'is where are the carriages we ordered?'

'I don't know,' said Gerald, 'but I'll find out. But we ought to be moving,' he added; 'you see, the performance is over, and they want to shut up the house and put the lights out. Let's be moving.'

'Eh – ech e oo-ig,' repeated the respectable Ugly-Wugly, and stepped towards the front door.

'Oo um oo,' said the flower-wreathed one; and Gerald assures me that her vermilion lips stretched in a smile.

'I shall be delighted,' said Gerald with earnest courtesy, 'to do anything, of course. Things do happen so awkwardly when you least expect it. I could go with you, and get you a lodging, if you'd only wait a few moments in the – in the yard. It's quite a superior sort of yard,' he went on, as a wave of surprised disdain passed over their white paper faces – 'not a common yard, you know; the pump,' he added madly, 'has just been painted green all over, and the dustbin is enamelled iron.'

The Ugly-Wuglies turned to each other in consultation, and Gerald gathered that the greenness of the pump and the enamelled character of the dustbin made, in their opinion, all the difference.

'I'm awfully sorry,' he urged eagerly, 'to have to ask you to wait, but you see I've got an uncle who's quite mad, and I have to give him his gruel at half-past nine. He won't feed out of any hand but mine.' Gerald did not mind what he said. The only people one is allowed to tell lies to are the Ugly-Wuglies; they are all clothes and have no insides, because they are not human beings, but only a sort of very real visions, and therefore cannot be really deceived, though they may seem to be.

Through the back door that has the blue, yellow, red, and green glass in it, down the iron steps into the yard, Gerald led the way, and the Ugly-Wuglies trooped after him. Some of them had boots, but the ones whose feet were only broomsticks or umbrellas found the open-work iron stairs very awkward.

'If you wouldn't *mind*,' said Gerald, 'just waiting *under* the balcony? My uncle is so *very* mad. If he were to see – see any strangers – I mean, even aristocratic ones – I couldn't answer for the consequences.'

'Perhaps,' said the flower-hatted lady nervously, 'it would be better for us to try and find a lodging ourselves?'

'I wouldn't advise you to,' said Gerald as grimly as he knew how; 'the police here arrest *all* strangers. It's the new law the Liberals have just made,' he added convincingly, 'and you'd get the sort of lodging you wouldn't care for– I couldn't bear to think of you in a prison dungeon,' he added tenderly.

'I ah wi oo er papers,' said the respectable Ugly-Wugly, and added something that sounded like 'disgraceful state of things.'

However, they ranged themselves under the iron balcony. Gerald gave one last look at them and wondered, in his secret heart, why he was not frightened, though in his outside mind he was congratulating himself on his bravery. For the things did look rather horrid. In that light it was hard to believe that they were really only clothes and pillows and sticks – with no insides. As he went up the steps he heard them talking among themselves – in that strange language of theirs, all oo's and ah's; and he thought he distinguished the voice of the respectable Ugly-Wugly saying, 'Most gentlemanly lad,' and the wreathed-hatted lady answering warmly: 'Yes, indeed.'

The coloured-glass door closed behind him. Behind him was the yard, peopled by seven impossible creatures. Before him lay the silent house, peopled, as he knew very well, by five human beings as frightened as human beings could be. You think, perhaps, that Ugly-Wuglies are nothing to be frightened of. That's only because you have never seen one come alive. You must make one – any old suit of your father's, and a hat that he isn't wearing, a bolster or two, a painted paper face, a few sticks and a pair of boots will do the trick; get your father to lend you a wishing ring, give it back to him when it has done its work, and see how you feel then.

Of course the reason why Gerald was not afraid was that he had the ring; and, as you have seen, the wearer of that is not frightened by *anything* unless he touches that thing. But Gerald knew well enough how the others must be feeling. That was why he stopped for a moment in the hall to try and imagine what would have been most soothing to him if he had been as terrified as he knew they were.

'Cathy! I say! What ho, Jimmy! Mabel ahoy!' he cried in a loud, cheerful voice that sounded very unreal to himself.

The dining-room door opened a cautious inch.

'I say – such larks!' Gerald went on, shoving gently at the door with his shoulder. 'Look out! what are you keeping the door shut for?'

'Are you – alone?' asked Kathleen in hushed, breathless tones.

'Yes, of course. Don't be a duffer!'

The door opened, revealing three scared faces and the disarranged chairs where that odd audience had sat.

'Where are they? Have you unwished them? We heard them talking. Horrible!'

'They're in the yard,' said Gerald with the best imitation of joyous excitement that he could manage. 'It *is* such fun! They're just like real people, quite kind and jolly. It's the most ripping lark. Don't let on to Mademoiselle and Eliza. I'll square *them*. Then Kathleen and Jimmy must go to bed, and I'll see Mabel home, and as soon as we get outside I must find some sort of lodging for the Ugly-Wuglies – they *are* such fun though. I *do* wish you could all go with me.'

'Fun?' echoed Kathleen dismally and doubting.

'Perfectly killing,' Gerald asserted resolutely. 'Now, you just listen to what I say to Mademoiselle and Eliza, and back me up for all you're worth.'

'But,' said Mabel, 'you can't mean that you're going to leave me alone directly we get out, and go off with those horrible creatures. They look like fiends.'

'You wait till you've seen them close,' Gerald advised. 'Why, they're just *ordinary* – the first thing one of them did was to ask me to recommend it to a good hotel! I couldn't understand it at first, because it has no roof to its mouth, of course.'

It was a mistake to say that, Gerald knew it at once.

Mabel and Kathleen were holding hands in a way that plainly showed how a few moments ago they had been clinging to each other in an agony of terror. Now they clung again. And Jimmy, who was sitting on the edge of what had been the stage, kicking his boots against the pink counterpane, shuddered visibly.

'It doesn't *matter*,' Gerald explained – 'about the roofs, I mean; you soon get to understand. I heard them say I was a gentlemanly lad as I was coming away. They wouldn't have cared to notice a little thing like that if they'd been fiends, you know.'

'It doesn't matter how gentlemanly they think you; if you don't see me home you *aren't*, that's all. Are you going to?' Mabel demanded.

'Of course I am. We shall have no end of a lark. Now for Mademoiselle.'

He had put on his coat as he spoke and now ran up the stairs. The others, herding in the hall, could hear his light-hearted there's-nothing-unusual-the-matter-whatever-did-you-bolt-like-that-for knock at Mademoiselle's door, the reassuring 'It's only me – Gerald, you know,' the pause, the opening of the door, and the low-voiced parley that followed; then Mademoiselle and Gerald at Eliza's door, voices of reassurance; Eliza's terror, bluntly voluble, tactfully soothed.

'Wonder what lies he's telling them,' Jimmy grumbled.

'Oh! not *lies*,' said Mabel; 'he's only telling them as much of the truth as it's good for them to know.'

'If you'd been a man,' said Jimmy witheringly, 'you'd have been a beastly Jesuit, and hid up chimneys.'

'If I were only just a boy,' Mabel retorted, 'I shouldn't be scared out of my life by a pack of old coats.'

'I'm *so* sorry you were frightened,' Gerald's honeyed tones floated down the staircase; 'we didn't think about you being frightened. And it *was* a good trick, wasn't it?'

'There!' whispered Jimmy, 'he's been telling her it was a trick of ours.'

'Well, so it was,' said Mabel stoutly.

'It was indeed a wonderful trick,' said Mademoiselle; 'and how did you move the mannikins?'

'Oh, we've often done it – with strings, you know,' Gerald explained.

'That's true, too,' Kathleen whispered.

'Let us see you do once again this trick so remarkable,' said Mademoiselle, arriving at the bottom-stair mat.

'Oh, I've cleared them all out,' said Gerald. ('So he has,' from Kathleen aside to Jimmy.) 'We were so sorry you were startled; we thought you wouldn't like to see them again.'

'Then,' said Mademoiselle brightly, as she peeped

into the untidy dining-room and saw that the figures
had indeed vanished, 'if we supped and discoursed of
your beautiful piece of theatre?'

Gerald explained fully how much his brother and
sister would enjoy this. As for him – Mademoiselle
would see that it was his duty to escort Mabel home,
and kind as it was of Mademoiselle to ask her to stay
the night, it could not be, on account of the frenzied
and anxious affection of Mabel's aunt. And it was
useless to suggest that Eliza should see Mabel home,

because Eliza was nervous at night unless accompanied by her gentleman friend.

So Mabel was hatted with her own hat and cloaked with a cloak that was not hers; and she and Gerald went out by the front door, amid kind last words and appointments for the morrow.

The moment that front door was shut Gerald caught Mabel by the arm and led her briskly to the corner of the side street which led to the yard. Just round the corner he stopped.

'Now,' he said, 'what I want to know is – are you an idiot or aren't you?'

'Idiot yourself!' said Mabel, but mechanically, for she saw that he was in earnest.

'Because *I'm* not frightened of the Ugly-Wuglies. They're as harmless as tame rabbits. But an idiot might be frightened, and give the whole show away. If you're an idiot, say so, and I'll go back and tell them you're afraid to walk home, and that I'll go and let your aunt know you're stopping.'

'I'm not an idiot,' said Mabel; 'and,' she added, glaring round her with the wild gaze of the truly terror-stricken, 'I'm not afraid of *anything*.'

'I'm going to let you share my difficulties and dangers,' said Gerald; 'at least, I'm inclined to let you. I wouldn't do as much for my own brother, I can tell you. And if you queer my pitch I'll never speak to you again or let the others either.'

'You're a beast, that's what you are! I don't need to be threatened to make me brave. I *am*.'

'Mabel,' said Gerald, in low, thrilling tones, for he saw that the time had come to sound another note, 'I *know* you're brave. I *believe* in you. That's why I've arranged it like this. I'm certain you've got the heart of a lion under that black-and-white exterior. Can I trust you? To the death?'

Mabel felt that to say anything but 'Yes' was to throw away a priceless reputation for courage. So 'Yes' was what she said.

'Then wait here. You're close to the lamp. And when you see me coming with *them* remember they're as harmless as serpents – I mean doves. Talk to them just like you would to anyone else. See?'

He turned to leave her, but stopped at her natural question:

'What hotel did you say you were going to take them to?'

'Oh, Jimminy!' the harassed Gerald caught at his hair with both hands. 'There! you see, Mabel, you're a help already;' he had, even at that moment, some tact left. 'I clean forgot! I meant to ask you – isn't there any lodge or anything in the Castle grounds where I could put them for the night! The charm will break, you know, some time, like being invisible did, and they'll just be a pack of coats and things that we can easily carry home any day. Is there a lodge or anything?'

'There's a secret passage,' Mabel began – but at the moment the yard-door opened and an Ugly-Wugly put out its head and looked anxiously down the street.

'Righto!' – Gerald ran to meet it. It was all Mabel could do not to run in an opposite direction with an opposite motive. It was all she could do, but she did it, and was proud of herself as long as ever she remembered that night.

And now, with all the silent precaution necessitated by the near presence of an extremely insane uncle, the Ugly-Wuglies, a grisly band, trooped out of the yard door.

'Walk on your toes, dear,' the bonneted Ugly-Wugly whispered to the one with a wreath; and even at that thrilling crisis Gerald wondered how she could, since the toes of one foot were but the end of a golf club and of the other the end of a hockey-stick.

Mabel felt that there was no shame in retreating to the lamp-post at the street corner, but, once there, she made herself halt – and no one but Mabel will ever know how much making that took. Think of it – to stand there, firm and quiet, and wait for those hollow, unbelievable things to come up to her, clattering on the pavement with their stumpy feet or borne along noiselessly, as in the case of the flower-hatted lady, by a skirt that touched the ground, and had, Mabel knew very well, nothing at all inside it.

She stood very still; the insides of her hands grew cold and damp, but still she stood, saying over and over again: 'They're not true – they can't be true. It's only a dream – they aren't really true. They can't be.' And then Gerald was there, and all the Ugly-Wuglies crowding round, and Gerald saying:

'This is one of our friends, Mabel – the Princess in the play, you know. Be a man!' he added in a whisper for her ear alone.

Mabel, all her nerves stretched tight as banjo strings, had an awful instant of not knowing whether she would be able to be a man or whether she would be merely a shrieking and running little mad girl. For the respectable Ugly-Wugly shook her limply by the hand

('He *can't* be true,' she told herself), and the rose-wreathed one took her arm with a soft-padded glove at the end of an umbrella arm, and said:

'You dear, clever little thing! *Do* walk with me!' in a gushing, girlish way, and in speech almost wholly lacking in consonants.

Then they all walked up the High Street as if, as Gerald said, they were anybody else.

It was a strange procession, but Liddlesby goes early to bed, and the Liddlesby police, in common with those of most other places, wear boots that one can hear a mile off. If such boots had been heard, Gerald would have had time to turn back and head them off. He felt now that he could not resist a flush of pride in Mabel's courage as he heard her polite rejoinders to the still more polite remarks of the amiable Ugly-Wuglies. He did not know how near she was to the scream that would throw away the whole thing and bring the police and the residents out to the ruin of everybody.

They met no one, except one man, who murmured, 'Guy Fawkes, swelp me!' and crossed the road hurriedly; and when, next day, he told what he had seen, his wife disbelieved him, and also said it was a judgement on him, which was unreasonable.

Mabel felt as though she were taking part in a very completely arranged nightmare, but Gerald was in it too, Gerald, who had asked if she was an idiot. Well, she wasn't. But she soon would be, she felt. Yet she went on answering the courteous vowel-talk of these impossible people. She had often heard her aunt speak of impossible people. Well, now she knew what they were like.

Summer twilight had melted into summer moonlight. The shadows of the Ugly-Wuglies on the white
road were much more horrible than their more solid
selves. Mabel wished it had been a dark night, and
then corrected the wish with a hasty shudder.

Gerald, submitting to a searching interrogatory
from the tall-hatted Ugly-Wugly as to his schools,
his sports, pastimes, and ambitions, wondered how
long the spell would last. The ring seemed to work
in sevens. Would these things have seven hours' life
– or fourteen – or twenty-one? His mind lost itself
in the intricacies of the seven-times table (a teaser at
the best of times) and only found itself with a shock
when the procession found *itself* at the gates of the
Castle grounds.

Locked – of course.

'You see,' he explained, as the Ugly-Wuglies vainly

shook the iron gates with incredible hands; 'it's so very late. There *is* another way. But you have to climb through a hole.'

'The ladies,' the respectable Ugly-Wugly began objecting; but the ladies with one voice affirmed that they loved adventures. 'So frightfully thrilling,' added the one who wore roses.

So they went round by the road, and coming to the hole – it was a little difficult to find in the moonlight, which always disguises the most familiar things – Gerald went first with the bicycle lantern which he had snatched as his pilgrims came out of the yard; the shrinking Mabel followed, and then the Ugly-Wuglies, with hollow rattlings of their wooden limbs against the stone, crept through, and with strange vowel-sounds of general amazement, manly courage, and feminine nervousness, followed the light along the passage through the fern-hung cutting and under the arch.

When they emerged on the moonlit enchantment of the Italian garden a quite intelligible 'Oh!' of surprised admiration broke from more than one painted paper lip; and the respectable Ugly-Wugly was understood to say that it must be quite a show-place – by George, sir! yes.

Those marble terraces and artfully serpentining gravel walks surely never had echoed to steps so strange. No shadows so wildly unbelievable had, for all its enchantments, ever fallen on those smooth, grey, dewy lawns. Gerald was thinking this, or something like it (what he really thought was, 'I bet there never was such ado as this, even here!'), when he saw the statue of Hermes leap from its pedestal and run towards him and his company with all the lively curiosity of a street boy eager to be in at a street fight. He saw, too, that he was the only one who perceived that white advancing presence. And he knew that it was the ring that let him see what by others could not be seen. He slipped it from his finger. Yes; Hermes was on his pedestal, still as the snow man you make in the Christmas holidays. He put the ring on again, and there was Hermes, circling round the group and gazing deep in each unconscious Ugly-Wugly face.

'This seems a very superior hotel,' the tall-hatted Ugly-Wugly was saying; 'the grounds are laid out with what you might call taste.'

'We should have to go in by the back door,' said Mabel suddenly. 'The front door's locked at half-past nine.'

A short, stout Ugly-Wugly in a yellow and blue cricket cap, who had hardly spoken, muttered something about an escapade, and about feeling quite young again.

And now they had skirted the marble-edged pool where the gold fish swam and glimmered, and where the great prehistoric beast had come down to bathe and drink. The water flashed white diamonds in the moonlight, and Gerald alone of them all saw that the scaly-plated vast lizard was even now rolling and wallowing there among the lily pads.

They hastened up the steps of the Temple of Flora. The back of it, where no elegant arch opened to the air, was against one of those sheer hills, almost cliffs, that diversified the landscape of that garden. Mabel passed behind the statue of the goddess, fumbled a little, and then Gerald's lantern, flashing like a searchlight, showed a very high and very narrow doorway: the stone that was the door, and that had closed it, revolved slowly under the touch of Mabel's fingers.

'This way,' she said, and panted a little. The back of her neck felt cold and goose-fleshy.

'You lead the way, my lad, with the lantern,' said the suburban Ugly-Wugly in his bluff, agreeable way.

'I – I must stay behind to close the door,' said Gerald.

'The Princess can do that. *We'll* help her,' said the wreathed one with effusion; and Gerald thought her horribly officious.

He insisted gently that he would be the one responsible for the safe shutting of that door.

'You wouldn't like me to get into trouble, I'm sure,' he urged; and the Ugly-Wuglies, for the last time kind and reasonable, agreed that this, of all things, they would most deplore.

'*You* take it,' Gerald urged, pressing the bicycle lamp on the elderly Ugly-Wugly; 'you're the natural leader. Go straight ahead. Are there any steps?' he asked Mabel in a whisper.

'Not for ever so long,' she whispered back. 'It goes on for ages, and then twists round.'

'Whispering,' said the smallest Ugly-Wugly suddenly, 'ain't manners.'

'*He* hasn't any, anyhow,' whispered the lady Ugly-Wugly; 'don't mind him – quite a self-made man,' and squeezed Mabel's arm with horrible confidential flabbiness.

The respectable Ugly-Wugly leading with the lamp, the others following trustfully, one and all disappeared into that narrow doorway; and Gerald and Mabel standing without, hardly daring to breathe lest a breath should retard the procession, almost sobbed with relief. Prematurely, as it turned out. For suddenly there was a rush and a scuffle inside the passage, and as they strove to close the door the Ugly-Wuglies fiercely pressed to open it again. Whether they saw something in the dark passage that alarmed them, whether they took it into their empty heads that this could not be the back way to any really respectable hotel, or whether a convincing sudden instinct warned them that they were being tricked, Mabel and Gerald never knew. But they knew that the Ugly-Wuglies were no longer friendly and commonplace, that a fierce change had come over them. Cries of 'No, No!' 'We won't go on!' 'Make *him* lead!' broke the dreamy stillness of the perfect night. There were screams from ladies' voices, the hoarse, determined shouts of strong Ugly-Wuglies roused to resistance, and, worse than all, the steady pushing open of that narrow stone door that had almost closed upon the ghastly crew. Through the chink of it they could be seen, a writhing black crowd against the light of the bicycle lamp; a padded hand reached round the door; stick-boned arms stretched out angrily towards the world that that door, if it closed, would shut them off from for ever. And the tone of their consonantless speech was no longer conciliatory and ordinary; it was threatening, full of the menace of unbearable horrors.

The padded hand fell on Gerald's arm, and instantly all the terrors that he had, so far, only known in imagination became real to him, and he saw, in the sort of flash that shows drowning people their past lives, what it was that he had asked of Mabel, and that she had given.

'Push, push for your life!' he cried, and setting his heel against the pedestal of Flora, pushed manfully.

'I can't any more – oh, I can't!' moaned Mabel, and tried to use her heel likewise, but her legs were too short.

'They mustn't get out, they mustn't!' Gerald panted.

'You'll know it when we do,' came from inside the door in tones which fury and mouth-rooflessness would have made unintelligible to any ears but those sharpened by the wild fear of that unspeakable moment.

'What's up, there?' cried suddenly a new voice – a voice with all its consonants comforting, clean-cut, and ringing, and abruptly a new shadow fell on the marble floor of Flora's temple.

'Come and help push!' Gerald's voice only just reached the newcomer. 'If they get out they'll kill us all.'

A strong, velveteen-covered shoulder pushed suddenly between the shoulders of Gerald and Mabel; a stout man's heel sought the aid of the goddess's pedestal; the heavy, narrow door yielded slowly, it closed, its spring clicked, and the furious, surging, threatening mass of Ugly-Wuglies was shut in, and Gerald and Mabel – oh, incredible relief! – were shut out. Mabel threw herself on the marble floor, sobbing slow, heavy sobs of achievement and exhaustion. If I had been there I should have looked the other way, so as not to see whether Gerald yielded himself to the same abandonment.

The newcomer – he appeared to be a gamekeeper, Gerald decided later – looked down on – well, certainly on Mabel, and said:

'Come on, don't be a little duffer.' (He may have said, 'a couple of little duffers'.) 'Who is it, and what's it all about?'

'I can't possibly tell you,' Gerald panted.

'We shall have to see about that, shan't we,' said the newcomer amiably. 'Come out into the moonlight and let's review the situation.'

Gerald, even in that topsy-turvy state of his world, found time to think that a gamekeeper who used such words as that had most likely a romantic past. But at the same time he saw that such a man would be far less easy to 'square' with an unconvincing tale than Eliza, or Johnson, or even Mademoiselle. In fact, he seemed, with the only tale that they had to tell, practically unsquarable.

Gerald got up – if he was not up already, or still up – and pulled at the limp and now hot hand of the sobbing Mabel; and as he did so the unsquarable one took *his* hand, and thus led both children out from under the shadow of Flora's dome into the bright white moonlight that carpeted Flora's steps. Here he sat down, a child on each side of him, drew a hand of each through his velveteen arm, pressed them to his velveteen sides in a friendly, reassuring way, and said: 'Now then! Go ahead!'

Mabel merely sobbed. We must excuse her. She had been very brave, and I have no doubt that all heroines, from Joan of Arc to Grace Darling, have had their sobbing moments.

But Gerald said: 'It's no use. If I made up a story you'd see through it.'

'That's a compliment to my discernment, anyhow,' said the stranger. 'What price telling me the truth?'

'If we told you the truth,' said Gerald, 'you wouldn't believe it.'

'Try me,' said the velveteen one. He was clean-shaven, and had large eyes that sparkled when the moonlight touched them.

'I *can't*,' said Gerald, and it was plain that he spoke the truth. 'You'd either think we were mad, and get us shut up, or else – oh, it's no good. Thank you for helping us, and do let us go home.'

'I wonder,' said the stranger musingly, 'whether you have any imagination.'

'Considering that we invented them,' Gerald hotly began, and stopped with late prudence.

'If by "them" you mean the people whom I helped you to imprison in yonder tomb,' said the Stranger, loosing Mabel's hand to put his arm round her, 'remember that I saw and heard them. And with all respect to your imagination, I doubt whether any invention of yours would be quite so convincing.'

Gerald put his elbows on his knees and his chin in his hands.

'Collect yourself,' said the one in velveteen; 'and while you are collecting, let me just put the thing from my point of view. I think you hardly realize my position. I come down from London to take care of a big estate.'

'I *thought* you were a gamekeeper,' put in Gerald.

Mabel put her head on the stranger's shoulder. 'Hero in disguise, then, *I* know,' she sniffed.

'Not at all,' said he; 'bailiff would be nearer the mark. On the very first evening I go out to take the moonlit air, and approaching a white building, hear sounds of an agitated scuffle, accompanied by frenzied appeals for assistance. Carried away by the enthusiasm of the moment, I *do* assist and shut up goodness knows who behind a stone door. Now, is it unreasonable that I should ask who it is that I've shut up – helped to shut up, I mean, and who it is that I've assisted?'

'It's reasonable enough,' Gerald admitted.

'Well then,' said the stranger.

'Well then,' said Gerald, 'the fact is – No,' he added after a pause, 'the fact is, I simply can't tell you.'

'Then I must ask the other side,' said Velveteens. 'Let me go – I'll undo that door and find out for myself.'

'Tell him,' said Mabel, speaking for the first time. 'Never mind if he believes or not. We can't have them let out.'

'Very well,' said Gerald, 'I'll tell him. Now look here, Mr Bailiff, will you promise us on an English gentleman's word of honour – because, of course, I can see you're *that*, bailiff or not – will you promise that you won't tell any one what we tell you and that you won't have us put in a lunatic asylum, however mad we sound?'

'Yes,' said the stranger, 'I think I can promise that. But if you've been having a sham fight or anything and shoved the other side into that hole, don't you think you'd better let them out? They'll be most awfully frightened, you know. After all, I suppose they are only children.'

'Wait till you hear,' Gerald answered. 'They're not

children – not much! Shall I just tell about them or begin at the beginning?'

'The beginning, of course,' said the stranger.

Mabel lifted her head from his velveteen shoulder and said, 'Let me begin, then. I found a ring, and I said it would make me invisible. I said it in play. And it *did*. I was invisible twenty-one hours. Never mind where I got the ring. Now, Gerald, you go on.'

Gerald went on; for quite a long time he went on, for the story was a splendid one to tell.

'And so,' he ended, 'we got them in there; and when seven hours are over, or fourteen, or twenty-one, or something with a seven in it, they'll just be old coats again. They came alive at half-past nine. *I* think they'll stop being it in seven hours – that's half-past four. *Now* will you let us go home?'

'I'll see you home,' said the stranger in a quite new tone of exasperating gentleness. 'Come – let's be going.'

'You don't believe us,' said Gerald. 'Of course you don't. Nobody could. But I could make you believe if I chose.'

All three stood up, and the stranger stared in Gerald's eyes till Gerald answered his thought.

'No, I don't look mad, do I?'

'No, you aren't. But, come, you're an extraordinarily sensible boy; don't you think you may be sickening for a fever or something?'

'And Cathy and Jimmy and Mademoiselle and Eliza, and the man who said "Guy Fawkes, swelp me!" and *you*, you saw them move – you heard them call out. Are you sickening for anything?'

'No – or at least not for anything but information. Come, and I'll see you home.'

'Mabel lives at the Towers,' said Gerald, as the stranger turned into the broad drive that leads to the big gate.

'No relation to Lord Yalding,' said Mabel hastily – 'housekeeper's niece.' She was holding on to his hand all the way. At the servants' entrance she put up her face to be kissed, and went in.

'Poor little thing!' said the bailiff, as they went down the drive towards the gate.

He went with Gerald to the door of the school.

'Look here,' said Gerald at parting. 'I know what you're going to do. You're going to try to undo that door.'

'Discerning!' said the stranger.

'Well – don't. Or, any way, wait till daylight and let us be there. We can get there by ten.'

'All right – I'll meet you there by ten,' answered the stranger. 'By George! you're the rummest kids I ever met.'

'We are rum,' Gerald owned, 'but so would you be if – Good-night.'

As the four children went over the smooth lawn towards Flora's Temple they talked, as they had talked all the morning, about the adventures of last night and of Mabel's bravery. It was not ten, but half-past twelve; for Eliza, backed by Mademoiselle, had insisted on their 'clearing up', and clearing up very thoroughly, the 'litter' of last night.

'You're a Victoria Cross heroine, dear,' said Cathy warmly. 'You ought to have a statue put up to you.'

'It would come alive if you put it here,' said Gerald grimly.

'*I* shouldn't have been afraid,' said Jimmy.

'By daylight,' Gerald assured him, 'everything looks so jolly different.'

'I do hope he'll be there,' Mabel said; 'he *was* such a dear, Cathy – a perfect bailiff, with the soul of a gentleman.'

'He isn't there, though,' said Jimmy. 'I believe you just dreamed him, like you did the statues coming alive.'

They went up the marble steps in the sunshine, and

it was difficult to believe that this was the place where only in last night's moonlight fear had laid such cold hands on the hearts of Mabel and Gerald.

'Shall we open the door,' suggested Kathleen, 'and begin to carry home the coats?'

'Let's listen first,' said Gerald; 'perhaps they aren't only coats yet.'

They laid ears to the hinges of the stone door, behind which last night the Ugly-Wuglies had shrieked and threatened. All was still as the sweet morning itself. It was as they turned away that they saw the man they had come to meet. He was on the other side of Flora's pedestal. But he was not standing up. He lay there, quite still, on his back, his arms flung wide.

'Oh, look!' cried Cathy, and pointed. His face was a queer greenish colour, and on his forehead there was a cut; its edges were blue, and a little blood had trickled from it on to the white of the marble.

At the same time Mabel pointed too – but she did not cry out as Cathy had done. And what she pointed at was a big glossy-leaved rhododendron bush, from which a painted pointed paper face peered out – very white, very red, in the sunlight – and, as the children gazed, shrank back into the cover of the shining leaves.

8

It was but too plain. The unfortunate bailiff must have opened the door before the spell had faded, while yet the Ugly-Wuglies were something more than mere coats and hats and sticks. They had rushed out upon him, and had done this. He lay there insensible – was it a golf-club or a hockey-stick that had made that horrible cut on his forehead? Gerald wondered. The girls had rushed to the sufferer; already his head was in Mabel's lap. Kathleen had tried to get it on to hers, but Mabel was too quick for her.

Jimmy and Gerald both knew what was the first thing needed by the unconscious, even before Mabel impatiently said: 'Water! water!'

'What in?' Jimmy asked, looking doubtfully at his hands, and then down the green slope to the marble-bordered pool where the water-lilies were.

'Your hat – anything,' said Mabel.

The two boys turned away.

'Suppose they come after us,' said Jimmy.

'*What* come after us?' Gerald snapped rather than asked.

'The Ugly-Wuglies,' Jimmy whispered.

'Who's afraid?' Gerald inquired.

But he looked to right and left very carefully, and

chose the way that did not lead near the bushes. He scooped water up in his straw hat and returned to Flora's Temple, carrying it carefully in both hands. When he saw how quickly it ran through the straw he pulled his handkerchief from his breast pocket with his teeth and dropped it into the hat. It was with this that the girls wiped the blood from the bailiff's brow.

'We ought to have smelling salts,' said Kathleen, half in tears. 'I know we ought.'

'They would be good,' Mabel owned.

'Hasn't your aunt any?'

'Yes, but –'

'Don't be a coward,' said Gerald; 'think of last night. *They* wouldn't hurt you. He must have insulted them or something. Look here, you run. We'll see that nothing runs after you.'

There was no choice but to relinquish the head of the interesting invalid to Kathleen; so Mabel did it, cast one glaring glance round the rhododendron bordered slope, and fled towards the castle.

The other three bent over the still unconscious bailiff.

'He's not dead, is he?' asked Jimmy anxiously.

'No,' Kathleen reassured him, 'his heart's beating. Mabel and I felt it in his wrist, where doctors do. How frightfully good-looking he is!'

'Not so dusty,' Gerald admitted.

'I never know what you mean by good-looking,' said Jimmy, and suddenly a shadow fell on the marble beside them and a fourth voice spoke – not Mabel's; her hurrying figure, though still in sight, was far away.

'Quite a personable young man,' it said.

The children looked up – into the face of the eldest of the Ugly-Wuglies, the respectable one. Jimmy and Kathleen screamed. I am sorry, but they did.

'Hush!' said Gerald savagely: he was still wearing the ring. 'Hold your tongues! I'll get him away,' he added in a whisper.

'Very sad affair this,' said the respectable Ugly-Wugly. He spoke with a curious accent; there was something odd about his r's, and his m's and n's were those of a person labouring under an almost intolerable cold in the head. But it was not the dreadful 'oo' and 'ah' voice of the night before. Kathleen and Jimmy stooped over the bailiff. Even that prostrate form, being human, seemed some little protection. But Gerald, strong in the fearlessness that the ring gave to its wearer, looked full into the face of the Ugly-Wugly – and started. For though the face was almost the same as the face he had himself painted on the school drawing-paper, it was not the same. For it was no longer paper. It was a real face, and the hands, lean and almost transparent as they were, were real hands. As it moved a little to get a better view of the bailiff it was plain that it had legs, arms – live legs and arms, and a self-supporting backbone. It was alive indeed – with a vengeance.

'How did it happen?' Gerald asked with an effort at calmness – a successful effort.

'Most regrettable,' said the Ugly-Wugly. 'The others must have missed the way last night in the passage. They never found the hotel.'

'Did *you*?' asked Gerald blankly.

'Of course,' said the Ugly-Wugly. 'Most respectable, exactly as you said. Then when I came away – I didn't come the front way because I wanted to revisit this sylvan scene by daylight, and the hotel people didn't seem to know how to direct me to it – I found the others all at this door, very angry. They'd been here all night, trying to get out. Then the door opened – this gentleman must have opened it – and before I could protect him, that underbred man in the high hat – you remember –'

Gerald remembered.

'Hit him on the head, and he fell where you see him. The others dispersed, and I myself was just going for assistance when I saw you.'

Here Jimmy was discovered to be in tears and Kathleen white as any drawing-paper.

'What's the matter, my little man?' said the respectable Ugly-Wugly kindly. Jimmy passed instantly from tears to yells.

'Here, take the ring!' said Gerald in a furious whisper, and thrust it on to Jimmy's hot, damp, resisting finger. Jimmy's voice stopped short in the middle of a howl. And Gerald in a cold flash realized what it was that Mabel had gone through the night before. But it was daylight, and Gerald was not a coward.

'We must find the others,' he said.

'I imagine,' said the elderly Ugly-Wugly, 'that they have gone to bathe. Their clothes are in the wood.'

He pointed stiffly.

'You two go and see,' said Gerald. 'I'll go on dabbing this chap's head.'

In the wood Jimmy, now fearless as any lion, discovered four heaps of clothing, with broomsticks, hockey-sticks, and masks complete, all that had gone to make up the gentlemen Ugly-Wuglies of the night before. On a stone seat well in the sun sat the two lady Ugly-Wuglies, and Kathleen approached them gingerly. Valour is easier in the sunshine than at night, as we all know. When she and Jimmy came close to the bench, they saw that the Ugly-Wuglies were only Ugly-Wuglies such as they had often made. There was no life in them. Jimmy shook them to pieces, and a sigh of relief burst from Kathleen.

'The spell's broken, you see,' she said; 'and that old gentleman, he's real. He only happens to be like the Ugly-Wugly we made.'

'He's got the coat that hung in the hall on, anyway,' said Jimmy.

'No, it's only like it. Let's get back to the unconscious stranger.'

They did, and Gerald begged the elderly Ugly-Wugly to retire among the bushes with Jimmy; 'because,' said he, 'I think the poor bailiff's coming round, and it might upset him to see strangers – and Jimmy'll keep you company. He's the best one of us to go with you,' he added hastily.

And this, since Jimmy had the ring, was certainly true.

So the two disappeared behind the rhododendrons. Mabel came back with the salts just as the bailiff opened his eyes.

'It's just like life,' she said; 'I might just as well not have gone. However –' She knelt down at once and held the bottle under the sufferer's nose till he sneezed and feebly pushed her hand away with the faint question:

'What's up now?'

H. R. MILLAR '7

'You've hurt your head,' said Gerald. 'Lie still.'

'No – more – smelling-bottle,' he said weakly, and lay.

Quite soon he sat up and looked round him. There was an anxious silence. Here was a grown-up who knew last night's secret, and none of the children were at all sure what the utmost rigour of the law might be in a case where people, no matter how young, made Ugly-Wuglies, and brought them to life – dangerous, fighting, angry life. What would he say – what would he do? He said: 'What an odd thing! Have I been insensible long?'

'Hours,' said Mabel earnestly.

'Not long,' said Kathleen.

'We don't know. We found you like it,' said Gerald.

'I'm all right now,' said the bailiff, and his eye fell on the blood-stained handkerchief. 'I say, I did give my head a bang. And you've been giving me first aid. Thank you most awfully. But it is rum.'

'What's rum?' politeness obliged Gerald to ask.

'Well, I suppose it isn't really rum – I expect I saw you just before I fainted, or whatever it was – but I've dreamed the most extraordinary dream while I've been insensible and you were in it.'

'Nothing but us?' asked Mabel breathlessly.

'Oh, lots of things – impossible things – but *you* were real enough.'

Everyone breathed deeply in relief. It was indeed, as they agreed later, a lucky let-off.

'Are you *sure* you're all right?' they all asked, as he got on his feet.

'Perfectly, thank you.' He glanced behind Flora's statue as he spoke. 'Do you know, I dreamed there was a door there, but of course there isn't. I don't know how to thank you,' he added, looking at them with what the girls called his beautiful, kind eyes; 'it's lucky for me you came along. You come here whenever you like, you know,' he added. 'I give you the freedom of the place.'

'You're the new bailiff, aren't you?' said Mabel.

'Yes. How did you know?' he asked quickly; but they did not tell him how they knew. Instead, they found out which way he was going, and went the other way after warm handshakes and hopes on both sides that they would meet again soon.

'I'll tell you what,' said Gerald, as they watched the tall, broad figure of the bailiff grow smaller across the hot green of the grass slope, 'have you got any idea of how we're going to spend the day? Because I have.'

The others hadn't.

'We'll get rid of that Ugly-Wugly – oh, we'll find a way right enough – and directly we've done it we'll go home and seal up the ring in an envelope so that its teeth'll be drawn and it'll be powerless to have unforeseen larks with us. Then we'll get out on the roof, and have a quiet day – books and apples. I'm about fed up with adventures, so I tell you.'

The others told him the same thing.

'Now, *think*,' said he – 'think as you never thought before – how to get rid of that Ugly-Wugly.'

Everyone thought, but their brains were tired with anxiety and distress, and the thoughts they thought were, as Mabel said, not worth thinking, let alone saying.

'I suppose Jimmy's all right,' said Kathleen anxiously.

'Oh, *he's* all right: he's got the ring,' said Gerald.

'I hope he won't go wishing anything rotten,' said Mabel, but Gerald urged her to shut up and let him think.

'I think I think best sitting down,' he said, and sat; 'and sometimes you can think best aloud. The Ugly-Wugly's *real* – don't make any mistake about that. And he got made real inside that passage. If we could get him back there he might get changed again, and then we could take the coats and things back.'

'Isn't there any other way?' Kathleen asked; and Mabel, more candid, said bluntly: 'I'm not going into that passage, so there!'

'Afraid! In broad daylight,' Gerald sneered.

'It wouldn't be broad daylight in there,' said Mabel, and Kathleen shivered.

'If we went to him and suddenly tore his coat off,' said she – 'he *is* only coats – he couldn't go on being real then.'

'*Couldn't* he!' said Gerald. 'You don't know what he's like under the coat.'

Kathleen shivered again. And all this time the sun was shining gaily and the white statues and the green trees and the fountains and terraces looked as cheerfully romantic as a scene in a play.

'Anyway,' said Gerald, 'we'll try to get him back, and shut the door. That's the most we can hope for. And then apples, and *Robinson Crusoe* or the *Swiss Family*, or any book you like that's got no magic in it. Now, we've just got to do it. And he's not horrid now; *really* he isn't. He's real, you see.'

'I suppose that makes all the difference,' said Mabel, and tried to feel that perhaps it did.

'And it's broad daylight – just look at the sun,' Gerald insisted. 'Come on!'

He took a hand of each, and they walked resolutely towards the bank of rhododendrons behind which Jimmy and the Ugly-Wugly had been told to wait, and as they went Gerald said: 'He's real' – 'The sun's shining' – 'It'll all be over in a minute.' And he said these things again and again, so that there should be no mistake about them.

As they neared the bushes the shining leaves rustled, shivered, and parted, and before the girls had time to begin to hang back Jimmy came blinking out into the sunlight. The boughs closed behind him, and they did not stir or rustle for the appearance of anyone else. Jimmy was alone.

'Where is it?' asked the girls in one breath.

'Walking up and down in a fir-walk,' said Jimmy, 'doing sums in a book. He says he's most frightfully rich, and he's got to get up to town to the Stocks or something – where they change papers into gold if you're clever, he says. I should like to go to the Stocks-change, wouldn't you?'

'I don't seem to care very much about changes,' said Gerald. 'I've had enough. Show us where he is – we must get rid of him.'

'He's got a motor-car,' Jimmy went on, parting the warm varnished-looking rhododendron leaves, 'and a garden with a tennis-court and a lake and a carriage and pair, and he goes to Athens for his holiday sometimes, just like other people go to Margate.'

'The best thing,' said Gerald, following through the bushes, 'will be to tell him the shortest way out is through that hotel that he thinks he found last night. Then we get him into the passage, give him a push, fly back, and shut the door.'

'He'll starve to death in there,' said Kathleen, 'if he's really real.'

'I expect it doesn't last long, the ring magics don't – anyway, it's the only thing I can think of.'

'He's frightfully rich,' Jimmy went on unheeding amid the cracking of the bushes; 'he's building a public library for the people where he lives, and having his portrait painted to put in it. He thinks they'll like that.'

The belt of rhododendrons was passed, and the

children had reached a smooth grass walk bordered by tall pines and firs of strange different kinds. 'He's just round that corner,' said Jimmy. 'He's simply rolling in money. He doesn't know what to do with it. He's been building a horse-trough and drinking fountain with a bust of himself on top. Why doesn't he build a private swimming-bath close to his bed, so that he can just roll off into it of a morning? I wish *I* was rich; I'd soon show him –'

'That's a sensible wish,' said Gerald. 'I wonder we didn't think of doing that. Oh, criky!' he added, and with reason. For there, in the green shadows of the pine-walk, in the woodland silence, broken only by rustling leaves and the agitated breathing of the three unhappy others, Jimmy got his wish. By quick but perfectly plain-to-be-seen degrees Jimmy became rich. And the horrible thing was that though they could see it happening they did not know what was happening, and could not have stopped it if they had. All they could see was Jimmy, their own Jimmy, whom they had larked with and quarrelled with and made it up with ever since they could remember, Jimmy continuously and horribly growing old. The whole thing was over in a few seconds. Yet in those few seconds they saw him grow to a youth, a young man, a middle-aged man; and then, with a sort of shivering shock, unspeakably horrible and definite, he seemed to settle down into an elderly gentleman, handsomely but rather dowdily dressed, who was looking down at them through spectacles and asking them the nearest way to the railway-station. If they had not seen the change take place, in all its awful details, they would never have guessed that this stout, prosperous, elderly gentleman with the high hat, the frock-coat, and the large red seal dangling from the curve of a portly waistcoat, was their own Jimmy. But, as they *had* seen it, they knew the dreadful truth.

'Oh, Jimmy, *don't*!' cried Mabel desperately.

Gerald said: 'This is perfectly beastly,' and Kathleen broke into wild weeping.

'Don't cry, little girl!' said That-which-had-been Jimmy; 'and you, boy, can't you give a civil answer to a civil question?'

'He doesn't know us!' wailed Kathleen.

'Who doesn't know you?' said That-which-had-been impatiently.

'You – y-*you* don't!' Kathleen sobbed.

'I certainly don't,' returned That-which – 'but surely that need not distress you so deeply.'

'Oh, Jimmy, Jimmy, Jimmy!' Kathleen sobbed louder than before.

'He *doesn't* know us,' Gerald owned, 'or – look here, Jimmy, y-you aren't kidding, are you? Because if you are it's simply abject rot –'

'My name is Mr —,' said That-which-had-been-Jimmy, and gave the name correctly. By the way, it will perhaps be shorter to call this elderly stout person who was Jimmy grown rich by some simpler name than I have just used. Let us call him 'That' – short for 'That-which-had-been Jimmy'.

'What *are* we to do?' whispered Mabel, awestruck; and aloud she said: 'Oh, Mr James, or whatever you call yourself, *do* give me the ring.' For on That's finger the fatal ring showed plain.

'Certainly not,' said That firmly. 'You appear to be a very grasping child.'

'But what are you going to *do*?' Gerald asked in the flat tones of complete hopelessness.

'Your interest is very flattering,' said That. 'Will you tell me, or won't you, the way to the nearest railway-station?'

'No,' said Gerald, 'we won't.'

'Then,' said That, still politely, though quite plainly furious, 'perhaps you'll tell me the way to the nearest lunatic asylum?'

'Oh, no, no, no!' cried Kathleen. 'You're not so bad as that.'

'Perhaps not. But *you* are,' That retorted; 'if you're not lunatics you're idiots. However, I see a gentleman ahead who is perhaps sane. In fact, I seem to recognize him.' A gentleman, indeed, was now to be seen approaching. It was the elderly Ugly-Wugly.

'Oh! don't you remember Jerry?' Kathleen cried, 'and Cathy, your own Cathy Puss Cat? Dear, dear Jimmy, *don't* be so silly!'

'Little girl,' said That, looking at her crossly through his spectacles, 'I am sorry you have not been better brought up.' And he walked stiffly towards the Ugly-Wugly. Two hats were raised, a few words were exchanged, and two elderly figures walked side by side down the green pine-walk, followed by three miserable children, horrified, bewildered, alarmed, and, what is really worse than anything, quite at their wits' end.

'He wished to be rich, so of course he is,' said Gerald; 'he'll have money for tickets and every-thing.'

'And when the spell breaks – it's sure to break, isn't it? – he'll find himself somewhere awful –

perhaps in a really good hotel – and not know how he got there.'

'I wonder how long the Ugly-Wuglies lasted,' said Mabel.

'Yes,' Gerald answered, 'that reminds me. You two *must* collect the coats and things. Hide them, anywhere you like, and we'll carry them home tomorrow – if there *is* any tomorrow,' he added darkly.

'Oh, don't!' said Kathleen, once more breathing

heavily on the verge of tears: 'you wouldn't think everything *could* be so awful, and the sun shining like it does.'

'Look here,' said Gerald, 'of course I must stick to Jimmy. You two must go home to Mademoiselle and tell her Jimmy and I have gone off in the train with a gentleman – say he looked like an uncle. He does – some kind of uncle. There'll be a beastly row afterwards, but it's got to be done.'

'It all seems thick with lies,' said Kathleen; 'you don't seem to be able to get a word of truth in edgewise hardly.'

'Don't you worry,' said her brother; 'they aren't lies – they're as true as anything else in this magic rot we've got mixed up in. It's like telling lies in a dream; you can't help it.'

'Well, all I know is I wish it would stop.'

'Lot of use your wishing *that* is,' said Gerald, exasperated. 'So long. I've *got* to go, and you've *got* to stay. If it's any comfort to you, I don't believe *any* of it's real: it can't be; it's too thick. Tell Mademoiselle Jimmy and I will be back to tea. If we don't happen to be I can't help it. I can't help *anything*, except perhaps Jimmy.' He started to run, for the girls had lagged, and the Ugly-Wugly and That (late Jimmy) had quickened their pace.

The girls were left looking after them.

'We've *got* to find these clothes,' said Mabel, 'simply got to. I used to want to be a heroine. It's different when it really comes to being, isn't it?'

'Yes, very,' said Kathleen. 'Where shall we hide the clothes when we've got them? Not – not that passage?'

'Never!' said Mabel firmly; 'we'll hide them inside the great stone dinosaurus. He's hollow.'

'He comes alive – in his stone,' said Kathleen.

'Not in the sunshine he doesn't,' Mabel told her confidently, 'and not without the ring.'

'There won't be any apples and books today,' said Kathleen.

'No, but we'll do the babiest thing we *can* do the minute we get home. We'll have a dolls' tea-party. That'll make us feel as if there wasn't really any magic.'

'It'll have to be a very strong tea party, then,' said Kathleen doubtfully.

And now we see Gerald, a small but quite determined figure, paddling along in the soft white dust of the sunny road, in the wake of two elderly gentlemen. His hand, in his trousers pocket, buries itself with a feeling of satisfaction in the heavy mixed coinage that is his share of the profits of his conjuring at the fair. His noiseless tennis-shoes bear him to the station, where, unobserved, he listens at the ticket office to the voice of That-which-was-James. 'One first London,' it says and Gerald, waiting till That and the Ugly-Wugly have strolled on to the platform, politely conversing of politics and the Kaffir market, takes a third return to London. The train strides in, squeaking and puffing. The watched take their seats in a carriage blue-lined. The watcher springs into a yellow wooden compartment. A whistle sounds, a flag is waved. The train pulls itself together, strains, jerks, and starts.

'I don't understand,' says Gerald, alone in his third-class carriage, 'how railway trains and magic *can* go on at the same time.'

And yet they do.

Mabel and Kathleen, nervously peering among the rhododendron bushes and the bracken and the fancy fir-trees, find six several heaps of coats, hats, skirts, gloves, golf-clubs, hockey- sticks, broom-handles. They carry them, panting and damp, for the mid-day sun is pitiless, up the hill to where the stone dinosaurus looms immense among a forest of larches. The dinosaurus has a hole in his stomach. Kathleen shows Mabel how to 'make a back' and climbs up on it into the cold, stony inside of the monster. Mabel hands up the clothes and the sticks.

'There's lots of room,' says Kathleen; 'its tail goes down into the ground. It's like a secret passage.'

'Suppose something comes out of it and jumps out at you,' says Mabel, and Kathleen hurriedly descends.

The explanations to Mademoiselle promise to be difficult, but, as Kathleen said afterwards, any little thing is enough to take a grown-up's attention off. A figure passes the window just as they are explaining that it really did look exactly like an uncle that the boys have gone to London with.

'Who's that?' says Mademoiselle suddenly, pointing, too, which everyone knows is not manners.

It is the bailiff coming back from the doctor's with antiseptic plaster on that nasty cut that took so long a-bathing this morning. They tell her it is the bailiff at Yalding Towers, and she says, 'Sky!' (*Ciel!*) and asks no more awkward questions about the boys. Lunch – very late – is a silent meal. After lunch Mademoiselle

goes out, in a hat with many pink roses, carrying a rose-lined parasol. The girls, in dead silence, organize a dolls' tea-party, with real tea. At the second cup Kathleen bursts into tears. Mabel, also weeping, embraces her.

'I wish,' sobs Kathleen, 'oh, I do wish I knew where the boys were! It *would* be such a comfort.'

Gerald knew where the boys were, and it was no comfort to him at all. If you come to think of it, he was the only person who could know where they were, because Jimmy didn't know that he was a boy – and indeed he wasn't really – and the Ugly-Wugly couldn't be expected to know anything real, such as where boys were. At the moment when the second cup of dolls' tea – very strong, but not strong enough to drown care in – was being poured out by the trembling hand of Kathleen, Gerald was lurking – there really is no other

word for it – on the staircase of Aldermanbury Build-
ings, Old Broad Street. On the floor below him was a
door bearing the legend 'MR U. W. UGLI, Stock and
Share Broker. And at the Stock Exchange', and on the
floor above was another door, on which was the name
of Gerald's little brother, now grown suddenly rich in
so magic and tragic a way. There were no explaining
words under Jimmy's name. Gerald could not guess
what walk in life it was to which That (which had been
Jimmy) owed its affluence. He had seen, when the
door opened to admit his brother, a tangle of clerks
and mahogany desks. Evidently That had a large
business.

What was Gerald to do? What *could* he do?

It is almost impossible, especially for one so young
as Gerald, to enter a large London office and explain
that the elderly and respected head of it is not what he
seems, but is really your little brother, who has been
suddenly advanced to age and wealth by a tricky wishing ring. If you think it's a possible thing, try it, that's
all. Nor could he knock at the door of Mr U. W. Ugli,
Stock and Share Broker (and at the Stock Exchange),
and inform *his* clerks that their chief was really nothing
but old clothes that had accidentally come alive, and
by some magic, which he couldn't attempt to explain,
become real during a night spent at a really good hotel
which had no existence.

The situation bristled, as you see, with difficulties.
And it was so long past Gerald's proper dinner-time
that his increasing hunger was rapidly growing to
seem the most important difficulty of all. It is quite
possible to starve to death on the staircase of a London
building if the people you are watching for only stay

long enough in their offices. The truth of this came home to Gerald more and more painfully.

A boy with hair like a new front door mat came whistling up the stairs. He had a dark blue bag in his hands.

'I'll give you a tanner for yourself if you'll get me a tanner's worth of buns,' said Gerald, with that prompt decision common to all great commanders.

'Show us yer tanners,' the boy rejoined with at least equal promptness. Gerald showed them. 'All right; hand over.'

'Payment on delivery,' said Gerald, using words from the drapers which he had never thought to use.

The boy grinned admiringly.

'Knows 'is wy abaht,' he said; 'ain't no flies on 'im.'

'Not many,' Gerald owned with modest pride. 'Cut along, there's a good chap. I've *got* to wait here. I'll take care of your bag if you like.'

'Nor yet there ain't no flies on me neither,' remarked the boy, shouldering it. 'I been up to the confidence trick for years – ever since I was your age.'

With this parting shot he went, and returned in due course bun-laden. Gerald gave the sixpence and took the buns. When the boy, a minute later, emerged from the door of Mr U. W. Ugli, Stock and Share Broker (and at the Stock Exchange), Gerald stopped him.

'What sort of chap's that?' he asked, pointing the question with a jerk of an explaining thumb.

'Awful big pot,' said the boy; 'up to his eyes in oof. Motor and all that.'

'Know anything about the one on the next landing?'

'He's bigger than what this one is. Very old firm – special cellar in the Bank of England to put his chink in – all in bins like against the wall at the corn-chandler's. Jimminy, I wouldn't mind 'alf an hour in there, and the doors open and the police away at a beano. Not much! Neither. You'll bust if you eat all them buns.'

'Have one?' Gerald responded, and held out the bag.

'They say in our office,' said the boy, paying for the bun honourably with unasked information, 'as these two is all for cutting each other's throats – oh, only in the way of business – been at it for years.'

Gerald wildly wondered what magic and how much had been needed to give history and a past to these two things of yesterday, the rich Jimmy and the Ugly-Wugly. If he could get them away would all memory of them fade – in this boy's mind, for instance, in the minds of all the people who did business with them in the City? Would the mahogany-and-clerk-furnished offices fade away? Were the clerks real? Was the mahogany? Was he himself real? Was the boy?

'Can you keep a secret?' he asked the other boy. 'Are you on for a lark?'

'I ought to be getting back to the office,' said the boy.

'Get then!' said Gerald.

'Don't you get stuffy,' said the boy. 'I was just a-going to say it didn't matter. I know how to make my nose bleed if I'm a bit late.'

Gerald congratulated him on this accomplishment, at once so useful and so graceful, and then said:

'Look here. I'll give you five bob – honest.'

'What for?' was the boy's natural question.

'If you'll help me.'

'Fire ahead.'

'I'm a private inquiry,' said Gerald.

'Tec? You don't look it.'

'What's the good of being one if you look it?' Gerald asked impatiently, beginning on another bun. 'That old chap on the floor above – he's *wanted*.'

'Police?' asked the boy with fine carelessness.

'No – sorrowing relations.'

'"Return to,"' said the boy; '"all forgotten and forgiven." I see.'

'And I've got to get him to them, somehow. Now, if you could go in and give him a message from someone who wanted to meet him on business –'

'Hold on!' said the boy. 'I know a trick worth two of that. You go in and see old Ugli. He'd give his ears to have the old boy out of the way for a day or two. They were saying so in our office only this morning.'

'Let me think,' said Gerald, laying down the last bun on his knee expressly to hold his head in his hands.

'Don't you forget to think about my five bob,' said the boy.

Then there was a silence on the stairs, broken only by the cough of a clerk in That's office, and the clickety-clack of a typewriter in the office of Mr U. W. Ugli.

Then Gerald rose up and finished the bun.

'You're right,' he said. 'I'll chance it. Here's your five bob.'

He brushed the bun crumbs from his front, cleared his throat, and knocked at the door of Mr U. W. Ugli. It opened and he entered.

The door-mat boy lingered, secure in his power to account for his long absence by means of his well-trained nose, and his waiting was rewarded. He went down a few steps, round the bend of the stairs, and heard the voice of Mr U. W. Ugli, so well known on that staircase (and on the Stock Exchange) say in soft, cautious accents:

'Then I'll ask him to let me look at the ring – and I'll drop it. You pick it up. But remember, it's a pure accident, and you don't know me. I can't have my name mixed up in a thing like this. You're *sure* he's really unhinged?'

'Quite,' said Gerald; 'he's quite mad about that ring. He'll follow it anywhere. I know he will. And think of his sorrowing relations.'

'I do – I do,' said Mr Ugli kindly; 'that's all I *do* think of, of course.'

He went up the stairs to the other office, and Gerald heard the voice of That telling his clerks that he was going out to lunch. Then the horrible Ugly-Wugly and Jimmy, hardly less horrible in the eyes of Gerald, passed down the stairs where, in the dusk of the lower landing, two boys were making themselves as undistinguishable as possible, and so out into the street, talking of stocks and shares, bears and bulls. The two boys followed.

'I say,' the door-mat-headed boy whispered admiringly, 'whatever are you up to?'

'You'll see,' said Gerald recklessly. 'Come on!'

'You tell me. I must be getting back.'

'Well, I'll tell you, but you won't believe me. That old gentleman's not really old at all – he's my young brother suddenly turned into what you see. The other's not real at all. He's only just old clothes and nothing inside.'

'He looks it, I must say,' the boy admitted; 'but I say – you do stick it on, don't you?'

'Well, my brother was turned like that by a magic ring.'

'There ain't no such thing as magic,' said the boy. 'I learnt that at school.'

'All right,' said Gerald. 'Good-bye.'

'Oh, go ahead!' said the boy; 'you do stick it on, though.'

'Well, that magic ring. If I can get hold of it I shall just wish we were all in a certain place. And we shall be. And then I can deal with both of them.'

'Deal?'

'Yes, the ring won't *unwish* anything you've wished. That undoes itself with time, like a spring uncoiling. But it'll give you a brand-new wish – I'm almost certain of it. Anyhow, I'm going to chance it.'

'You are a rotter, aren't you?' said the boy respectfully.

'You wait and see,' Gerald repeated.

'I say, you aren't going into this swell place! You *can't*?'

The boy paused, appalled at the majesty of Pym's.

'Yes, I am – they can't turn us out as long as we behave. You come along, too. I'll stand lunch.'

I don't know why Gerald clung so to this boy. He wasn't a very nice boy. Perhaps it was because he was the only person Gerald knew in London, to speak to –

except That-which-had-been-Jimmy and the Ugly-Wugly; and he did not want to talk to either of them.

What happened next happened so quickly that, as Gerald said later, it was 'just like magic'. The restaurant was crowded – busy men were hastily bolting the food hurriedly brought by busy waitresses. There was a clink of forks and plates, the gurgle of beer from bottles, the hum of talk, and the smell of many good things to eat.

'Two chops, please,' Gerald had just said, playing with a plainly shown handful of money, so as to leave no doubt of his honourable intentions. Then at the next table he heard the words, 'Ah, yes, curious old family heirloom,' the ring was drawn off the finger of That, and Mr U. W. Ugli, murmuring something about a unique curio, reached his impossible hand out for it. The door-mat-headed boy was watching breathlessly.

'There's a ring right enough,' he owned. And then the ring slipped from the hand of Mr U. W. Ugli and skidded along the floor. Gerald pounced on it like a greyhound on a hare. He thrust the dull circlet on his finger and cried out aloud in that crowded place:

'I wish Jimmy and I were inside that door behind the statue of Flora.'

It was the only safe place he could think of.

The lights and sounds and scents of the restaurant died away as a wax-drop dies in fire – a rain-drop in water. I don't know, and Gerald never knew, what happened in that restaurant. There was nothing about it in the papers, though Gerald looked anxiously for 'Extraordinary Disappearance of well-known City Man'. What the door-mat-headed boy did or thought

I don't know either. No more does Gerald. But he would like to know, whereas I don't care tuppence. The world went on all right, anyhow, whatever he thought or did. The lights and the sounds and the scents of Pym's died out. In place of the light there was darkness; in place of the sounds there was silence; and in place of the scent of beef, pork, mutton, fish, veal, cabbage, onions, carrots, beer, and tobacco there was the musty, damp scent of a place underground that has been long shut up.

Gerald felt sick and giddy, and there was something at the back of his mind that he knew would make him feel sicker and giddier as soon as he should have the sense to remember what it was. Meantime it was important to think of proper words to soothe the City man that had once been Jimmy – to keep him quiet till Time, like a spring uncoiling, should bring the reversal of the spell – make all things as they were and as they ought to be. But he fought in vain for words. There were none. Nor were they needed. For through the deep darkness came a voice – and it was not the voice of that City man who had been Jimmy, but the voice of that very Jimmy who was Gerald's little brother, and who had wished that unlucky wish for riches that could only be answered by changing all that was Jimmy, young and poor, to all that Jimmy, rich and old, would have been. Another voice said: 'Jerry, Jerry! Are you awake? – I've had such a rum dream.'

And then there was a moment when nothing was said or done.

Gerald felt through the thick darkness, and the thick silence, and the thick scent of old earth shut up, and he got hold of Jimmy's hand.

'It's all right, Jimmy, old chap,' he said; 'it's not a dream now. It's that beastly ring again. I had to wish us here, to get you back at all out of your dream.'

'Wish us where?' Jimmy held on to the hand in a way that in the daylight of life he would have been the first to call babyish.

'Inside the passage – behind the Flora statue,' said Gerald, adding, 'it's all right, really.'

'Oh, I dare say it's all right,' Jimmy answered through the dark, with an irritation not strong enough to make him loosen his hold of his brother's hand. *'But how are we going to get out?'*

Then Gerald knew what it was that was waiting to make him feel more giddy than the lightning flight from Cheapside to Yalding Towers had been able to make him. But he said stoutly:

'I'll wish us out, of course.' Though all the time he knew that the ring would not undo its given wishes.

It didn't.

Gerald wished. He handed the ring carefully to Jimmy, through the thick darkness. And Jimmy wished.

And there they still were, in that black passage behind Flora, that had led – in the case of one Ugly-Wugly at least – to 'a good hotel'. And the stone door was shut. And they did not know even which way to turn to it.

'If I only had some matches!' said Gerald.

'Why didn't you leave me in the dream?' Jimmy almost whimpered. 'It was light there, and I was just going to have salmon and cucumber.'

'I,' rejoined Gerald in gloom, 'was just going to have steak and fried potatoes.'

The silence, and the darkness, and the earthy scent were all they had now.

'I always wondered what it would be like,' said Jimmy in low, even tones, 'to be buried alive. And now I know! Oh!' his voice suddenly rose to a shriek, 'it isn't true, it isn't! It's a dream – that's what it is!'

There was a pause while you could have counted ten. Then –

'Yes,' said Gerald bravely, through the scent and the silence and the darkness, 'it's just a dream, Jimmy, old chap. We'll just hold on, and call out now and then just for the lark of the thing. But it's really only a dream, of course.'

'Of course,' said Jimmy in the silence and the darkness and the scent of old earth.

9

There is a curtain, thin as gossamer, clear as glass, strong as iron, that hangs for ever between the world of magic and the world that seems to us to be real. And when once people have found one of the little weak spots in that curtain which are marked by magic rings, and amulets, and the like, almost anything may happen. Thus it is not surprising that Mabel and Kathleen, conscientiously conducting one of the dullest dolls' tea-parties at which either had ever assisted, should suddenly, and both at once, have felt a strange, unreasonable, but quite irresistible desire to return instantly to the Temple of Flora – even at the cost of leaving the dolls' tea-service in an unwashed state, and only half the raisins eaten. They went – as one has to go when the magic impulse drives one – against their better judgement, against their wills almost.

And the nearer they came to the Temple of Flora, in the golden hush of the afternoon, the more certain each was that they could not possibly have done otherwise.

And this explains exactly how it was that when Gerald and Jimmy, holding hands in the darkness of the passage, uttered their first concerted yell, 'just for the lark of the thing', that yell was instantly answered from outside.

A crack of light showed in that part of the passage where they had least expected the door to be. The stone door itself swung slowly open, and they were out of it, in the Temple of Flora, blinking in the good daylight, an unresisting prey to Kathleen's embraces and the questionings of Mabel.

'And you left that Ugly-Wugly loose in London,' Mabel pointed out; 'you might have wished it to be with you, too.'

'It's all right where it is,' said Gerald. 'I couldn't think of everything. And besides, no, thank you! Now we'll go home and seal up the ring in an envelope.'

'*I* haven't done anything with the ring yet,' said Kathleen.

'I shouldn't think you'd want to when you see the sort of things it does with you,' said Gerald.

'It wouldn't do things like that if *I* was wishing with it,' Kathleen protested,

'Look here,' said Mabel, 'let's just put it back in the treasure-room and have done with it. I oughtn't ever to have taken it away, really. It's a sort of stealing. It's quite as bad, really, as Eliza borrowing it to astonish her gentleman friend with.'

'I don't mind putting it back if you like,' said Gerald, 'only if any of us do think of a sensible wish you'll let us have it out again, of course?'

'Of course, of course,' Mabel agreed.

So they trooped up to the castle, and Mabel once more worked the spring that let down the panelling and showed the jewels, and the ring was put back among the odd dull ornaments that Mabel had once said were magic.

'How innocent it looks!' said Gerald. 'You wouldn't think there was any magic about it. It's just like an old silly ring. I wonder if what Mabel said about the other things is true! Suppose we try.'

'*Don't!*' said Kathleen. 'I think magic things are spiteful. They just enjoy getting you into tight places.'

'I'd like to try,' said Mabel, 'only – well, everything's been rather upsetting, and I've forgotten what I said anything was.'

So had the others. Perhaps that was why, when Gerald said that a bronze buckle laid on the foot would have the effect of seven-league boots, it didn't; when Jimmy, a little of the City man he had been clinging to him still, said that the steel collar would ensure your always having money in your pockets, his own remained empty; and when Mabel and Kathleen invented qualities of the most delightful nature for various rings and chains and brooches, nothing at all happened.

'It's only the ring that's magic,' said Mabel at last; 'and, I say!' she added, in quite a different voice.

'What?'

'Suppose even the ring isn't!'

'But we know it is.'

'I don't,' said Mabel. 'I believe it's not today at all. I believe it's the other day – we've just dreamed all these things. It's the day I made up that nonsense about the ring.'

'No, it isn't,' said Gerald; 'you were in your Princess-clothes then.'

'What Princess-clothes?' said Mabel, opening her dark eyes very wide.

'Oh, don't be silly,' said Gerald wearily.

'I'm not silly,' said Mabel; 'and I think it's time you went. I'm sure Jimmy wants his tea.'

'Of course I do,' said Jimmy. 'But you had got the Princess-clothes that day. Come along; let's shut up the shutters and leave the ring in its long home.'

'What ring?' said Mabel.

'Don't take any notice of her,' said Gerald. 'She's only trying to be funny.'

'No, I'm not,' said Mabel; 'but I'm inspired like a Python or a Sibylline lady. What ring?'

'The wishing-ring,' said Kathleen; 'the invisibility ring.'

'Don't you see *now*,' said Mabel, her eyes wider than ever, 'the ring's what you *say* it is? That's how it came to make us invisible – I just said it. Oh, we can't leave it here, if that's what it is. It isn't stealing, really, when it's as valuable as that, you see. Say what it is.'

'It's a wishing-ring,' said Jimmy.

'We've had that before and you had your silly wish,' said Mabel, more and more excited. 'I say it isn't a wishing-ring. I say it's a ring that makes the wearer four yards high.'

She had caught up the ring as she spoke, and even as she spoke the ring showed high above the children's heads on the finger of an impossible Mabel, who was, indeed, twelve feet high.

'Now you've done it!' said Gerald – and he was right. It was in vain that Mabel asserted that the ring was a wishing-ring. It quite clearly wasn't; it was what she had said it was.

'And you can't tell at all how long the effect will last,' said Gerald. 'Look at the invisibleness.' This is difficult to do, but the others understood him.

'It may last for days,' said Kathleen. 'Oh, Mabel, it *was* silly of you!'

'That's right, rub it in,' said Mabel bitterly; 'you should have believed me when I said it was what I said it was. Then I shouldn't have had to show you, and I shouldn't be this silly size. What am I to do now, I should like to know?'

'We must conceal you till you get your right size again – that's all,' said Gerald practically.

'Yes – but *where*?' said Mabel, stamping a foot twenty-four inches long.

'In one of the empty rooms. You wouldn't be afraid?'

'Of course not,' said Mabel. 'Oh, I do wish we'd just put the ring back and left it.'

'Well, it wasn't us that didn't,' said Jimmy, with more truth than grammar.

'I shall put it back now,' said Mabel, tugging at it.

'I wouldn't if I were you,' said Gerald thoughtfully. 'You don't want to stay that length, do you? And unless the ring's on your finger when the time's up, I dare say it wouldn't act.'

The exalted Mabel sullenly touched the spring. The panels slowly slid into place, and all the bright jewels were hidden. Once more the room was merely eight-sided, panelled, sunlit, and unfurnished.

'Now,' said Mabel, 'where am I to hide? It's a good thing auntie gave me leave to stay the night with you. As it is, one of you will have to stay the night with me. I'm not going to be left alone, the silly height I am.'

Height was the right word; Mabel had said 'four yards high' – and she *was* four yards high. But she was hardly any thicker than when her height was four feet seven, and the effect was, as Gerald remarked, 'wonderfully worm-like'. Her clothes had, of course, grown with her, and she looked like a little girl reflected in one of those long bent mirrors at Rosherville Gardens, that make stout people look so happily slender, and slender people so sadly scraggy. She sat down suddenly on the floor, and it was like a four-fold foot-rule folding itself up.

'It's no use sitting there, girl,' said Gerald.

'I'm not sitting here,' retorted Mabel; 'I only got down so as to be able to get through the door. It'll have to be hands and knees through most places for me now, I suppose.'

'Aren't you hungry?' Jimmy asked suddenly.

'I don't know,' said Mabel desolately; 'it's – it's such a long way off!'

'Well, I'll scout,' said Gerald; 'if the coast's clear –'

'Look here,' said Mabel, 'I think I'd rather be out of doors till it gets dark.'

'You *can't*. Someone's certain to see you.'

'Not if I go through the yew-hedge,' said Mabel. 'There's a yew-hedge with a passage along its inside like the box-hedge in *The Luck of the Vails*.'

'In *what*?'

'*The Luck of the Vails*. It's a ripping book. It was that book first set me on to hunt for hidden doors in panels and things. If I crept along that on my front, like a serpent – it comes out amongst the rhododendrons, close by the dinosaurus – we could camp there.'

'There's tea,' said Gerald, who had had no dinner.

'That's just what there isn't,' said Jimmy, who had had none either.

'Oh, you *won't* desert me!' said Mabel. 'Look here – I'll write to auntie. She'll give you the things for a picnic, if she's there and awake. If she isn't, one of the maids will.'

So she wrote on a leaf of Gerald's invaluable pocket-book: –

'DEAREST AUNTIE, –

'Please may we have some things for a picnic? Gerald will bring them. I would come myself, but I am a little tired. I think I have been growing rather fast. – Your loving niece,

'MABEL.

'P.S. – Lots, please, because some of us are very hungry.'

It was found difficult, but possible, for Mabel to creep along the tunnel in the yew-hedge. Possible, but slow, so that the three had hardly had time to settle themselves among the rhododendrons and to wonder bitterly what on earth Gerald was up to, to be such a time gone, when he returned, panting under the weight of a covered basket. He dumped it down on the fine grass carpet, groaned, and added, 'But it's worth it. Where's our Mabel?'

The long, pale face of Mabel peered out from rhododendron leaves, very near the ground.

'I look just like anybody else like this, don't I?' she asked anxiously; 'all the rest of me's miles away, under different bushes.'

'We've covered up the bits between the bushes with

bracken and leaves,' said Kathleen, avoiding the question; 'don't wriggle, Mabel, or you'll waggle them off.'

Jimmy was eagerly unpacking the basket. It was a generous tea. A long loaf, butter in a cabbage-leaf, a bottle of milk, a bottle of water, cake, and large, smooth, yellow gooseberries in a box that had once held an extra-sized bottle of somebody's matchless something for the hair and moustache. Mabel cautiously advanced her incredible arms from the rhododendron and leaned on one of her spindly elbows, Gerald cut bread and butter, while Kathleen obligingly ran round, at Mabel's request, to see that the green coverings had not dropped from any of the remoter parts of Mabel's person. Then there was a happy, hungry silence, broken only by those brief, impassioned suggestions natural to such an occasion:

'More cake, please.'

'Milk ahoy, there.'

'Chuck us the goosegogs.'

Everyone grew calmer – more contented with their lot. A pleasant feeling, half tiredness and half restfulness, crept to the extremities of the party. Even the unfortunate Mabel was conscious of it in her remote feet, that lay crossed under the third rhododendron to the north-north-west of the tea-party. Gerald did but voice the feelings of the others when he said, not without regret:

'Well, I'm a new man, but I couldn't eat so much as another goosegog if you paid me.'

'*I* could,' said Mabel; 'yes, I know they're all gone, and I've had my share. But I *could*. It's me being so long, I suppose.'

A delicious after-food peace filled the summer air. At a little distance the green-lichened grey of the vast stone dinosaurus showed through the shrubs. He, too, seemed peaceful and happy. Gerald caught his stone eye through a gap in the foliage. His glance seemed somehow sympathetic.

'I dare say he liked a good meal in his day,' said Gerald, stretching luxuriously.

'Who did?'

'The dino what's-his-name,' said Gerald.

'He had a meal today,' said Kathleen, and giggled.

'Yes – didn't he?' said Mabel, giggling also.

'You mustn't laugh lower than your chest,' said Kathleen anxiously, 'or your green stuff will joggle off.'

'What do you mean – a meal?' Jimmy asked suspiciously. 'What are you sniggering about?'

'He had a meal. Things to put in his inside,' said Kathleen, still giggling.

'Oh, be funny if you want to,' said Jimmy, suddenly cross. 'We don't want to know – do we, Jerry?'

'I do,' said Gerald witheringly; 'I'm *dying* to know. Wake me, you girls, when you've finished pretending you're not going to tell.'

He tilted his hat over his eyes, and lay back in the attitude of slumber.

'Oh, don't be stupid!' said Kathleen hastily. 'It's only that we fed the dinosaurus through the hole in his stomach with the clothes the Ugly-Wuglies were made of!'

'We can take them home with us, then,' said Gerald, chewing the white end of a grass stalk, 'so that's all right.'

'Look here,' said Kathleen suddenly; 'I've got an idea. Let me have the ring a bit. I won't say what the idea is, in case it doesn't come off, and then you'd say I was silly. I'll give it back before we go.'

'Oh, but you aren't going yet!' said Mabel, pleading. She pulled off the ring. 'Of course,' she added earnestly, 'I'm only too glad for you to try any idea, however silly it is.'

Now, Kathleen's idea was quite simple. It was only that perhaps the ring would change its powers if someone else renamed it – someone who was not under the power of its enchantment. So the moment it had passed from the long, pale hand of Mabel to one of her own fat, warm, red paws, she jumped up, crying, 'Let's go and empty the dinosaurus *now*,' and started to run swiftly towards that prehistoric monster. She had a good start. She wanted to say aloud, yet so that the others could not hear her, 'This is a wishing-ring. It gives you any wish you choose.' And she did say it. And no one heard her, except the birds and a squirrel or two, and perhaps a stone faun, whose pretty face seemed to turn a laughing look on her as she raced past its pedestal.

The way was uphill; it was sunny, and Kathleen had run her hardest, though her brothers caught her up before she reached the great black shadow of the dino-saurus. So that when she did reach that shadow she was very hot indeed and not in any state to decide calmly on the best wish to ask for.

'I'll get up and move the things down, because I know exactly where I put them,' she said.

Gerald made a back, Jimmy assisted her to climb up, and she disappeared through the hole into the dark inside of the monster. In a moment a shower began to descend from the opening – a shower of empty waist-coats, trousers with wildly waving legs, and coats with sleeves uncontrolled.

'Heads below!' called Kathleen, and down came walking-sticks and golf-sticks and hockey-sticks and broom-sticks, rattling and chattering to each other as they came.

'Come on,' said Jimmy.

'Hold on a bit,' said Gerald. 'I'm coming up.' He caught the edge of the hole above in his hands and jumped. Just as he got his shoulders through the opening and his knees on the edge he heard Kathleen's boots on the floor of the dinosaurus's inside, and Kathleen's voice saying:

'Isn't it jolly cool in here? I suppose statues are always cool. I do wish I was a statue. Oh!'

The 'oh' was a cry of horror and anguish. And it seemed to be cut off very short by a dreadful stony silence.

'What's up?' Gerald asked. But in his heart he knew. He climbed up into the great hollow. In the little light that came up through the hole he could see something white against the grey of the creature's sides. He felt in his pockets, still kneeling, struck a match, and when the blue of its flame changed to clear yellow he looked up to see what he had known he would see – the face of Kathleen, white, stony, and lifeless. Her hair was white, too, and her hands, clothes, shoes – everything was white, with the hard, cold whiteness of marble. Kathleen had her wish: she was a statue. There was a long moment of perfect stillness in the inside of the dinosaurus. Gerald could not speak. It was too sudden, too terrible. It was worse than anything that had happened yet. Then he turned and spoke down out of that cold, stony silence to Jimmy, in the green, sunny, rustling, live world outside.

'Jimmy,' he said, in tones perfectly ordinary and matter of fact, 'Kathleen's gone and said that ring was a wishing-ring. And so it was, of course. I see now what she was up to, running like that. And then the young duffer went and wished she was a statue.'

'And she is?' asked Jimmy, below.

'Come up and have a look,' said Gerald. And Jimmy came, partly with a pull from Gerald and partly with a jump of his own.

'She's a statue, right enough,' he said, in awestruck tones. 'Isn't it awful!'

'Not at all,' said Gerald firmly. 'Come on – let's go and tell Mabel.'

To Mabel, therefore, who had discreetly remained with her long length screened by rhododendrons, the two boys returned and broke the news. They broke it as one breaks a bottle with a pistol-shot.

'Oh, my goodness!' said Mabel, and writhed through her long length so that the leaves and fern tumbled off in little showers, and she felt the sun suddenly hot on the backs of her legs. 'What next? Oh, my goodness!'

'She'll come all right,' said Gerald, with outward calm.

'Yes; but what about *me*?' Mabel urged. 'I haven't got the ring. And my time will be up before hers is. Couldn't you get it back? Can't you get it off her hand? I'd put it back on her hand the very minute I was my right size again – faithfully I would.'

'Well, it's nothing to blub about,' said Jimmy, answering the sniffs that had served her in this speech for commas and full-stops; 'not for you, any-way.'

'Ah! you don't know,' said Mabel; 'you don't know what it is to be as long as I am. Do – do try and get the ring. After all, it is my ring more than any of the rest of yours, anyhow, because I did find it, and I did say it was magic.'

The sense of justice always present in the breast of Gerald awoke to this appeal.

'I expect the ring's turned to stone – her boots have, and all her clothes. But I'll go and see. Only if I can't, I can't, and it's no use your making a silly fuss.'

The first match lighted inside the dinosaurus showed the ring dark on the white hand of the Statuesque Kathleen.

H. R. MILLAR. 1907.

The fingers were stretched straight out. Gerald took hold of the ring, and, to his surprise, it slipped easily off the cold, smooth marble finger.

'I say, Cathy, old girl, I am sorry,' he said, and gave the marble hand a squeeze. Then it came to him that perhaps she could hear him. So he told the statue exactly what he and the others meant to do. This helped to clear up his ideas as to what he and the others did mean to do. So that when, after thumping the statue hearteningly on its marble back, he returned to the rhododendrons, he was able to give his orders with the clear precision of a born leader, as he later said. And since the others had, neither of them, thought of any plan, his plan was accepted, as the plans of born leaders are apt to be.

'Here's your precious ring,' he said to Mabel. 'Now you're not frightened of anything, are you?'

'No,' said Mabel, in surprise. 'I'd forgotten that. Look here, I'll stay here or farther up in the wood if you'll leave me all the coats, so that I sha'n't be cold in the night. Then I shall be here when Kathleen comes out of the stone again.'

'Yes,' said Gerald, 'that was exactly the born leader's idea.'

'You two go home and tell Mademoiselle that Kathleen's staying at the Towers. She is.'

'Yes,' said Jimmy, 'she certainly is.'

'The magic goes in seven-hour lots,' said Gerald; 'your invisibility was twenty-one hours, mine fourteen, Eliza's seven. When it was a wishing-ring it began with seven. But there's no knowing what number it will be really. So there's no knowing which of you will come right first. Anyhow, we'll sneak out by the cistern

window and come down the trellis, after we've said good night to Mademoiselle, and come and have a look at you before we go to bed. I think you'd better come close up to the dinosaurus and we'll leaf you over before we go.'

Mabel crawled into cover of the taller trees, and there stood up looking as slender as a poplar and as unreal as the wrong answer to a sum in long division. It was to her an easy matter to crouch beneath the dinosaurus, to put her head up through the opening, and thus to behold the white form of Kathleen.

'It's all right, dear,' she told the stone image; 'I shall be quite close to you. You call me as soon as you feel you're coming right again.'

The statue remained motionless, as statues usually do, and Mabel withdrew her head, lay down, was covered up, and left. The boys went home. It was the only reasonable thing to do. It would never have done for Mademoiselle to become anxious and set the police on their track. Everyone felt that. The shock of discovering the missing Kathleen, not only in a dinosaurus's stomach, but, further, in a stone statue of herself, might well have unhinged the mind of any constable, to say nothing of the mind of Mademoiselle, which, being foreign, would necessarily be a mind more light and easy to upset. While as for Mabel –

'Well, to look at her as she is now,' said Gerald, 'why, it would send any one off their chump – except us.'

'We're different,' said Jimmy; 'our chumps have had to jolly well get used to things. It would take a lot to upset us now.'

'Poor old Cathy! all the same,' said Gerald.

'Yes, of course,' said Jimmy.

The sun had died away behind the black trees and the moon was rising. Mabel, her preposterous length covered with coats, waistcoats, and trousers laid along it, slept peacefully in the chill of the evening. Inside the dinosaurus Kathleen, alive in her marble, slept too. She had heard Gerald's words – had seen the lighted matches. She was Kathleen just the same as ever only she was Kathleen in a case of marble that would not let her move. It would not have let her cry, even if she wanted to. But she had not wanted to cry. Inside, the marble was not cold or hard. It seemed,

somehow, to be softly lined with warmth and pleasant-
ness and safety. Her back did not ache with stooping.
Her limbs were not stiff with the hours that they had
stayed moveless. Everything was well – better than
well. One had only to wait quietly and quite comfortably and one would come out of this stone case, and
once more be the Kathleen one had always been used
to being. So she waited happily and calmly, and presently waiting changed to not waiting – to not anything;
and, close held in the soft inwardness of the marble,
she slept as peacefully and calmly as though she had
been lying in her own bed.

She was awakened by the fact that she was not lying
in her own bed – was not, indeed, lying at all – by the
fact that she was standing and that her feet had pins
and needles in them. Her arms, too, held out in that
odd way, were stiff and tired. She rubbed her eyes,
yawned, and remembered. She had been a statue, a
statue inside the stone dinosaurus.

'Now I'm alive again,' was her instant conclusion,
'and I'll get out of it.'

She sat down, put her feet through the hole that
showed faintly grey in the stone beast's underside, and
as she did so a long, slow lurch threw her sideways on
the stone where she sat. *The dinosaurus was moving!*

'*Oh!*' said Kathleen inside it, 'how dreadful! It
must be moonlight, and it's come alive, like Gerald
said.'

It was indeed moving. She could see through the
hole the changing surface of grass and bracken and
moss as it waddled heavily along. She dared not drop
through the hole while it moved, for fear it should
crush her to death with its gigantic feet. And with that

thought came another: where was Mabel? Somewhere
– somewhere *near*? Suppose one of the great feet
planted itself on some part of Mabel's inconvenient
length? Mabel being the size she was now it would be
quite difficult not to step on some part or other of her,
if she should happen to be in one's way – quite difficult, however much one tried. And the dinosaurus
would not try: Why should it? Kathleen hung in an
agony over the round opening. The huge beast swung
from side to side. It was going faster; it was no good,
she dared not jump out. Anyhow, they must be quite
away from Mabel by now. Faster and faster went the
dinosaurus. The floor of its stomach sloped. They
were going downhill. Twigs cracked and broke as it
pushed through a belt of evergreen oaks; gravel
crunched, ground beneath its stony feet. Then stone
met stone. There was a pause. A splash! They were
close to water – the lake where by moonlight Hermes
fluttered and Janus and the dinosaurus swam together.
Kathleen dropped swiftly through the hole on to the
flat marble that edged the basin, rushed sideways, and
stood panting in the shadow of a statue's pedestal.
Not a moment too soon, for even as she crouched the
monster lizard slipped heavily into the water, drowning
a thousand smooth, shining lily pads, and swam away
towards the central island.

'Be still, little lady. I leap!' The voice came from the
pedestal, and next moment Phoebus had jumped from
the pedestal in his little temple, clearing the steps, and
landing a couple of yards away.

'You are new,' said Phoebus over his graceful shoulder. 'I should not have forgotten you if once I had
seen you.'

'I am,' said Kathleen, 'quite, quite new. And I didn't know you could talk.'

'Why not?' Phoebus laughed. 'You can talk.'

'But I'm alive.'

'Am not I?' he asked.

'Oh, yes, I suppose so,' said Kathleen, distracted, but not afraid; 'only I thought you had to have the ring on before one could even see you move.'

Phoebus seemed to understand her, which was rather to his credit, for she had certainly not expressed herself with clearness.

'Ah! that's for mortals,' he said. '*We* can hear and

see each other in the few moments when life is ours. That is a part of the beautiful enchantment.'

'But I am a mortal,' said Kathleen.

'You are as modest as you are charming,' said Phoebus Apollo absently; 'the white water calls me! I go,' and the next moment rings of liquid silver spread across the lake, widening and widening, from the spot where the white joined hands of the Sun-god had struck the water as he dived.

Kathleen turned and went up the hill towards the rhododendron bushes. She must find Mabel, and they must go home at once. If only Mabel was of a size that one could conveniently take home with one! Most likely, at this hour of enchantments, she was. Kathleen, heartened by the thought, hurried on. She passed through the rhododendron bushes, remembered the pointed painted paper face that had looked out from the glossy leaves, expected to be frightened – and wasn't. She found Mabel easily enough, and much more easily than she would have done had Mabel been as she wished to find her. For quite a long way off in the moonlight, she could see that long and worm-like form, extended to its full twelve feet – and covered with coats and trousers and waistcoats. Mabel looked like a drain-pipe that has been covered in sacks in frosty weather. Kathleen touched her long cheek gently, and she woke.

'What's up?' she said sleepily.

'It's only me,' Kathleen explained.

'How cold your hands are!' said Mabel.

'Wake up,' said Kathleen, 'and let's talk.'

'Can't we go home now? I'm awfully tired, and it's so long since tea-time.'

'*You're* too long to go home yet,' said Kathleen sadly, and then Mabel remembered.

She lay with closed eyes – then suddenly she stirred and cried out:

'Oh! Cathy, I feel so funny – like one of those horn snakes when you make it go short to get it into its box. I am – yes – I know I am –'

She was; and Kathleen, watching her, agreed that it was exactly like the shortening of a horn spiral snake between the closing hands of a child. Mabel's distant feet drew near – Mabel's long, lean arms grew shorter – Mabel's face was no longer half a yard long.

'You're coming right – you are! Oh, I am so glad!' cried Kathleen.

'I know *I* am,' said Mabel; and as she said it she became once more Mabel, not only in herself which, of course, she had been all the time, but in her outward appearance.

'You are all right. Oh, hooray! hooray! I *am* so glad!' said Kathleen kindly; 'and now we'll go home at once, dear.'

'Go home?' said Mabel, slowly sitting up and staring at Kathleen with her big dark eyes. 'Go home – like that?'

'Like what?' Kathleen asked impatiently.

'Why, *you*,' was Mabel's odd reply.

'I'm all right,' said Kathleen. 'Come on.'

'Do you mean to say you don't know?' said Mabel. 'Look at yourself – your hands – your dress – everything.'

Kathleen looked at her hands. They were of marble whiteness. Her dress, too – her shoes, her stockings,

even the ends of her hair. She was white as new-fallen snow.

'What is it?' she asked, beginning to tremble. 'What am I all this horrid colour for?'

'Don't you see? Oh, Cathy, don't you see? You've *not* come right. You're a statue still.'

'I'm not – I'm alive – I'm talking to you.'

'I know you are, darling,' said Mabel, soothing her as one soothes a fractious child. 'That's because it's moonlight.'

'But you can see I'm alive.'

'Of course I can. I've got the ring.'

'But I'm all right; I *know* I am.'

'Don't you see,' said Mabel gently, taking her white marble hand, 'you're not all right? It's moonlight, and you're a statue, and you've just come alive with all the other statues. And when the moon goes down you'll just be a statue again. *That's* the difficulty, dear, about our going home again. You're just a statue still, only you've come alive with the other marble things. Where's the dinosaurus?'

'In his bath,' said Kathleen, 'and so are all the other stone beasts.'

'Well,' said Mabel, trying to look on the bright side of things, 'then we've got one thing, at any rate, to be thankful for!'

10

'If,' said Kathleen, sitting disconsolate in her marble, 'if I am really a statue come alive, I wonder you're not afraid of me.'

'I've got the ring,' said Mabel with decision. 'Cheer up, dear! you will soon be better. Try not to think about it.'

She spoke as you speak to a child that has cut its finger, or fallen down on the garden path, and rises up with grazed knees to which gravel sticks intimately.

'I know,' Kathleen absently answered.

'And I've been thinking,' said Mabel brightly, 'we might find out a lot about this magic place, if the other statues aren't too proud to talk to us.'

'They aren't,' Kathleen assured her; 'at least, Phoebus wasn't. He was most awfully polite and nice.'

'Where is he?' Mabel asked.

'In the lake – he was,' said Kathleen.

'Then let's go down there,' said Mabel. 'Oh, Cathy! it is jolly being your own proper thickness again.' She jumped up, and the withered ferns and branches that had covered her long length and had been gathered closely upon her as she shrank to her proper size fell as forest leaves do when sudden storms tear them. But the white Kathleen did not move.

The two sat on the grey moonlit grass with the quiet of the night all about them. The great park was still as a painted picture; only the splash of the fountains and the far-off whistle of the Western express broke the silence, which, at the same time, then deepened.

'What cheer, little sister!' said a voice behind them – a golden voice. They turned quick, startled heads, as birds, surprised, might turn. There in the moonlight stood Phoebus, dripping still from the lake, and smiling at them, very gentle, very friendly.

'Oh, it's you!' said Kathleen.

'None other,' said Phoebus cheerfully. 'Who is your friend, the earth-child?'

'This is Mabel,' said Kathleen.

Mabel got up and bowed, hesitated, and held out a hand.

'I am your slave, little lady,' said Phoebus, enclosing it in marble fingers. 'But I fail to understand how you can see us, and why you do not fear.'

Mabel held up the hand that wore the ring.

'Quite sufficient explanation,' said Phoebus; 'but since you have that, why retain your mottled earthy appearance? Become a statue, and swim with us in the lake.'

'I can't swim,' said Mabel evasively.

'Nor yet me,' said Kathleen.

'*You* can,' said Phoebus. 'All Statues that come to life are proficient in all athletic exercises. And you, child of the dark eyes and hair like night, wish yourself a statue and join our revels.'

'I'd rather not, if you will excuse me,' said Mabel cautiously. 'You see . . . this ring . . . you wish for things, and you never know how long they're going to last. It would be jolly and all that to be a statue *now*, but in the morning I should wish I hadn't.'

'Earth-folk often do, they say,' mused Phoebus. 'But, child, you seem ignorant of the powers of your ring. Wish exactly, and the ring will exactly perform. If you give no limit of time, strange enchantments woven by Arithmos the outcast god of numbers will creep in and spoil the spell. Say thus: "I wish that till the dawn I may be a statue of living marble, even as my child friend, and that after that time I may be as before, Mabel of the dark eyes and night-coloured hair."'

'Oh, yes, do, it would be so jolly!' cried Kathleen. 'Do, Mabel! And if we're both statues, shall we be afraid of the dinosaurus?'

'In the world of living marble fear is not,' said Phoebus. 'Are we not brothers, we and the dinosaurus, brethren alike wrought of stone and life?'

'And could I swim if I did?'

'Swim, and float, and dive – and with the ladies of Olympus spread the nightly feast, eat of the food of the gods, drink their cup, listen to the song that is undying, and catch the laughter of immortal lips.'

'A feast!' said Kathleen. 'Oh, Mabel, do! You would if you were as hungry as I am.'

'But it won't be real food,' urged Mabel.

'It will be real to you, as to us,' said Phoebus; 'there is no other realness even in your many-coloured world.'

Still Mabel hesitated. Then she looked at Kathleen's legs and suddenly said:

'Very well, I will. But first I'll take off my shoes and stockings. Marble boots look simply awful – especially

the laces. And a marble stocking that's coming down –
and mine *do*!'

She had pulled off shoes and stockings and pinafore.

'Mabel has the sense of beauty,' said Phoebus approv-
ingly. 'Speak the spell, child, and I will lead you to the
ladies of Olympus.'

Mabel, trembling a little, spoke it, and there were
two little live statues in the moonlit glade. Tall Phoebus took a hand of each.

'Come – run!' he cried. And they ran.

'Oh – it is jolly!' Mabel panted. 'Look at my white
feet in the grass! I thought it would feel stiff to be a
statue, but it doesn't.'

'There is no stiffness about the immortals,' laughed
the Sun-god. 'For tonight you are one of us.'

And with that they ran down the slope to the lake.

'Jump!' he cried, and they jumped, and the water
splashed up round three white, gleaming shapes.

'Oh! I *can* swim!' breathed Kathleen.

'So can I,' said Mabel.

'Of course you can,' said Phoebus. 'Now three times
round the lake, and then make for the island.'

Side by side the three swam, Phoebus swimming
gently to keep pace with the children. Their marble
clothes did not seem to interfere at all with their
swimming, as your clothes would if you suddenly
jumped into the basin of the Trafalgar Square fountains and tried to swim there. And they swam most
beautifully, with that perfect ease and absence of effort
or tiredness which you must have noticed about your
own swimming – in dreams. And it was the most
lovely place to swim in; the water-lilies, whose long,
snaky stalks are so inconvenient to ordinary swimmers,

did not in the least interfere with the movements of marble arms and legs. The moon was high in the clear sky-dome. The weeping willows, cypresses, temples, terraces, banks of trees and shrubs, and the wonderful old house, all added to the romantic charm of the scene.

'This is the nicest thing the ring has brought us yet,' said Mabel, through a languid but perfect side-stroke.

'I thought you'd enjoy it,' said Phoebus kindly; 'now once more round, and then the island.'

They landed on the island amid a fringe of rushes, yarrow, willow-herb, loose-strife, and a few late, scented, powdery, creamy heads of meadow-sweet. The island was bigger than it looked from the bank, and it seemed covered with trees and shrubs. But when, Phoebus leading the way, they went into the shadow of these, they perceived that beyond the trees lay a light, much nearer to them than the other side of the island could possibly be. And almost at once they were through the belt of trees, and could see where the light came from. The trees they had just passed among made a dark circle round a big cleared space, standing up thick and dark, like a crowd round a football field, as Kathleen remarked.

First came a wide, smooth ring of lawn, then marble steps going down to a round pool, where there were no water-lilies, only gold and silver fish that darted here and there like flashes of quicksilver and dark flames. And the enclosed space of water and marble and grass was lighted with a clear, white, radiant light, seven times stronger than the whitest moonlight, and in the still waters of the pool seven moons lay reflected. One could see that they were only reflections by the way their shape broke and changed as the gold and silver fish rippled the water with moving fin and tail that steered.

The girls looked up at the sky, almost expecting to see seven moons there. But no, the old moon shone alone, as she had always shone on them.

'There are seven moons,' said Mabel blankly, and pointed, which is not manners.

'Of course,' said Phoebus kindly; 'everything in our world is seven times as much so as in yours.'

'But there aren't seven of you,' said Mabel.

'No, but I am seven times as much,' said the Sun-god. 'You see, there's numbers, and there's quantity, to say nothing of quality. You see that, I'm sure.'

'Not quite,' said Kathleen.

'Explanations always weary me,' Phoebus interrupted. 'Shall we join the ladies?'

On the further side of the pool was a large group, so white that it seemed to make a great white hole in the trees. Some twenty or thirty figures there were in the group – all statues and all alive. Some were dipping their white feet among the gold and silver fish, and sending ripples across the faces of the seven moons. Some were pelting each other with roses – roses so sweet that the girls could smell them even across the pool. Others were holding hands and dancing in a ring, and two were sitting on the steps playing cat's-cradle – which is a very ancient game indeed – with a thread of white marble.

As the new-comers advanced a shout of greeting and gay laughter went up.

'Late again, Phoebus!' someone called out. And another: 'Did one of your horses cast a shoe?' And yet another called out something about laurels.

'I bring two guests,' said Phoebus, and instantly the statues crowded round, stroking the girls' hair, patting their cheeks, and calling them the prettiest love-names.

'Are the wreaths ready, Hebe?' the tallest and most splendid of the ladies called out. 'Make two more!'

And almost directly Hebe came down the steps, her round arms hung thick with rose-wreaths. There was one for each marble head.

Everyone now looked seven times more beautiful than before, which, in the case of the gods and goddesses, is saying a good deal. The children remembered how at the raspberry vinegar feast Mademoiselle had said that gods and goddesses always wore wreaths for meals.

Hebe herself arranged the roses on the girls' heads – and Aphrodite Urania, the dearest lady in the world, with a voice like mother's at those moments when you love her most, took them by the hands and said:

'Come, we must get the feast ready. Eros – Psyche – Hebe – Ganymede – all you young people can arrange the fruit.'

'I don't see any fruit,' said Kathleen, as four slender forms disengaged themselves from the white crowd and came towards them.

'You will though,' said Eros, a really nice boy, as the girls instantly agreed; 'you've only got to pick it.'

'Like this,' said Psyche, lifting her marble arms to a willow branch. She reached out her hand to the children – it held a ripe pomegranate.

'I see,' said Mabel. 'You just –' She laid her fingers to the willow branch and the firm softness of a big peach was within them.

'Yes, just that,' laughed Psyche, who was a darling, as any one could see.

After this Hebe gathered a few silver baskets from a convenient alder, and the four picked fruit industriously. Meanwhile the elder statues were busy plucking golden goblets and jugs and dishes from the branches of ash-trees and young oaks and filling them with everything nice to eat and drink that anyone could possibly want, and these were spread on the steps. It was a celestial picnic. Then everyone sat or lay down and the feast began. And oh! the taste of the food served on those dishes, the sweet wonder of the drink that melted from those gold cups on the white lips of the company! And the fruit – there is no fruit like it grown on earth, just as there is no laughter like the laughter of those lips, no songs like the songs that stirred the silence of that night of wonder.

'Oh!' cried Kathleen, and through her fingers the juice of her third peach fell like tears on the marble steps. 'I do wish the boys were here!'

'I do wonder what they're doing,' said Mabel.

'At this moment,' said Hermes, who had just made a

wide ring of flight, as a pigeon does, and come back into the circle – 'at this moment they are wandering desolately near the home of the dinosaurus, having escaped from their home by a window, in search of you. They fear that you have perished, and they would weep if they did not know that tears do not become a man, however youthful.'

Kathleen stood up and brushed the crumbs of ambrosia from her marble lap.

'Thank you all very much,' she said. 'It was very kind of you to have us, and we've enjoyed ourselves very much, but I think we ought to go now, please.'

'If it is anxiety about your brothers,' said Phoebus obligingly, 'it is the easiest thing in the world for them to join you. Lend me your ring a moment.'

He took it from Kathleen's half-reluctant hand, dipped it in the reflection of one of the seven moons, and gave it back. She clutched it. 'Now,' said the Sun-god, 'wish for them that which Mabel wished for herself. Say –'

'I know,' Kathleen interrupted. 'I wish that the boys may be statues of living marble like Mabel and me till dawn, and afterwards be like they are now.'

'If you hadn't interrupted,' said Phoebus – 'but there, we can't expect old heads on shoulders of young marble. You should have wished them *here* – and – but no matter. Hermes, old chap, cut across and fetch them, and explain things as you come.'

He dipped the ring again in one of the reflected moons before he gave it back to Kathleen.

'There,' he said, 'now it's washed clean ready for the next magic.'

'It is not our custom to question guests,' said Hera

H.R. MILLAR
1907.

the queen, turning her great eyes on the children; but that ring excites, I am sure, the interest of us all.'

'It is *the* ring,' said Phoebus.

'That, of course,' said Hera; 'but if it were not inhospitable to ask questions I should ask, How came it into the hands of these earth-children?'

'That,' said Phoebus, 'is a long tale. After the feast the story, and after the story the song.'

Hermes seemed to have 'explained everything' quite fully; for when Gerald and Jimmy in marble whiteness arrived, each clinging to one of the god's winged feet, and so borne through the air, they were certainly quite at ease. They made their best bows to the goddesses and took their places as unembarrassed as though they had had Olympian suppers every night of their lives. Hebe had woven wreaths of roses ready for them, and as Kathleen watched them eating and drinking, perfectly at home in their marble, she was very glad that amid the welling springs of immortal peach-juice she had not forgotten her brothers.

'And now,' said Hera, when the boys had been supplied with everything they could possibly desire, and more than they could eat – 'now for the story.'

'Yes,' said Mabel intensely; and Kathleen said, 'Oh *yes*; now for the story. How splendid!'

'The story,' said Phoebus unexpectedly, 'will be told by our guests.'

'Oh *no*!' said Kathleen, shrinking.

'The lads, maybe, are bolder,' said Zeus the king, taking off his rose-wreath, which was a little tight, and rubbing his compressed ears.

'I really can't,' said Gerald; 'besides, I don't know any stories.'

'Nor yet me,' said Jimmy.

'It's the story of how we got the ring that they want,' said Mabel in a hurry. 'I'll tell it if you like. Once upon a time there was a little girl called Mabel,' she added yet more hastily, and went on with the tale – all the tale of the enchanted castle, or almost all, that you have read in these pages. The marble Olympians listened enchanted – almost as enchanted as the castle itself, and the soft moonlit moments fell past like pearls dropping into a deep pool.

'And so,' Mabel ended abruptly, 'Kathleen wished for the boys and the Lord Hermes fetched them and here we all are.'

A burst of interested comment and question blossomed out round the end of the story, suddenly broken off short by Mabel.

'But,' said she, brushing it aside, as it grew thinner, 'now we want *you* to tell *us*.'

'To tell you –?'

'How you come to be alive, and how you know about the ring – and everything you *do* know.'

'Everything I know?' Phoebus laughed – it was to him that she had spoken – and not his lips only but all the white lips curled in laughter. 'The span of your life, my earth-child, would not contain the words I should speak, to tell you all I know.'

'Well, about the ring anyhow, and how you come alive,' said Gerald; 'you see, it's very puzzling to us.'

'Tell them, Phoebus,' said the dearest lady in the world; 'don't tease the children.'

So Phoebus, leaning back against a heap of leopard-

skins that Dionysus had lavishly plucked from a spruce
fir, told.

'All statues,' he said, 'can come alive when the moon
shines, if they so choose. But statues that are placed in
ugly cities do not choose. Why should they weary
themselves with the contemplation of the hideous?'

'Quite so,' said Gerald politely, to fill the pause.

'In your beautiful temples,' the Sun-god went on,
'the images of your priests and of your warriors who
lie cross-legged on their tombs come alive and walk in
their marble about their temples, and through the
woods and fields. But only on one night in all the year
can any see them. You have beheld us because you
held the ring, and are of one brotherhood with us
in your marble, but on that one night all may behold
us.'

'And when is that?' Gerald asked, again polite, in a
pause.

'At the festival of the harvest,' said Phoebus. 'On
that night as the moon rises it strikes one beam of
perfect light on to the altar in certain temples. One of
these temples is in Hellas, buried under the fall of a
mountain which Zeus, being angry, hurled down upon
it. One is in this land; it is in this great garden.'

'Then,' said Gerald, much interested, 'if we were to
come up to that temple on that night, we could see
you, even without being statues or having the ring?'

'Even so,' said Phoebus. 'More, any question asked
by a mortal we are on that night bound to answer.'

'And the night is – when?'

'Ah!' said Phoebus, and laughed. 'Wouldn't you like
to know!'

Then the great marble King of the Gods yawned,

stroked his long beard, and said: 'Enough of stories, Phoebus. Tune your lyre.'

'But the ring,' said Mabel in a whisper, as the Sungod tuned the white strings of a sort of marble harp that lay at his feet – 'about how you know all about the ring?'

'Presently,' the Sun-god whispered back. 'Zeus must be obeyed; but ask me again before dawn, and I will tell you all I know of it.' Mabel drew back, and leaned against the comfortable knees of one Demeter – Kathleen and Psyche sat holding hands. Gerald and Jimmy lay at full length, chins on elbows, gazing at the Sungod; and even as he held the lyre, before ever his fingers began to sweep the strings, the spirit of music hung in the air, enchanting, enslaving, silencing all thought but the thought of itself, all desire but the desire to listen to it.

Then Phoebus struck the strings and softly plucked melody from them, and all the beautiful dreams of all the world came fluttering close with wings like doves' wings; and all the lovely thoughts that sometimes hover near, but not so near that you can catch them, now came home as to their nests in the hearts of those who listened. And those who listened forgot time and space, and how to be sad, and how to be naughty, and it seemed that the whole world lay like a magic apple in the hand of each listener, and that the whole world was good and beautiful.

And then, suddenly, the spell was shattered. Phoebus struck a broken chord, followed by an instant of silence; then he sprang up, crying, 'The dawn! the dawn! To your pedestals, O gods!'

In an instant the whole crowd of beautiful marble

people had leaped to its feet, had rushed through the belt of wood that cracked and rustled as they went, and the children heard them splash in the water beyond. They heard, too, the gurgling breathing of a great beast, and knew that the dinosaurus, too, was returning to his own place.

Only Hermes had time, since one flies more swiftly than one swims, to hover above them for one moment, and to whisper with a mischievous laugh:

'In fourteen days from now, at the Temple of Strange Stones.'

'What's the secret of the ring?' gasped Mabel.

'The ring is the heart of the magic,' said Hermes. 'Ask at the moonrise on the fourteenth day, and you shall know all.'

With that he waved the snowy caduceus and rose in the air supported by his winged feet. And as he went the seven reflected moons died out and a chill wind began to blow, a grey light grew and grew, the birds stirred and twittered, and the marble slipped away from the children like a skin that shrivels in fire, and they were statues no more, but flesh and blood children as they used to be, standing knee-deep in brambles and long coarse grass. There was no smooth lawn, no marble steps, no seven-mooned fish-pond. The dew lay thick on the grass and the brambles, and it was very cold.

'We ought to have gone with them,' said Mabel with chattering teeth. 'We can't swim now we're not marble. And I suppose this *is* the island?'

It was – and they couldn't swim.

They knew it. One always knows those sort of things somehow without trying. For instance, you know perfectly that you can't fly. There are some things that there is no mistake about.

The dawn grew brighter and the outlook more black every moment.

'There isn't a boat, I suppose?' Jimmy asked.

'No,' said Mabel, 'not on this side of the lake; there's one in the boat-house, of course – if you could swim there.'

'You know I can't,' said Jimmy.

'Can't anyone think of anything?' Gerald asked, shivering.

'When they find we've disappeared they'll drag all the water for miles round,' said Jimmy hopefully, 'in case we've fallen in and sunk to the bottom. When they come to drag this we can yell and be rescued.'

'Yes, dear, that *will* be nice,' was Gerald's bitter comment.

'Don't be so disagreeable,' said Mabel with a tone so strangely cheerful that the rest stared at her in amazement.

'The ring,' she said. 'Of course we've only got to wish ourselves home with it. Phoebus washed it in the moon ready for the next wish.'

'You didn't tell us about that,' said Gerald in accents of perfect good temper. 'Never mind. Where *is* the ring?'

'*You* had it,' Mabel reminded Kathleen.

'I know I had,' said that child in stricken tones, 'but I gave it to Psyche to look at – and – and she's got it on her finger!'

Everyone tried not to be angry with Kathleen. All partly succeeded.

'If we ever get off this beastly island,' said Gerald,

'I suppose you can find Psyche's statue and get it off again?'

'No I can't,' Mabel moaned. 'I don't know where the statue is. I've never seen it. It may be in Hellas, wherever that is – or anywhere, for anything *I* know.'

No one had anything kind to say, and it is pleasant to record that nobody said anything. And now it was grey daylight, and the sky to the north was flushing in pale pink and lavender.

The boys stood moodily, hands in pockets. Mabel and Kathleen seemed to find it impossible not to cling together, and all about their legs the long grass was icy with dew.

A faint sniff and a caught breath broke the silence.

'Now, look here,' said Gerald briskly, 'I won't have it. Do you hear? Snivelling's no good at all. No, I'm not a pig. It's for your own good. Let's make a tour of the island. Perhaps there's a boat hidden somewhere among the overhanging boughs.'

'How could there be?' Mabel asked.

'Someone might have left it there, I suppose,' said Gerald.

'But how would they have got off the island?'

'In another boat, of course,' said Gerald; 'come on.'

Downheartedly, and quite sure that there wasn't and couldn't be any boat, the four children started to explore the island. How often each one of them had dreamed of islands, how often wished to be stranded on one! Well, now they were. Reality is sometimes quite different from dreams, and not half so nice. It was worst of all for Mabel, whose shoes and stockings were far away on the mainland. The coarse grass and brambles were very cruel to bare legs and feet.

They stumbled through the wood to the edge of the water, but it was impossible to keep close to the edge of the island, the branches grew too thickly. There was a narrow, grassy path that wound in and out among the trees, and this they followed, dejected and mournful. Every moment made it less possible for them to hope to get back to the school-house unnoticed. And if they were missed and beds found in their present unslept-in state – well, there would be a row of some sort, and, as Gerald said, 'Farewell to liberty!'

'Of course we can get off all right,' said Gerald. 'Just all shout when we see a gardener or a keeper on the mainland. But if we do, concealment is at an end and all is absolutely up!'

'Yes,' said everyone gloomily.

'Come, buck up!' said Gerald, the spirit of the born general beginning to reawaken in him. 'We shall get out of this scrape all right, as we've got out of others; you know we shall. See, the sun's coming out. You feel all right and jolly now, don't you?'

'Yes, oh yes!' said everyone, in tones of unmixed misery.

The sun was now risen, and through a deep cleft in the hills it sent a strong shaft of light straight at the island. The yellow light, almost level, struck through the stems of the trees and dazzled the children's eyes. This, with the fact that he was not looking where he was going, as Jimmy did not fail to point out later, was enough to account for what now happened to Gerald, who was leading the melancholy little procession. He stumbled, clutched at a tree-trunk, missed his clutch, and disappeared, with a yell and a clatter; and Mabel, who came next, only pulled herself up just in time not to fall down a steep flight of moss-grown steps that seemed to open suddenly in the ground at her feet.

'Oh, Gerald!' she called down the steps; 'are you hurt?'

'No,' said Gerald, out of sight and crossly, for he *was* hurt, rather severely; 'it's steps, and there's a passage.'

'There always is,' said Jimmy.

'I knew there was a passage,' said Mabel; 'it goes under the water and comes out at the Temple of Flora. Even the gardeners know that, but they won't go down, for fear of snakes.'

'Then we can get out that way – I do think you might have said so,' Gerald's voice came up to say.

'I didn't think of it,' said Mabel. 'At least – And I suppose it goes past the place where the Ugly-Wugly found its good hotel.'

'I'm not going,' said Kathleen positively, 'not in the dark, I'm not. So I tell you!'

'Very well, baby,' said Gerald sternly, and his head appeared from below very suddenly through interlacing brambles. 'No one asked you to go in the dark. We'll leave you here if you like, and return and rescue you with a boat. Jimmy, the bicycle lamp!' He reached up a hand for it.

Jimmy produced from his bosom, the place where lamps are always kept in fairy stories – see Aladdin and others – a bicycle lamp.

'We brought it,' he explained, 'so as not to break our shins over bits of long Mabel among the rhododendrons.'

'Now,' said Gerald very firmly, striking a match and opening the thick, rounded glass front of the bicycle lamp, 'I don't know what the rest of you are going to do, but I'm going down these steps and along this passage. If we find the good hotel – a good hotel never hurt anyone yet.'

'It's no good, you know,' said Jimmy weakly; 'you know jolly well you can't get out of that Temple of Flora door, even if you get to it.'

'I *don't* know,' said Gerald, still brisk and commander-like; 'there's a secret spring inside that door most likely. We hadn't a lamp last time to look for it, remember.'

'If there's one thing I do hate its undergroundness,' said Mabel.

'*You're* not a coward,' said Gerald, with what is known as diplomacy. '*You're* brave, Mabel. Don't I know it! You hold Jimmy's hand and I'll hold Cathy's. Now then.'

'I won't have *my* hand held,' said Jimmy, of course. 'I'm not a kid.'

'Well, Cathy will. Poor little Cathy! Nice brother Jerry'll hold poor Cathy's hand.'

Gerald's bitter sarcasm missed fire here, for Cathy gratefully caught the hand he held out in mockery. She was too miserable to read his mood, as she mostly did. 'Oh, thank you, Jerry dear,' she said gratefully; 'you *are* a dear, and I *will* try not to be frightened.' And for quite a minute Gerald shamedly felt that he had not been quite, quite kind.

So now, leaving the growing goldness of the sunrise, the four went down the stone steps that led to the underground and underwater passage, and everything seemed to grow dark and then to grow into a poor pretence of light again, as the splendour of dawn gave place to the small dogged lighting of the bicycle lamp. The steps did indeed lead to a passage, the beginnings of it choked with the drifted dead leaves of many old autumns. But presently the passage took a turn, there were more steps, down, down, and then the passage was empty and straight – lined above and below and on each side with slabs of marble, very clear and clean. Gerald held Cathy's hand with more of kindness and less of exasperation than he had supposed possible.

And Cathy, on her part, was surprised to find it possible to be so much less frightened than she expected.

The flame of the bull's-eye threw ahead a soft circle of misty light – the children followed it silently. Till, silently and suddenly, the light of the bull's-eye behaved as the flame of a candle does when you take it out into the sunlight to light a bonfire, or explode a train of gunpowder, or what not. Because now, with feelings mixed indeed, of wonder, and interest, and awe, but no fear, the children found themselves in a great hall, whose arched roof was held up by two rows of round pillars, and whose every corner was filled with a soft, searching, lovely light, filling every cranny, as water fills the rocky secrecies of hidden sea-caves.

'How beautiful!' Kathleen whispered, breathing hard into the tickled ear of her brother, and Mabel caught the hand of Jimmy and whispered, 'I must hold your hand – I must hold on to something silly, or I shan't believe it's real.'

For this hall in which the children found themselves was the most beautiful place in the world. I won't describe it, because it does not look the same to any

two people, and you wouldn't understand me if I tried
to tell you how it looked to any one of these four. But
to each it seemed the most perfect thing possible. I
will only say that all round it were great arches. Kathleen saw them as Moorish, Mabel as Tudor, Gerald as
Norman, and Jimmy as Churchwarden Gothic. (If you
don't know what these are, ask your uncle who collects
brasses, and he will explain, or perhaps Mr Millar will
draw the different kinds of arches for you.) And
through these arches one could see many things – oh!
but many things. Through one appeared an olive
garden, and in it two lovers who held each other's
hands, under an Italian moon; through another a wild
sea, and a ship to whom the wild, racing sea was slave.
A third showed a king on his throne, his courtiers
obsequious about him; and yet a fourth showed a
really good hotel, with the respectable Ugly-Wugly
sunning himself on the front doorsteps. There was a
mother, bending over a wooden cradle. There was an
artist gazing entranced on the picture his wet brush
seemed to have that moment completed, a general
dying on a field where Victory had planted the stand-
ard he loved, and these things were not pictures, but
the truest truths, alive, and, as anyone could see,
immortal.

Many other pictures there were that these arches
framed. And all showed some moment when life had
sprung to fire and flower – the best that the soul
of man could ask or man's destiny grant. And the really
good hotel had its place here too, because there are
some souls that ask no higher thing of life than 'a
really good hotel'.

'Oh, I am glad we came; I am, I am!' Kathleen

murmured, and held fast to her brother's hand.

They went slowly up the hall, the ineffectual bull's-eye, held by Jimmy, very crooked indeed, showing almost as a shadow in this big, glorious light.

And then, when the hall's end was almost reached, the children saw where the light came from. It glowed and spread itself from one place, and in that place stood the one statue that Mabel 'did not know where to find' – the statue of Psyche. They went on, slowly, quite happy, quite bewildered. And when they came close to Psyche they saw that on her raised hand the ring showed dark.

Gerald let go Kathleen's hand, put his foot on the pediment, his knee on the pedestal. He stood up, dark and human, beside the white girl with the butterfly wings.

'I do hope you don't mind,' he said, and drew the ring off very gently. Then, as he dropped to the ground, 'Not here,' he said. 'I don't know why, but not here.'

And they all passed behind the white Psyche, and once more the bicycle lamp seemed suddenly to come to life again as Gerald held it in front of him, to be the pioneer in the dark passage that led from the Hall of — , but they did not know, then, what it was the Hall of.

Then, as the twisting passage shut in on them with a darkness that pressed close against the little light of the bicycle lamp, Kathleen said, 'Give me the ring. I know exactly what to say.'

Gerald gave it with not extreme readiness.

'I wish,' said Kathleen slowly, 'that no one at home may know that we've been out tonight, and I wish we were safe in our own beds, undressed, and in our nightgowns, and asleep.'

And the next thing any of them knew, it was good, strong, ordinary daylight – not just sunrise, but the kind of daylight you are used to being called in, and all were in their own beds. Kathleen had framed the wish most sensibly. The only mistake had been in saying 'in our own beds', because, of course, Mabel's own bed was at Yalding Towers, and to this day Mabel's drab-haired aunt cannot understand how Mabel, who was staying the night with that child in the town she was so taken up with, hadn't come home at eleven, when the aunt locked up, and yet she was in her bed in the morning. For though not a clever woman, she was not stupid enough to be able to believe any one of the eleven fancy explanations which the distracted Mabel offered in the course of the morning. The first (which makes twelve) of these explanations was The Truth, and of course the aunt was far too clever to believe That!

11

It was show-day at Yalding Castle, and it seemed good
to the children to go and visit Mabel, and, as Gerald
put it, to mingle unsuspected with the crowd; to gloat
over all the things which they knew and which the
crowd didn't know about the castle and the sliding
panels, the magic ring and the statues that came alive.
Perhaps one of the pleasantest things about magic
happenings is the feeling which they give you of knowing what other people not only don't know but
wouldn't, so to speak, believe if they did.

On the white road outside the gates of the castle was
a dark spattering of breaks and wagonettes and dog-
carts. Three or four waiting motor-cars puffed fatly
where they stood, and bicycles sprawled in heaps along
the grassy hollow by the red brick wall. And the
people who had been brought to the castle by the
breaks and wagonettes, and dog-carts and bicycles and
motors, as well as those who had walked there on their
own unaided feet, were scattered about the grounds,
or being shown over those parts of the castle which
were, on this one day of the week, thrown open to
visitors.

There were more visitors than usual today because
it had somehow been whispered about that Lord Yald-

ing was down, and that the holland covers were to be taken off the state furniture so that a rich American who wished to rent the castle, to live in, might see the place in all its glory.

It certainly did look very splendid. The embroidered satin, gilded leather and tapestry of the chairs, which had been hidden by brown holland, gave to the rooms a pleasant air of being lived in. There were flowering plants and pots of roses here and there on tables or window-ledges. Mabel's aunt prided herself on her tasteful touch in the home, and had studied the arrangement of flowers in a series of articles in *Home Drivel* called 'How to Make Home High-class on Nine-pence a Week'.

The great crystal chandeliers, released from the bags that at ordinary times shrouded them, gleamed with grey and purple splendour. The brown linen sheets had been taken off the state beds, and the red ropes that usually kept the low crowd in its proper place had been rolled up and hidden away.

'It's exactly as if we were calling on the family,' said the grocer's daughter from Salisbury to her friend who was in the millinery.

'If the Yankee doesn't take it, what do you say to you and me setting up here when we get spliced?' the draper's assistant asked his sweetheart. And she said: 'Oh, Reggie, how can you! you are *too* funny.'

All the afternoon the crowd in its smart holiday clothes, pink blouses, and light-coloured suits, flowery hats, and scarves beyond description passed through and through the dark hall, the magnificent drawing-rooms and boudoirs and picture-galleries. The chattering crowd was awed into something like quiet by the calm, stately bedchambers, where men had been born, and died; where royal guests had lain in long-ago summer nights, with big bow-pots of elder-flowers set on the hearth to ward off fever and evil spells. The terrace, where in old days dames in ruffs had sniffed the sweet-brier and southernwood of the borders below, and ladies, bright with rouge and powder and brocade, had walked in the swing of their hooped skirts – the terrace now echoed to the sound of brown boots, and the tap-tap of high-heeled shoes at two and eleven three, and high laughter and chattering voices that said nothing that the children wanted to hear. These spoiled for them the quiet of the enchanted castle, and outraged the peace of the garden of enchantments.

'It isn't such a lark after all,' Gerald admitted, as from the window of the stone summer-house at the end of the terrace they watched the loud colours and heard the loud laughter. 'I do hate to see all these people in *our* garden.'

'I said that to that nice bailiff-man this morning,' said Mabel, setting herself on the stone floor, 'and he said it wasn't much to let them come once a week. He said Lord Yalding ought to let them come when they liked – said he would if he lived there.'

'That's all he knows!' said Jimmy. 'Did he say anything else?'

'Lots,' said Mabel. 'I do like him! I told him –'

'You didn't!'

'Yes. I told him lots about our adventures. The humble bailiff is a beautiful listener.'

'We shall be locked up for beautiful lunatics if you let your jaw get the better of you, my Mabel child.'

'Not us!' said Mabel. 'I told it – you know the way – every word true, and yet so that nobody believes any of it. When I'd quite done he said I'd got a real littery talent, and I promised to put his name on the beginning of the first book I write when I grow up.'

'You don't know his name,' said Kathleen. 'Let's do something with the ring.'

'Imposs!' said Gerald. 'I forgot to tell you, but I met Mademoiselle when I went back for my garters – and she's coming to meet us and walk back with us.'

'What did you say?'

'I said,' said Gerald deliberately, 'that it was very kind of her. And so it was. Us not wanting her doesn't make it not kind her coming –'

'It may be kind, but it's sickening too,' said Mabel, 'because now I suppose we shall have to stick here and wait for her; and I promised we'd meet the bailiff-man. He's going to bring things in a basket and have a picnic-tea with us.'

'Where?'

'Beyond the dinosaurus. He said he'd tell me all about the anteddy-something animals – it means before Noah's Ark; there are lots besides the dinosaurus – in return for me telling him my agreeable fictions. Yes, he called them that.'

'When?'

'As soon as the gates shut. That's five.'

'We might take Mademoiselle along,' suggested Gerald.

'She'd be too proud to have tea with a bailiff, I expect; you never know how grown-ups will take the simplest things.' It was Kathleen who said this.

'Well, I'll tell you what,' said Gerald, lazily turning

on the stone bench. 'You all go along, and meet your bailiff. A picnic's a picnic. And I'll wait for Mademoiselle.'

Mabel remarked joyously that this was jolly decent of Gerald, to which he modestly replied: 'Oh, rot!'

Jimmy added that Gerald rather liked sucking-up to people.

'Little boys don't understand diplomacy,' said Gerald calmly; 'sucking-up is simply silly. But it's better to be good than pretty and –'

'How do you know?' Jimmy asked.

'And,' his brother went on, 'you never know when a grown-up may come in useful. Besides, they *like* it. You must give them *some* little pleasures. Think how awful it must be to be old. My hat!'

'I hope *I* shan't be an old maid,' said Kathleen.

'I don't *mean* to be,' said Mabel briskly. 'I'd rather marry a travelling tinker.'

'It would be rather nice,' Kathleen mused, 'to marry the Gipsy King and go about in a caravan telling fortunes and hung round with baskets and brooms.'

'Oh, if I could choose,' said Mabel, 'of course I'd marry a brigand, and live in his mountain fastnesses, and be kind to his captives and help them to escape and –'

'You'll be a real treasure to your husband,' said Gerald.

'Yes,' said Kathleen, 'or a sailor would be nice. You'd watch for his ship coming home and set the lamp in the dormer window to light him home through the storm; and when he was drowned at sea you'd be most frightfully sorry, and go every day to lay flowers on his daisied grave.'

'Yes,' Mabel hastened to say, 'or a soldier, and then you'd go to the wars with short petticoats and a cocked hat and a barrel round your neck like a St Bernard dog. There's a picture of a soldier's wife on a song auntie's got. It's called "The Veevandyear".'

'When I marry –' Kathleen quickly said.

'When I marry,' said Gerald, 'I'll marry a dumb girl, or else get the ring to make her so that she can't speak unless she's spoken to. Let's have a squint.'

He applied his eye to the stone lattice.

'They're moving off,' he said. 'Those pink and purple hats are nodding off in the distant prospect; and the funny little man with the beard like a goat is going a different way from everyone else – the gardeners will have to head him off. I don't see Mademoiselle, though. The rest of you had better bunk. It doesn't do to run any risks with picnics. The deserted hero of our tale, alone and unsupported, urged on his brave followers to pursue the commissariat waggons, he himself remaining at the post of danger and difficulty, because he was born to stand on burning decks whence all but he had fled, and to lead forlorn hopes when despaired of by the human race!'

'I think I'll marry a dumb husband,' said Mabel, 'and there shan't be any heroes in my books when I write them, only a heroine. Come on, Cathy.'

Coming out of that cool, shadowy summer-house into the sunshine was like stepping into an oven, and the stone of the terrace was burning to the children's feet.

'I know now what a cat on hot bricks feels like,' said Jimmy.

The antediluvian animals are set in a beech-wood on

a slope at least half a mile across the park from the castle. The grandfather of the present Lord Yalding had them set there in the middle of last century, in the great days of the late Prince Consort, the Exhibition of 1851, Sir Joseph Paxton, and the Crystal Palace. Their stone flanks, their wide, ungainly wings, their lozenged crocodile-like backs show grey through the trees a long way off.

Most people think that noon is the hottest time of the day. They are wrong. A cloudless sky gets hotter and hotter all the afternoon, and reaches its very hottest at five. I am sure you must all have noticed this when you are going out to tea anywhere in your best clothes, especially if your clothes are starched and you happen to have a rather long and shadeless walk.

Kathleen, Mabel, and Jimmy got hotter and hotter, and went more and more slowly. They had almost reached that stage of resentment and discomfort when one 'wishes one hadn't come' before they saw, below the edge of the beech-wood, the white waved handker-chief of the bailiff.

That banner, eloquent of tea, shade, and being able to sit down, put new heart into them. They mended their pace, and a final desperate run landed them among the drifted coppery leaves and bare grey and green roots of the beech-wood.

'Oh, glory!' said Jimmy, throwing himself down. 'How do you do?'

The bailiff looked very nice, the girls thought. He was not wearing his velveteens, but a grey flannel suit that an Earl need not have scorned; and his straw hat would have done no discredit to a Duke; and a Prince could not have worn a prettier green tie. He welcomed the children warmly. And there were two baskets dumped heavy and promising among the beech-leaves.

He was a man of tact. The hot, instructive tour of the stone antediluvians, which had loomed with ever-lessening charm before the children, was not even mentioned.

'You must be desert-dry,' he said, 'and you'll be hungry, too, when you've done being thirsty. I put on the kettle as soon as I discerned the form of my fair romancer in the extreme offing.'

The kettle introduced itself with puffings and bubblings from the hollow between two grey roots where it sat on a spirit-lamp.

'Take off your shoes and stockings, won't you?' said the bailiff in matter-of-course tones, just as old ladies ask each other to take off their bonnets; 'there's a little baby canal just over the ridge.'

The joys of dipping one's feet in cool running water after a hot walk have yet to be described. I could write pages about them. There was a mill-stream when I was young with little fishes in it, and dropped leaves that spun round, and willows and alders that leaned over it and kept it cool, and – but this is not the story of *my* life.

When they came back, on rested, damp, pink feet, tea was made and poured out, delicious tea with as much milk as ever you wanted, out of a beer bottle with a screw top, and cakes, and gingerbread, and plums, and a big melon with a lump of ice in its heart – a tea for the gods!

This thought must have come to Jimmy, for he said suddenly, removing his face from inside a wide-bitten crescent of melon-rind:

'Your feast's as good as the feast of the Immortals, almost.'

'Explain your recondite allusion,' said the grey-flannelled host; and Jimmy, understanding him to say, 'What do you mean?' replied with the whole tale of that wonderful night when the statues came alive, and a banquet of unearthly splendour and deliciousness was plucked by marble hands from the trees of the lake island.

When he had done the bailiff said:

'Did you get all this out of a book?'

'No,' said Jimmy, 'it happened.'

'You are an imaginative set of young dreamers, aren't you?' the bailiff asked, handing the plums to Kathleen, who smiled, friendly but embarrassed. Why couldn't Jimmy have held his tongue?

'No, we're not,' said that indiscreet one obstinately; 'everything I've told you *did* happen, and so did the things Mabel told you.'

The bailiff looked a little uncomfortable. 'All right, old chap,' he said. And there was a short, uneasy silence. 'Look here,' said Jimmy, who seemed for once to have got the bit between his teeth, 'do you believe me or not?'

'Don't be silly, Jimmy!' Kathleen whispered. 'Because, if you don't I'll *make* you believe.'

'Don't!' said Mabel and Kathleen together.

'Do you or don't you?' Jimmy insisted, lying on his front with his chin on his hands, his elbows on a moss-cushion, and his bare legs kicking among the beech-leaves.

'I think you tell adventures awfully well,' said the bailiff cautiously.

'Very well,' said Jimmy, abruptly sitting up, 'you don't believe me. Nonsense, Cathy! he's a gentleman, even if he is a bailiff.'

'Thank you!' said the bailiff with eyes that twinkled.

'You won't tell, will you?' Jimmy urged.

'Tell what?'

'*Anything.*'

'Certainly not. I am, as you say, the soul of honour.'

'Then – Cathy, give me the ring.'

'Oh, *no!*' said the girls together.

Kathleen did not mean to give up the ring; Mabel did not mean that she should; Jimmy certainly used no force. Yet presently he held it in his hand. It was his hour. There are times like that for all of us, when what we say shall be done *is* done.

'Now,' said Jimmy, 'this is the ring Mabel told you about. I say it is a wishing-ring. And if you will put it on your hand and wish, whatever you wish will happen.'

'Must I wish out loud?'

'Yes – I think so.'

'Don't wish for anything silly,' said Kathleen, making the best of the situation, 'like its being fine on Tuesday or its being your favourite pudding for dinner tomorrow. Wish for something you really want.'

'I will,' said the bailiff. 'I'll wish for the only thing I really want. I wish my – I wish my friend were here.'

The three who knew the power of the ring looked round to see the bailiff's friend appear; a surprised man that friend would be, they thought, and perhaps a frightened one. They had all risen, and stood ready to soothe and reassure the newcomer. But no startled gentleman appeared in the wood, only, coming quietly through the dappled sun and shadow under the beech-trees, Mademoiselle and Gerald, Mademoiselle in a white gown, looking quite nice and like a picture, Gerald hot and polite.

'Good afternoon,' said that dauntless leader of forlorn hopes. 'I persuaded Mademoiselle –'

That sentence was never finished, for the bailiff and the French governess were looking at each other with the eyes of tired travellers who find, quite without expecting it, the desired end of a very long journey.

And the children saw that even if they spoke it would not make any difference.

'*You!*' said the bailiff.

'Mais . . . c'est donc vous,' said Mademoiselle, in a funny choky voice.

And they stood still and looked at each other, 'like stuck pigs', as Jimmy said later, for quite a long time.

'Is *she* your friend?' Jimmy asked.

'Yes – oh yes,' said the bailiff. 'You are my friend, are you not?'

'But yes,' Mademoiselle said softly. 'I am your friend.'

'There! you see,' said Jimmy, 'the ring *does* do what I said.'

'We won't quarrel about that,' said the bailiff. 'You can say it's the ring. For me – it's a coincidence – the happiest, the dearest –'

'Then you –?' said the French governess.

'Of course,' said the bailiff. 'Jimmy, give your brother some tea. Mademoiselle, come and walk in the woods: there are a thousand things to say.'

'Eat then, my Gerald,' said Mademoiselle, now grown young, and astonishingly like a fairy princess. 'I return all at the hour, and we re-enter together. It is that we must speak each other. It is long time that we have not seen us, me and Lord Yalding!'

'So he was Lord Yalding all the time,' said Jimmy, breaking a stupefied silence as the white gown and the grey flannels disappeared among the beech-trunks. 'Landscape painter sort of dodge – silly, I call it. And fancy her being a friend of his, and his wishing she was here! Different from us, eh? Good old ring!'

'His friend!' said Mabel with strong scorn; 'don't you see she's his lover? Don't you see she's the lady that was bricked up in the convent, because he was so poor, and he couldn't find her. And now the ring's made them live happy ever after. I *am* glad! Aren't you, Cathy?'

'Rather!' said Kathleen; 'it's as good as marrying a sailor or a bandit.'

'It's the ring did it,' said Jimmy. 'If the American takes the house he'll pay lots of rent, and they can live on that.'

'I wonder if they'll be married tomorrow!' said Mabel.

'Wouldn't if be fun if we were bridesmaids,' said Cathy.

'May I trouble you for the melon,' said Gerald. 'Thanks! Why didn't we know he was Lord Yalding? Apes and moles that we were!'

'*I've* known since last night,' said Mabel calmly; 'only I promised not to tell. I *can* keep a secret, can't I?'

'Too jolly well,' said Kathleen, a little aggrieved.

'He was disguised as a bailiff,' said Jimmy; 'that's why we didn't know.'

'Disguised as a fiddle-stick-end,' said Gerald. 'Ha, ha! I see something old Sherlock Holmes never saw, nor that idiot Watson, either. If you want a really impenetrable disguise, you ought to disguise yourself as what you really are. I'll remember that.'

'It's like Mabel, telling things so that you can't believe them,' said Cathy.

'I think Mademoiselle's jolly lucky,' said Mabel.

'She's not so bad. He might have done worse,' said Gerald. 'Plums, please!'

There was quite plainly magic at work. Mademoiselle next morning was a changed governess. Her cheeks were pink, her lips were red, her eyes were larger and brighter, and she had done her hair in an entirely new way, rather frivolous and very becoming.

'Mam'selle's coming out!' Eliza remarked.

Immediately after breakfast Lord Yalding called with a wagonette that wore a smart blue cloth coat, and was drawn by two horses whose coats were brown and shining and fitted them even better than the blue cloth coat fitted the wagonette, and the whole party drove in state and splendour to Yalding Towers.

Arrived there, the children clamoured for permission

to explore the castle thoroughly, a thing that had never yet been possible. Lord Yalding, a little absent in manner, but yet quite cordial, consented. Mabel showed the others all the secret doors and unlikely passages and stairs that she had discovered. It was a glorious morning. Lord Yalding and Mademoiselle went through the house, it is true, but in a rather half-hearted way. Quite soon they were tired, and went out through the French windows of the drawing-room and through the rose garden, to sit on the curved stone seat in the middle of the maze, where once, at the beginning of things, Gerald, Kathleen, and Jimmy had found the sleeping Princess who wore pink silk and diamonds.

The children felt that their going left to the castle a more spacious freedom, and explored with more than Arctic enthusiasm. It was as they emerged from the little rickety secret staircase that led from the powdering-room of the state suite to the gallery of the hall that they came suddenly face to face with the odd little man who had a beard like a goat and had taken the wrong turning yesterday.

'This part of the castle is private,' said Mabel, with great presence of mind, and shut the door behind her.

'I am aware of it,' said the goat-faced stranger, 'but I have the permission of the Earl of Yalding to examine the house *at* my leisure.'

'Oh!' said Mabel. 'I beg your pardon. We all do. We didn't know.'

'You are relatives of his lordship, I should surmise?' asked the goat-faced.

'Not exactly,' said Gerald. 'Friends.'

The gentleman was thin and very neatly dressed; he had small, merry eyes and a face that was brown and dry-looking.

'You are playing some game, I should suppose?'

'No, sir,' said Gerald, 'only exploring.'

'May a stranger propose himself as a member of your Exploring Expedition?' asked the gentleman, smiling a tight but kind smile.

The children looked at each other.

'You see,' said Gerald, 'it's rather difficult to explain – but – you see what I mean, don't you?'

'He means,' said Jimmy, 'that we can't take you into an exploring party without we know what you want to go for.'

'Are you a photographer?' asked Mabel, 'or is it some newspaper's sent you to write about the Towers?'

'I understand your position,' said the gentleman. 'I am not a photographer, nor am I engaged by any journal. I am a man of independent means, travelling in this country with the intention of renting a residence. My name is Jefferson D. Conway.'

'Oh!' said Mabel; 'then you're the American millionaire.'

'I do not like the description, young lady,' said Mr Jefferson D. Conway. 'I am an American citizen, and I am not without means. This is a fine property – a very fine property. If it were for sale –'

'It isn't, it can't be,' Mabel hastened to explain. 'The lawyers have put it in a tale, so Lord Yalding can't sell it. But you could take it to live in, and pay Lord Yalding a good millionairish rent, and then he could marry the French governess –'

'Shish!' said Kathleen and Mr Jefferson D. Conway together, and he added:

'Lead the way, please; and I should suggest that the exploration be complete and exhaustive.'

Thus encouraged, Mabel led the millionaire through all the castle. He seemed pleased, yet disappointed too.

'It is a fine mansion,' he said at last when they had come back to the point from which they had started; 'but I should suppose, in a house this size, there would mostly be a secret stairway, or a priests' hiding place, or a ghost?'

'There are,' said Mabel briefly, 'but I thought Americans didn't believe in anything but machinery and newspapers.' She touched the spring of the panel behind her, and displayed the little tottery staircase to the American. The sight of it worked a wonderul transformation in him. He became eager, alert, very keen.

'Say!' he cried, over and over again, standing in the door that led from the powdering-room to the state bed-chamber. 'But this is great – great!'

The hopes of everyone ran high. It seemed almost certain that the castle would be let for a millionairish rent and Lord Yalding be made affluent to the point of marriage.

'If there were a ghost located in this ancestral pile, I'd close with the Earl of Yalding today, now, on the nail,' Mr Jefferson D. Conway went on.

'If you were to stay till tomorrow, and sleep in this room, I expect you'd see the ghost,' said Mabel.

'There *is* a ghost located here then?' he said joyously.

'They say,' Mabel answered, 'that old Sir Rupert,

who lost his head in Henry the Eighth's time, walks of a night here, with his head under his arm. But we've not seen that. What we have seen is the lady in a pink dress with diamonds in her hair. She carries a lighted taper,' Mabel hastily added. The others, now suddenly aware of Mabel's plan, hastened to assure the American in accents of earnest truth that they had all seen the lady with the pink gown.

He looked at them with half-closed eyes that twinkled.

'Well,' he said, 'I calculate to ask the Earl of Yalding to permit me to pass a night in his ancestral best bed-chamber. And if I hear so much as a phantom foot-step, or hear so much as a ghostly sigh, I'll take the place.'

'I *am* glad!' said Cathy.

'You appear to be very certain of your ghost,' said the American, still fixing them with little eyes that shone. 'Let me tell you, young gentlemen, that I carry a gun, and when I see a ghost, I shoot.'

He pulled a pistol out of his hip-pocket, and looked at it lovingly.

'And I am a fair average shot,' he went on, walking across the shiny floor of the state bed-chamber to the open window. 'See that big red rose, like a tea-saucer?'

They saw.

The next moment a loud report broke the stillness, and the red petals of the shattered rose strewed balus-trade and terrace.

The American looked from one child to another. Every face was perfectly white.

'Jefferson D. Conway made his little pile by strict attention to business, and keeping his eyes skinned,' he added. 'Thank you for all your kindness.'

'Suppose you'd done it, and he'd shot you!' said Jimmy cheerfully. 'That *would* have been an adventure, wouldn't it?'

'I'm going to do it still,' said Mabel, pale and defiant. 'Let's find Lord Yalding and get the ring back.'

Lord Yalding had had an interview with Mabel's aunt, and lunch for six was laid in the great dark hall, among the armour and the oak furniture – a beautiful lunch served on silver dishes. Mademoiselle, becoming every moment younger and more like a Princess, was moved to tears when Gerald rose, lemonade-glass in hand, and proposed the health of 'Lord and Lady Yalding'.

When Lord Yalding had returned thanks in a speech full of agreeable jokes the moment seemed to Gerald propitious, and he said:

'The ring, you know – you don't believe in it, but we do. May we have it back?'

And got it.

Then, after a hasty council, held in the panelled jewel-room, Mabel said: 'This is a wishing-ring, and I wish all the American's weapons of all sorts were here.'

Instantly the room was full – six feet up the wall – of a tangle and mass of weapons, swords, spears, arrows, tomahawks, fowling pieces, blunderbusses, pistols, revolvers, scimitars, kreeses – every kind of weapon you can think of – and the four children wedged in among all these weapons of death hardly dared to breathe.

'He collects arms, I expect,' said Gerald, 'and the arrows are poisoned, I shouldn't wonder. Wish them back where they came from, Mabel, for goodness' sake, and try again.'

Mabel wished the weapons away, and at once the four children stood safe in a bare panelled room. But –

'No,' Mabel said, 'I can't stand it. We'll work the ghost another way. I wish the American may think he sees a ghost when he goes to bed. Sir Rupert with his head under his arm will do.'

'Is it tonight he sleeps there?'

'I don't know. I wish he may see Sir Rupert every night – that'll make it all serene.'

'It's rather dull,' said Gerald; 'we shan't know whether he's seen Sir Rupert or not.'

'We shall know in the morning, when he takes the house.'

This being settled, Mabel's aunt was found to be desirous of Mabel's company, so the others went home.

It was when they were at supper that Lord Yalding suddenly appeared, and said:

'Mr Jefferson Conway wants you boys to spend the night with him in the state chamber. I've had beds put up. You don't mind, do you? He seems to think you've got some idea of playing ghost-tricks on him.'

It was difficult to refuse, so difficult that it proved impossible.

Ten o'clock found the boys each in a narrow white bed that looked quite absurdly small in that high, dark chamber, and in face of that tall gaunt four-poster hung with tapestry and ornamented with funereal-looking plumes.

'I hope to goodness there isn't a *real* ghost,' Jimmy whispered.

'Not likely,' Gerald whispered back.

'But I don't want to see Sir Rupert's ghost with its head under its arm,' Jimmy insisted.

'You won't. The most you'll see'll be the millionaire seeing it. Mabel said he was to see it, not us. Very likely you'll sleep all night and not see anything. Shut your eyes and count up to a million and don't be a goat!'

But he was reckoning without Mabel and the ring.

As soon as Mabel had learned from her drab-haired aunt that this was indeed the night when Mr Jefferson D. Conway would sleep at the castle she had hastened to add a wish, 'that Sir Rupert and his head may appear tonight in the state bedroom'.

Jimmy shut his eyes and began to count a million. Before he had counted it he fell asleep. So did his brother.

They were awakened by the loud echoing bang of a pistol shot. Each thought of the shot that had been fired that morning, and opened eyes that expected to see a sunshiny terrace and red-rose petals strewn upon warm white stone.

Instead, there was the dark, lofty state chamber, lighted but little by six tall candles; there was the American in shirt and trousers, a smoking pistol in his hand; and there, advancing from the door of the powdering-room, a figure in doublet and hose, a ruff round its neck – and no head! The head, sure enough, was there; but it was under the right arm, held close in the slashed-velvet sleeve of the doublet. The face look-ing from under the arm wore a pleasant smile. Both boys, I am sorry to say, screamed. The American fired again. The bullet passed through Sir Rupert, who advanced without appearing to notice it.

Then, suddenly, the lights went out. The next thing the boys knew it was morning. A grey daylight shone blankly through the tall windows – and wild rain was beating upon the glass, and the American was gone.

'Where are we?' said Jimmy, sitting up with tangled hair and looking round him. 'Oh, I remember. Ugh! it was horrid. I'm about fed up with that ring, so I don't mind telling you.'

'Nonsense!' said Gerald. 'I enjoyed it. I wasn't a bit frightened, were you?'

'No,' said Jimmy, 'of course I wasn't.'

'We've done the trick,' said Gerald later when they learned that the American had breakfasted early with Lord Yalding and taken the first train to London; 'he's gone to get rid of his other house, and take this one. The old ring's beginning to do really useful things.'

*

'Perhaps you'll believe in the ring now,' said Jimmy to Lord Yalding, whom he met later on in the picture-gallery; 'it's all our doing that Mr Jefferson saw the ghost. He told us he'd take the house if he saw a ghost, so of course we took care he did see one.'

'Oh, you did, did you?' said Lord Yalding in rather an odd voice. 'I'm very much obliged, I'm sure.'

'Don't mention it,' said Jimmy kindly. 'I thought you'd be pleased and him too.'

'Perhaps you'll be interested to learn,' said Lord Yalding, putting his hands in his pockets and staring down at Jimmy, 'that Mr Jefferson D. Conway was so pleased with your ghost that he got me out of bed at six o'clock this morning to talk about it.'

'Oh, ripping!' said Jimmy. 'What did he say?'

'He said, as far as I can remember,' said Lord Yalding, still in the same strange voice – 'he said: "My lord, your ancestral pile is A1. It is, in fact, The Limit. Its luxury is palatial, its grounds are nothing short of Edenesque. No expense has been spared, I should surmise. Your ancestors were whole-hoggers. They have done the thing as it should be done – every detail attended to. I like your tapestry, and I like your oak, and I like your secret stairs. But I think your ancestors should have left well enough alone, and stopped at that." So I said they had, as far as I knew, and he shook his head and said:

'"No, Sir. Your ancestors take the air of a night with their heads under their arms. A ghost that sighed or glided or rustled I could have stood, and thanked you for it, and considered it in the rent. But a ghost that bullets go through while it stands grinning with a bare neck and its head loose under its own arm and little boys screaming and fainting in their beds – no! What I say is, If this is a British hereditary high-toned family ghost, excuse me!" And he went off by the early train.'

'I say,' the stricken Jimmy remarked, 'I *am* sorry, and I don't think we did faint, really I don't – but we thought it would be just what you wanted. And perhaps someone else will take the house.'

'I don't know anyone else rich enough,' said Lord Yalding. 'Mr Conway came the day before he said he would, or you'd never have got hold of him. And I don't know how you did it, and I don't want to know. It was a rather silly trick.'

There was a gloomy pause. The rain beat against the long windows.

'I say' – Jimmy looked up at Lord Yalding with the light of a new idea in his round face. 'I say, if you're hard up, why don't you sell your jewels?'

'I haven't any jewels, you meddlesome young duffer,' said Lord Yalding quite crossly; and taking his hands out of his pockets, he began to walk away.

'I mean the ones in the panelled room with the stars in the ceiling,' Jimmy insisted, following him.

'There aren't any,' said Lord Yalding shortly; 'and if this is some more ring-nonsense I advise you to be careful, young man. I've had about as much as I care for.'

'It's *not* ring-nonsense,' said Jimmy: 'there are shelves and shelves of beautiful family jewels. You can sell them and –'

'Oh, *no!*' cried Mademoiselle, appearing like an oleograph of a duchess in the door of the picture-gallery; 'don't sell the family jewels –'

'There aren't any, my lady,' said Lord Yalding, going towards her. 'I thought you were never coming.'

'Oh, aren't there!' said Mabel, who had followed Mademoiselle. 'You just come and see.'

'Let us see what they will to show us,' cried Mademoiselle, for Lord Yalding did not move; 'it should at least be amusing.'

'It is,' said Jimmy.

So they went, Mabel and Jimmy leading, while Mademoiselle and Lord Yalding followed, hand in hand.

'It's much safer to walk hand in hand,' said Lord Yalding; 'with these children at large one never knows what may happen next.'

12

It would be interesting, no doubt, to describe the
feelings of Lord Yalding as he followed Mabel and
Jimmy through his ancestral halls, but I have no means
of knowing at all what he felt. Yet one must suppose
that he felt something: bewilderment, perhaps, mixed
with a faint wonder, and a desire to pinch himself to
see if he were dreaming. Or he may have pondered the
rival questions, 'Am I mad?' 'Are they mad?' without
being at all able to decide which he ought to try to
answer, let alone deciding what, in either case, the
answer ought to be. You see, the children did seem to
believe in the odd stories they told – and the wish had
come true, and the ghost *had* appeared. He must have
thought – but all this is vain; I don't *really* know what
he thought any more than you do.

Nor can I give you any clue to the thoughts and
feelings of Mademoiselle. I only know that she was
very happy, but anyone would have known that if they
had seen her face. Perhaps this is as good a moment as
any to explain that when her guardian had put her in a
convent so that she should not sacrifice her fortune by
marrying a poor lord, her guardian had secured that
fortune (to himself) by going off with it to South
America. Then, having no money left, Mademoiselle

had to work for it. So she went out as governess, and took the situation she did take because it was near Lord Yalding's home. She wanted to see him, even though she thought he had forsaken her and did not love her any more. And now she had seen him. I dare say she thought about some of these things as she went along through his house, her hand held in his. But of course I can't be sure.

Jimmy's thoughts, of course, I can read like any old book. He thought, 'Now he'll *have* to believe me.' That Lord Yalding should believe him had become, quite unreasonably, the most important thing in the world to Jimmy. He wished that Gerald and Kathleen were there to share his triumph, but they were helping Mabel's aunt to cover the grand furniture up, and so were out of what followed. Not that they missed much, for when Mabel proudly said, 'Now you'll see,' and the others came close round her in the little panelled room, there was a pause, and then – nothing happened at all!

'There's a secret spring here somewhere,' said Mabel, fumbling with fingers that had suddenly grown hot and damp.

'Where?' said Lord Yalding.

'*Here*,' said Mabel impatiently, 'only I can't find it.'

And she couldn't. She found the spring of the secret panel under the window all right, but that seemed to everyone dull compared with the jewels that everyone had pictured and two at least had seen. But the spring that made the oak panelling slide away and displayed jewels plainly to any eye worth a king's ransom – this could not be found. More, it was simply not there. There could be no doubt of that. Every inch of the

panelling was felt by careful fingers. The earnest pro-
tests of Mabel and Jimmy died away presently in a
silence made painful by the hotness of one's ears, the
discomfort of not liking to meet anyone's eyes, and the
resentful feeling that the spring was not behaving in at
all a sportsmanlike way, and that, in a word, this was
not cricket.

'You see!' said Lord Yalding severely. 'Now you've
had your joke, if you call it a joke, and I've had
enough of the whole silly business. Give me the ring –
it's mine, I suppose, since you say you found it somewhere here – and don't let's hear another word about
all this rubbish of magic and enchantment.'

'Gerald's got the ring,' said Mabel miserably.

'Then go and fetch him,' said Lord Yalding – 'both
of you.'

The melancholy pair retired, and Lord Yalding
spent the time of their absence in explaining to
Mademoiselle how very unimportant jewels were compared with other things.

The four children came back together.

'We've had enough of this ring business,' said Lord
Yalding. 'Give it to me and we'll say no more about
it.'

'I – I can't get it off,' said Gerald. 'It – it always did
have a will of its own.'

'I'll soon get it off,' said Lord Yalding. But he
didn't. 'We'll try soap,' he said firmly. Four out of his
five hearers knew just exactly how much use soap
would be.

'They won't believe about the jewels,' wailed Mabel,
suddenly dissolved in tears, 'and I can't find the spring.
I've felt all over – we all have – it was just here, and –'

Her fingers felt it as she spoke; and as she ceased to speak the carved panels slid away, and the blue velvet shelves laden with jewels were disclosed to the unbelieving eyes of Lord Yalding and the lady who was to be his wife.

'Jove!' said Lord Yalding.

'*Miséricorde!*' said the lady.

'But why *now*?' gasped Mabel. 'Why not before?'

'I expect it's magic,' said Gerald. 'There's no real spring here, and it couldn't act because the ring wasn't here. You know Phoebus told us the ring was the heart of all the magic.'

'Shut it up and take the ring away and see.'

They did, and Gerald was (as usual, he himself pointed out) proved to be right. When the ring was away there was no spring; when the ring was in the room there (as Mabel urged) was the spring all right enough.

'So you see,' said Mabel to Lord Yalding.

'I see that the spring's very artfully concealed,' said that dense peer. 'I think it was very clever indeed of you to find it. And if those jewels are real –'

'Of course they're real,' said Mabel indignantly.

'Well, anyway,' said Lord Yalding, 'thank you all very much. I think it's clearing up. I'll send the wagonette home with you after lunch. And if you don't mind, I'll have the ring.'

Half an hour of soap and water produced no effect whatever, except to make the finger of Gerald very red and very sore. Then Lord Yalding said something very impatient indeed, and then Gerald suddenly became angry and said: 'Well, I'm sure I wish it would come off,' and of course instantly, 'slick as butter', as he later pointed out, off it came.

'Thank you,' said Lord Yalding.

'And I believe now he thinks I kept it on on pur-pose,' said Gerald afterwards when, at ease on the leads at home, they talked the whole thing out over a tin of preserved pineapple and a bottle of ginger-beer apiece. 'There's no pleasing some people. He wasn't in such a fiery hurry to order that wagonette after he found that Mademoiselle meant to go when we did. But I liked him better when he was a humble bailiff. Take him for all in all, he does not look as if we should like him again.'

'He doesn't know what's the matter with him,' said Kathleen, leaning back against the tiled roof; 'it's really the magic – it's like sickening with measles. Don't you remember how cross Mabel was at first about the invisibleness?'

'Rather!' said Jimmy.

'It's partly that,' said Gerald, trying to be fair, 'and partly it's the being in love. It always makes people like idiots – a chap at school told me. His sister was like that – quite rotten, you know. And she used to be quite a decent sort before she was engaged.'

At tea and at supper Mademoiselle was radiant – as attractive as a lady on a Christmas card, as merry as a marmoset, and as kind as you would always be yourself if you could take the trouble. At breakfast, an equal radiance, kindness, attraction, merriment. Then Lord Yalding came to see her. The meeting took place in the drawing-room; the children with deep discreetness remained shut in the school-room till Gerald, going up to his room for a pencil, surprised Eliza with her ear glued to the drawing-room key-hole.

After that Gerald sat on the top stair with a book.

He could not hear any of the conversation in the drawing-room, but he could command a view of the door, and in this way be certain that no one else heard any of it. Thus it was that when the drawing-room door opened Gerald was in a position to see Lord Yalding come out. 'Our young hero,' as he said later, 'coughed with infinite tact to show that he was there,' but Lord Yalding did not seem to notice. He walked in a blind sort of way to the hat-stand, fumbled clumsily with the umbrellas and macintoshes, found his straw hat and looked at it gloomily, crammed it on his head and went out, banging the door behind him in the most reckless way.

He left the drawing-room door open, and Gerald, though he had purposely put himself in a position where one could hear nothing from the drawing-room when the door was shut, could hear something quite plainly now that the door was open. That something, he noticed with deep distress and disgust, was the sound of sobs and sniffs. Mademoiselle was quite certainly crying.

'Jimminy!' he remarked to himself, 'they haven't lost much time. Fancy their beginning to quarrel *already*! I hope I'll never have to be anybody's lover.'

But this was no time to brood on the terrors of his own future. Eliza might at any time occur. She would not for a moment hesitate to go through that open door, and push herself into the very secret sacred heart of Mademoiselle's grief. It seemed to Gerald better that he should be the one to do this. So he went softly down the worn green Dutch carpet of the stairs and into the drawing-room, shutting the door softly and securely behind him.

'It is all over,' Mademoiselle was saying, her face buried in the beady arum-lilies on a red ground worked for a cushion cover by a former pupil: 'he will not marry me!'

Do not ask me how Gerald had gained the lady's confidence. He had, as I think I said almost at the beginning, very pretty ways with grown-ups, when he chose. Anyway, he was holding her hand, almost as affectionately as if she had been his mother with a headache, and saying 'Don't!' and 'Don't cry!' and 'It'll be all right, you see if it isn't' in the most comforting way you can imagine, varying the treatment with gentle thumps on the back and entreaties to her to tell him all about it.

This wasn't mere curiosity, as you might think. The entreaties were prompted by Gerald's growing certainty that whatever was the matter was somehow the fault of that ring. And in this Gerald was ('once more,' as he told himself) right.

The tale, as told by Mademoiselle, was certainly an unusual one. Lord Yalding, last night after dinner, had walked in the park 'to think of –'

'Yes, I know,' said Gerald; 'and he had the ring on. And he saw –'

'He saw the monuments become alive,' sobbed Mademoiselle; 'his brain was troubled by the ridiculous accounts of fairies that you tell him. He sees Apollon and Aphrodité alive on their marble. He remembers him of your story. He wish himself a statue. Then he becomes mad – imagines to himself that your story of the island is true, plunges in the lake, swims among the beasts of the Ark of Noé, feeds with gods on an island. At dawn the madness become less. He think the Panthéon vanish. But him, no – he thinks himself statue, hiding from gardeners in his garden till nine less a quarter. Then he thinks to wish himself no more a statue and perceives that he is flesh and blood. A bad dream, but he has lost the head with the tales you tell. He say it is no dream but he is fool – mad – how you say? And a mad man must not marry. There is no hope. I am at despair! And the life is vain!'

'There *is*,' said Gerald earnestly. 'I assure you there is – hope, I mean. And life's as right as rain really. And there's nothing to despair about. He's *not* mad, and it's *not* a dream. It's magic. It really and truly is.'

'The magic exists not,' Mademoiselle moaned; 'it is that he is mad. It is the joy to re-see me after so many days. Oh, la-la-la-la-la!'

'Did he talk to the gods?' Gerald asked gently.

'It is there the most mad of all his ideas. He say that Mercure give him rendezvous at some temple tomorrow when the moon raise herself.'

'Right,' cried Gerald, 'righto! Dear nice, kind, pretty Mademoiselle Rapunzel, don't be a silly little duffer' – he lost himself for a moment among the consoling endearments he was accustomed to offer to Kathleen in moments of grief and emotion, but hastily added: 'I mean, do not be a lady who weeps causelessly. Tomorrow he will go to that temple. I will go. Thou shalt go – he will go. We will go – you will go – let 'em all go! And, you see, it's going to be absolutely all right. He'll see he isn't mad, and you'll understand all about everything. Take my handkerchief, it's quite a clean one as it happens; I haven't even unfolded it. Oh! do stop crying, there's a dear, darling, long-lost lover.'

This flood of eloquence was not without effect. She took his handkerchief, sobbed, half smiled, dabbed at her eyes, and said: 'Oh, naughty! Is it some trick you play him, like the ghost?'

'I can't explain,' said Gerald, 'but I give you my word of honour – you know what an Englishman's word of honour is, don't you? even if you *are* French – that everything is going to be exactly what you wish. I've never told you a lie. Believe me!'

'It is curious,' said she, drying her eyes, 'but I do.' And once again, so suddenly that he could not have resisted, she kissed him. I think, however, that in this her hour of sorrow he would have thought it mean to resist.

'It pleases her and it doesn't hurt me – much,' would have been his thought.

And now it is near moonrise. The French governess, half-doubting, half-hoping, but wholly longing to be near Lord Yalding even if he be as mad as a March hare, and the four children – they have collected Mabel by an urgent letter-card posted the day before – are going over the dewy grass. The moon has not yet risen, but her light is in the sky mixed with the pink and purple of the sunset. The west is heavy with ink-clouds and rich colour, but the east, where the moon rises, is clear as a rock-pool.

They go across the lawn and through the beech-wood and come at last, through a tangle of underwood and bramble, to a little level tableland that rises out of the flat hill-top – one tableland out of another. Here is the ring of vast rugged stones, one pierced with a curious round hole, worn smooth at its edges. In the middle of the circle is a great flat stone, alone, desolate, full of meaning – a stone that is covered thick with the memory of old faiths and creeds long since forgotten. Something dark moves in the circle. The French girl breaks from the children, goes to it, clings to its arm. It is Lord Yalding, and he is telling her to go.

'Never of the life!' she cries. 'If you are mad I am mad too, for I believe the tale these children tell. And I am here to be with thee and see with thee – whatever the rising moon shall show us.'

The children, holding hands by the flat stone, more moved by the magic in the girl's voice than by any magic of enchanted rings, listen, trying not to listen.

'Are you not afraid?' Lord Yalding is saying.

'Afraid? With you?' she laughs. He put his arm round her. The children hear her sigh.

'Are you afraid,' he says, 'my darling?'

Gerald goes across the wide turf ring expressly to say:

'You can't be afraid if you are wearing the ring. And I'm sorry, but we can hear every word you say.'

She laughs again. 'It makes nothing,' she says 'you know already if we love each other.'

Then he puts the ring on her finger, and they stand together. The white of his flannel coat sleeve marks no line on the white of her dress; they stand as though cut out of one block of marble.

Then a faint greyness touches the top of that round hole, creeps up the side. Then the hole is a disc of light – a moonbeam strikes straight through it across the grey green of the circle that the stones mark, and as the moon rises the moonbeam slants downward. The children have drawn back till they stand close to the lovers. The moonbeam slants more and more; now it touches the far end of the stone, now it draws nearer and nearer to the middle of it, now at last it touches the very heart and centre of that central stone. And then it is as though a spring were touched, a fountain of light released. Everything changes. Or, rather, everything is revealed. There are no more secrets. The plan of the world seems plain, like an easy sum that one writes in big figures on a child's slate. One wonders how one can ever have wondered about anything. Space is not; every place that one has seen or dreamed of is here. Time is not; into this instant is crowded all that one has ever done or dreamed of doing. It is a moment and it is eternity. It is the centre of the universe and it is the universe itself. The eternal light rests on and illuminates the eternal heart of things.

None of the six human beings who saw that moonrising were ever able to think about it as having anything to do with time. Only for one instant could that moonray have rested full on the centre of that stone. And yet there was time for many happenings.

From that height one could see far out over the quiet park and sleeping gardens, and through the grey green of them shapes moved, approaching.

The great beasts came first, strange forms that were when the world was new – gigantic lizards with wings – dragons they lived as in men's memories – mammoths, strange vast birds, they crawled up the hill and ranged themselves outside the circle. Then, not from the garden but from very far away, came the stone gods of Egypt and Assyria – bull-bodied, bird-winged, hawk-headed, cat-headed, all in stone, and all alive and alert; strange, grotesque figures from the towers of cathedrals – figures of angels with folded wings, figures of beasts with wings wide spread; sphinxes; uncouth idols from Southern palm-fringed islands; and, last of all, the beautiful marble shapes of the gods and goddesses who had held their festival on the lake-island, and bidden Lord Yalding and the children to this meeting.

Not a word was spoken. Each stone shape came gladly and quietly into the circle of light and understanding, as children, tired with a long ramble, creep quietly through the open door into the firelit welcome of home.

The children had thought to ask many questions. And it had been promised that the questions should be answered. Yet now no one spoke a word, because all had come into the circle of the real magic where all things are understood without speech.

Afterwards none of them could ever remember at all what had happened. But they never forgot that they had been somewhere where everything was easy and beautiful. And people who can remember even that much are never quite the same again. And when they came to talk of it next day they found that to each some little part of that night's great enlightenment was left.

All the stone creatures drew closer round the stone – the light where the moonbeam struck it seemed to break away in spray such as water makes when it falls from a height. All the crowd was bathed in whiteness. A deep hush lay over the vast assembly.

Then a wave of intention swept over the mighty

crowd. All the faces, bird, beast, Greek statue, Babylo-
nian monster, human child and human lover, turned
upward, the radiant light illumined them and one
word broke from all.

'The light!' they cried, and the sound of their voice
was like the sound of a great wave; 'the light! the
light –'

And then the light was not any more, and, soft as
floating thistle-down, sleep was laid on the eyes of all
but the immortals.

The grass was chill and dewy and the clouds had
veiled the moon. The lovers and the children were
standing together, all clinging close, not for fear, but
for love.

'I want,' said the French girl softly, 'to go to the
cave on the island.'

Very quietly through the gentle brooding night they
went down to the boat-house, loosed the clanking
chain, and dipped oars among the drowned stars and
lilies. They came to the island, and found the steps.

'I brought candles,' said Gerald, 'in case.'

So, lighted by Gerald's candles, they went down
into the Hall of Psyche! and there glowed the light
spread from her statue, and all was as the children had
seen it before.

It is the Hall of Granted Wishes.

'The ring,' said Lord Yalding.

'The ring,' said his lover, 'is the magic ring given
long ago to a mortal, and it is what you say it is. It was
given to your ancestor by a lady of my house that he
might build her a garden and a house like her own
palace and garden in her own land. So that this place

is built partly by his love and partly by that magic. She never lived to see it; that was the price of the magic.'

It must have been English that she spoke, for otherwise how could the children have understood her? Yet the words were not like Mademoiselle's way of speaking.

'Except from children,' her voice went on, 'the ring exacts a payment. You paid for me, when I came by your wish, by this terror of madness that you have since known. Only one wish is free.'

'And that wish is –'

'The last,' she said. 'Shall I wish?'

'Yes – wish,' they said, all of them.

'I wish, then,' said Lord Yalding's lover, 'that all the magic this ring has wrought may be undone, and that the ring itself may be no more and no less than a charm to bind thee and me together for evermore.'

She ceased. And as she ceased the enchanted light died away, the windows of granted wishes went out, like magic-lantern pictures. Gerald's candle faintly lighted a rudely arched cave, and where Psyche's statue had been was a stone with something carved on it.

Gerald held the light low.

'It is her grave,' the girl said.

Next day no one could remember anything at all exactly. But a good many things were changed. There was no ring but the plain gold ring that Mademoiselle found clasped in her hand when she woke in her own bed in the morning. More than half the jewels in the panelled room were gone, and those that remained had no panelling to cover them; they just lay – bare on the velvet-covered shelves. There was no passage at the back of the Temple of Flora. Quite a lot of the secret passages and hidden rooms had disappeared. And there were not nearly so many statues in the garden as everyone had supposed. And large pieces of the castle were missing and had to be replaced at great expense. From which we may conclude that Lord Yalding's ancestor had used the ring a good deal to help him in his building.

However, the jewels that were left were quite enough to pay for everything.

The suddenness with which all the ring-magic was undone was such a shock to everyone concerned that they now almost doubt that any magic ever happened.

But it is certain that Lord Yalding married the French governess and that a plain gold ring was used in the ceremony, and this, if you come to think of it, could be no other than the magic ring, turned, by that last wish, into a charm to keep him and his wife together for ever.

Also, if all this story is nonsense and a make-up – if Gerald and Jimmy and Kathleen and Mabel have merely imposed on my trusting nature by a pack of unlikely inventions, how do you account for the paragraph which appeared in the evening papers the day after the magic of the moon-rising?

'MYSTERIOUS DISAPPEARANCE OF A
WELL-KNOWN CITY MAN,'

it said, and then went on to say how a gentleman, well known and much respected in financial circles, had vanished, leaving no trace.

'Mr U. W. Ugli,' the papers continued, 'had remained late, working at his office as was his occasional habit. The office door was found locked, and on its being broken open the clothes of the unfortunate gentleman were found in a heap on the floor, together with an umbrella, a walking stick, a golf club, and, curiously enough, a feather brush, such as housemaids use for dusting. Of his body, however, there was no trace. The police are stated to have a clue.'

If they have, they have kept it to themselves. But I do not think they can have a clue, because, of course, that respected gentleman was the Ugly-Wugly who became real when, in search of a really good hotel, he got into the Hall of Granted Wishes. And if none of this story ever happened, how is it that those four children are such friends with Lord and Lady Yalding, and stay at The Towers almost every holidays?

It is all very well for all of them to pretend that the whole of this story is my own invention: facts are facts, and you can't explain them away.

Also by E. Nesbit in Puffin Classics

THE MAGIC WORLD

A thoughtless boy is taught a lesson by his cat; a girl sent upstairs in disgrace is whisked to the world of her dreams; a magic telescope brings two boys a fortune; some very sensible princes and princesses outwit wicked fairies and usurpers . . . These twelve spellbinding stories open the door to the magic world of the imagination.

THE STORY OF THE AMULET

When Cyril, Robert, Anthea and Jane rescue their old friend the Psammead from a pet shop, the grateful sand fairy leads them to half an amulet which has the power to take them back in time in search of the other half – and the complete amulet can give them their heart's desire! But magic can cause problems in real life, especially when the Queen of Babylon visits the children in London . . .

FIVE CHILDREN AND IT

'It' is a Psammead, an ancient, ugly and irritable sand fairy the children find one day in a gravel pit and It grants them a wish a day, lasting until sunset. But they soon learn it is very hard to think of really sensible wishes, and each one gets them into unexpected difficulties. Magic, the children find, can be as awkward as it is enticing.

THE RAILWAY CHILDREN

When Father goes away unexpectedly, Roberta, Peter, Phyllis and their mother have to leave their happy life in London to go and live in a small cottage in the country. The children seek solace in the nearby railway station, and make friends with Perks the Porter and the Station Master himself. But the mystery remains: where is Father, and will he ever return?

THE STORY OF THE TREASURE SEEKERS

When their father's business fails, the six Bastable children decide to restore the family fortunes. But although they think of many ingenious ways to do so, their well-meant efforts are either more fun than profitable, or lead to trouble – until one adventure has quite unexpected results.

THE PHOENIX AND THE CARPET

It's startling enough to have a Phoenix hatch in your house, but even more startling when it tells you you have a magic carpet on the floor. Conceited it may be, but the Phoenix is also good-hearted, and obligingly accompanies the children on their adventures in time and space – which, magic being what it is, rarely turn out as they were meant . . .